Betrayal
A Contemporary Romance

Lesley Field

CROOKED
CAT

Discover us online:
www.crookedcatbooks.com

Join us on facebook:
www.facebook.com/crookedcat

Tweet a photo of yourself holding
this book to **@crookedcatbooks**
and something nice will happen.

For my mum and dad,
who would have been so proud.

To Neil for his continued
love and support.

And to my friends who
keep me firmly grounded.

About the Author

Lesley Field grew up on Teesside. She enjoyed riding and reading and later spent most of her working life pursuing legal cases. When retirement came she kicked off the restraints of the law and discovered her real self.

Lesley writes contemporary fiction which is set in Canada, and historical fiction set in London during the Regency period. She came into the Romantic Novelists Association under the New Writers Scheme and has progressed to full membership and is also a member of ROMNA.

Her first historical novel, "Dangerous Entrapment," (Book 1 in the Duchess in Danger series) was published in 2015 and was shortlisted for the Romantic Novelists Association's Historical Novel of the Year 2016. Book 2 in the series, "Dangerous Deception," was published in 2016. The next two books in the series, "Dangerous Desire," and "Dangerous Encounter," are due for publication in 2018.

Lesley's first contemporary romance, "Betrayal," set near Calgary, Canada, will be released on 27th February 2018.

Also due for publication in 2018/19 is the Saunders series, a trilogy of contemporary novels set in Banff, Canada. The first in the series is "Saunders-Lies and Deception," followed by, "Saunders-Endings and Beginnings," and finally, "Saunders-Sisters and Lovers."

Happily living on the North Yorkshire coast with her husband she spends her days enjoying life and writing.

Acknowledgements

To Laurence and Steph at Crooked Cat Books for taking a leap of faith with Betrayal. To Alice for her patience during editing. And to my fellow members of the Romantic Novelists Association, for their help and support. Especially the Northern Chapter (The Flying Ducks).

Betrayal
A Contemporary Romance

Chapter One

Jessica rested her elbows on the kitchen top and rubbed her fingers into her forehead. The pounding in her head was bad enough before, but now she felt as though it were about to explode. She could hear the angry voices along the hallway, but she didn't care what was going on in there. All she knew was that her life, the life she thought she had, was now crashing down about her ears and there was nothing she could do about it.

She couldn't believe what had happened. It seemed a lifetime ago since she had driven through the downtown Lethbridge traffic, grateful when their apartment block came into view. The headache she'd had all morning had turned into a migraine and it was only the insistence of her assistant, Anna, that had persuaded her to go home. She knew her fiancé, Tom, was meeting with some new clients out of the office so she'd had no option but to drive herself home. But at least that meant the apartment would be empty and all she wanted to do was to close the blinds and try and sleep.

Parking up, she had soon been inside the building, but even walking towards the elevator had been painful. Travelling up to the third floor, she stepped out into the spacious corridor. Despite the pain in her head she couldn't ignore the fact that she loved this building, which housed the apartment that had been her home for just over six months. It was Tom's apartment really but, when they got engaged, he'd asked her to move in with him. Since they were both lawyers working for the same firm it made sense to share a home rather than paying for two apartments, and it meant they could spend more time together.

She'd not noticed anything amiss when she'd opened the

door, nor when she'd slipped her shoes off and hung her coat in the closet. It was as she was walking along the hallway and into the lounge, with the intention of going through to the kitchen, that she thought she heard a noise. Crossing the lounge, she'd climbed the three steps up to the raised dining area. Ignoring the kitchen to her right she walked, or rather crept, along the hallway, leading off to the left of the dining area, which led to the bedrooms. She could only think that she or Tom had left the television in the bedroom on.

Passing the guest room and main bathroom, she'd moved cautiously along the hall. She could definitely hear something, and it sounded like voices. Approaching the master bedroom she saw the door was partly open, and then it became quite clear that it was not the television. Someone was inside.

By this time her heart had been thumping in her chest. *Did they have intruders? But if so, how did they get in?* Very cautiously and quietly she pushed the door further open and found herself looking at their large king size bed, now clearly occupied. She didn't think she would ever forget the next words she'd heard. She groaned as she remembered them, but couldn't stop her mind from re-playing the whole scene again.

"God, Christie stop gripping me, let me get all the way in first, you're so bloody eager all the time."

She'd frozen as she realised that the voice belonged to Tom, her fiancé, the person who was supposed to be out seeing a new client. His words were still resounding in her head, when his voice had again penetrated her brain.

"Ah, that's better. God, you were tight, but that's good now, baby, everything is just right, or at least it will be in a short while." As he spoke his bottom had moved back and then pushed forward and she'd heard the groan from underneath him. She saw him raise up on his hands and then start to move quickly back and forth. A pair of female legs appeared around his hips, dislodging the sheet and exposing his naked backside to her.

She had been frozen to the spot. He was screwing someone, in their bed, while he thought she was at work. *The bastard,* was her first thought, and in that moment all her hopes and dreams died and the anger started to course through her body. She backed away from the door, wanting to shut her ears to the words she could hear coming from the bed. "Harder, no harder. Oh God, screw me hard, Tom."

Then his voice. "If I screw you any harder I'll come out the top of your bloody head." A throaty laugh had reached her ears, and then an almighty scream, which seemed to suggest that the screwing had done its job and the recipient had just climaxed.

Unable to take any more, she had looked wildly about until her eyes alighted on the vase of roses. The ones he'd bought for her yesterday, that she'd put on the table in the hallway where it was cooler, and they could see them when they came in and out of the bedroom. Grabbing the vase, she'd stormed into the bedroom. That the female had climaxed she'd clearly heard, but he was still at it, pumping into her like there was no tomorrow, and she was screaming words of encouragement to him.

Whether he was about to come or not, Jessica didn't give a damn, she'd strode purposefully to the side of the bed and tipped the vase over the pair of them, showering them with cold water and thorny roses. The yells from them both, and his shout of, "bloody hell," were the only things that had given her any kind of satisfaction.

She had stood over them, keeping her eyes averted from his body, but the female she glared at. That was when she got her second shock. *Christie*. She wondered why the hell hadn't she realised when she heard the name, as she found herself looking down on the face of the daughter of the senior partner in their law firm.

She hadn't known what to say or what to do, so turned her head and looked Tom straight in the eye. "You bastard, you two-timing, screwing bastard." Turning back to the girl she drew herself up straight. "You want him, he's yours." With that, she'd turned and walked out of the room, registering for the first time that neither of them had managed to say a word. Which was probably just as well, as she would have taken great delight in ramming one of the roses down their throats.

Once back in the dining area, she didn't know what to do. The headache was now the least of her problems. Did she go, did she stay, and if she went, where would she go? And anyway, her things were in the bedroom, and she was damned if she was going back in there while it was still occupied. Moving into the kitchen, she'd automatically filled the coffee machine with shaking hands and turned it on, and now she was sitting on one of the breakfast stools, holding her throbbing head in her hands. She pulled her mind back to the present, and could still hear sounds and raised voices coming from the bedroom, as she poured a cup of coffee and sat and waited for what was to happen next.

Christie appeared first, and then Tom. Christie glared at Jessica and then stormed straight into the lounge without saying a word, and then out to the hallway with Tom following behind. Before he went into the hall he turned and called back, "Don't you leave, we need to talk."

"Too bloody right, we do," she shouted back, twisting her engagement ring around on her finger.

It was nearly an hour later before he returned, by which time she'd calmed and had her emotions in some kind of check. She waited for him to speak first.

"Sorry, Jess. I didn't mean for you to walk in on that. Anyway, what are you doing home?"

She couldn't believe that he'd just asked such a normal question after what she'd just seen. He sounded pathetic. "I bet you didn't," she threw at him. "And, not that's it's relevant, but I'm home because I wasn't feeling well. So how long has it been going on?"

"Oh God, Jessica, don't make a drama out of this. It's twenty-sixteen not nineteen-sixteen. You found me screwing someone, it's no big deal, we're not married," he said running his hand round the back of his neck.

He was struggling to cope with the situation, and she knew he hated being out of control. But she was astounded by what he'd just said.

"So you can screw around as long as we aren't married? What about when we are married, or isn't that on the cards? Is this a long engagement so you can have it at home, and have it away from home as well, when it suits?" She watched as his face flushed.

"It was a one-off. I met her as I was coming out of Starbucks this morning and she was upset. I couldn't leave her, she's the big boss's daughter, for Christ's sake." The excuse sounded lame, not only lame, she was certain it was a downright lie. "So you thought you'd bring her back here, to screw her happy?" she said.

"No, of course not. I brought her back until she felt able to go home but then she started coming on to me and…"

"And you just couldn't resist sticking your cock in it," she said, interrupting and using a word she hated, but which on this occasion seemed quite appropriate.

"Jessica," he shouted. "There's no need for crudeness."

"Isn't there? There were a lot of crude words being said in our bedroom." She watched as his eyes shifted away from her. "Yes, that's right, I was listening for quite a while before I came in." It was a small lie but she didn't believe a word of what he said about it being a one-off. His words earlier about Christie being eager all the time, told her he was lying. When he was avoiding the truth there was a small muscle in the side of his jaw that twitched, and right now it was dancing a jig.

"So where's your car, how come it's not in its parking bay where I would have seen it?" She watched his eyes slide away from her face. "Yes that's right, it's hidden isn't it, so nobody would know you were here, because this was all planned. Did you even wait until I'd driven away before you let her in? Why don't you just come clean, Tom, and admit how long it's been going on?" He looked back at her and she saw the anger in his face for the first time.

"The car's in the public car park, not that it's relevant, and it's been going on for a few months," he said angrily, hating to admit he was in the wrong.

She felt as though he'd slapped her. "So when you were out of the office, or I simply wasn't here, you had her in our bed."

"Yes, in our bed, which I might add, is in fact my bed. But

also in her bed in hotels, anywhere we could. Satisfied, now that you know?" he flung the words at her, furious he'd been caught out.

***

He'd been introduced to Christie shortly after he and Jessica had got engaged. It was at a business function and he'd been on his own, and she had made it quite clear that she was interested in him. She'd come into the office shortly after that to see her father and had bumped into him in the lobby. He was on his way to see a client and she had teased him about all work and no play, she had come on so hard to him that his pants were twitching by the time they reached his car. He ended up cancelling his appointment and spent the morning in her bed.

They'd both known what they wanted, and while she knew he was engaged, she told him it didn't matter. But it did to him, the boss's daughter was a big catch and it would do a lot for his career. That wasn't the only attraction, though; she was stunning and the sex was off the scale. Today had been a calmer episode but other times she was totally out of control, and that was something he found he enjoyed. So he'd cultivated their affair, made her want more than just the sex, and his plan had worked, Christie wanted them to be together. But he hadn't wanted to hurt Jessica so he'd persuaded her to keep the affair quiet for the time being.

His plan had been to slowly start picking fault with things at home and then break with Jessica, then a short time later he and Christie would start to date openly. He didn't want to be painted as the villain in the break-up and didn't want his reputation to suffer. Christie had been happy to wait as long as he was keeping her satisfied in bed. Now it had all blown up and he knew that he had to break with Jessica now. After today, Christie wouldn't wait, and he'd had a tense discussion with her in the car park. He'd persuaded her to go back to her apartment and wait for him, but she'd given him an ultimatum. He had to be with her by tonight or they were over, so he had to break this, and break it now. He looked at Jessica and felt guilty. She did look ill, but he couldn't turn back now.

***

"But you made love to me this morning?" she said in a shaky voice, as she remembered the way he'd come to her in the shower. She'd not expected it and was sitting on the shower seat washing her hair. She recalled how he'd lifted her leg onto his shoulder, fully exposing her and, without speaking, had entered her. No foreplay, just straight in, and he'd been rougher than usual, holding her wet hair firmly in one hand so that her head was held still. His teeth had ground into hers before his tongue had plundered her mouth. She'd been gasping for breath as he'd pounded into her and then, when she'd climaxed, he'd brought her back to the brink again, put her against the wall and had taken his fill of her body a second time. She'd never known him like that before. His actions had shocked her at the time, particularly as he'd not spoken one word to her while it took place, and then when it was over he'd kissed the top of her head and walked away. Now she was beginning to understand at least that part of his actions.

"I didn't make love to you this morning," he said calmly. "I screwed you. The way I've been screwing Christie. She likes it rough, not like you, you're so bloody predictable and reserved and you want it all soft and romantic. I was desperate for it this morning, even though I knew I was seeing her soon. She'd been sending me raunchy texts and photos and I needed it right then. So I thought I would give you a taste of rough this morning, but you didn't like, it did you? And that's part of the problem, you see, I've found out that I like it rough. I like it when she screams for more…"

"Shut up, shut up," she cried as she felt the tears gathering. "So you like it rough and I'm not up to it, am I?"

"No, you're not, Jessica. Look, I don't want to hurt you, but you don't satisfy me anymore, I don't think you ever did but I hadn't got Christie to compare you with until now. With us, it's always been so predictable. You wait for me to start it, and I can almost count the seconds to your first groan and then it's just like every other time, predictable, no excitement, no trying it differently. I want what she's offering, a hot body and sex like I've never known before."

He stopped speaking suddenly and stared at her, and Jessica felt the colour drain from her face. For a moment, she thought she was going to pass out. He wanted to finish it, end their relationship. But he was blowing it out of the water, and leaving her without even a lifejacket. She felt sick and had to take several deep breaths. The she looked at him, no longer knowing who he was. This was a stranger. This wasn't the man who'd said he loved her, who'd made love to her tenderly, and had asked her to marry him, to share his life with him. It was over, everything she'd hoped for was gone.

"I'll pack up and go," she said, suddenly sick of the whole thing.

"No, you stay here, at least for tonight. I'll go and give you time to sort your things out. Look, take as long as you need," he said guiltily.

"Going to her?" she couldn't stop herself asking the question.

"Yes," was his simple reply, as he turned and walked back into the bedroom.

He returned shortly, carrying a holdall, two suits and his briefcase. With a short goodbye, he walked out of the door and out of her life.

How she got through the rest of the day she didn't know. She packed her things up and left them in the guest bedroom, where she intended to sleep. Nothing would have got her back into their bedroom or their bed.

The headache that had sent her hurrying home had disappeared, and even that seemed to mock her, saying she should have stayed at work, then none of this would have happened. But it would have happened, he would still have been here with her, she just wouldn't have known about it.

The following morning, she arrived at the office and it didn't take Anna long to comment on her red eyes and notice that the ring wasn't on her finger. Saying they'd had a row was the only comment she made on its absence, but by mid-morning it was clearly the main topic of conversation. Tom kept himself in his office before leaving to go to court. She saw him go, and felt nothing but numbness inside.

By the end of the day, she realised that her position was untenable. She couldn't stay and work for the same firm as him, and probably watch him flaunt his relationship with Christie in the next few weeks. It would all be too humiliating. She sent him a text saying she needed a couple of days to sort things out and then she would be out of the apartment. He replied almost immediately saying to take as long as she needed.

Once she got home she phoned her cousin, Gemma, in Calgary and outlined to her what had happened, although she omitted the part about Christie, and just said they'd had a terrible row and had split up and she needed somewhere to stay for a short time until she could get another job and an apartment. As she'd hoped, Gemma was only too happy to have her stay, so that was her immediate plan.

The following morning, she handed in her resignation and told the firm she would use her outstanding holidays in lieu of notice. They weren't at all happy at first, until she spelled out quite plainly to them that she couldn't continue to work in the same firm as Tom, in view of what had happened. Before leaving, she went through her workload with one of her colleagues, and handed over her current files. She was both sad and angry that she would not be able to see these matters through, and that she was being forced to give up a job she loved through no fault of her own.

Having done that, she left a message for Tom on his cell phone to say that she would be out of the apartment first thing the following day. She had just finished the message when she remembered her ring. She rang back with a second message, to tell him that since she was having to leave because of him, and would be out of a job, she trusted he didn't want the ring returning as she intended to keep it in lieu of the damage he'd caused. "If you want it back, sue me," she said, ending the

11

call. He must have picked up the message straight away, as her phone went just as she was putting the last of her personal things in the box. Flicking it open, she looked at the text message. Two simple words. "Keep it." That was it. The final end of her engagement; and the end of her life and career in Lethbridge.

The following morning, she pulled out of her designated parking space and wondered how long it would be before Christie occupied it. Well, they wouldn't enjoy the bed tonight, she'd seen to that. The vase of flowers yesterday had done a reasonable job on it already, but this morning she'd suddenly been filled with a rage at what he'd done. Before she'd had time to think, she'd emptied three large pans of cold water on the bed, feeling some satisfaction as she'd watched the water soak through the sheets and then into the mattress.

Turning out of the complex and onto the road, it wasn't long before she was heading for the Crowsnest highway. *Twenty-six, single and unemployed, what more could I ask for?* she thought, as she turned onto the Deerfoot Trail, before hitting the Trans-Canada highway and driving towards a new life in Calgary.

Chapter Two

She couldn't believe it. This was the seventh interview she'd had in the past eight weeks and every one had at least twelve other applicants for it. When she'd applied for her position in Lethbridge, there had been three candidates including herself, and she'd had no problem in securing it. The present situation showed her how much things had changed and how many people were chasing each job.

Sitting in the waiting area, she could hear the gossip going on in the room behind. This was something else that she was sick of hearing, who was knocking off whom, and which partner had his eye on his PA. What the hell was happening in her profession? she wondered. Then she coloured slightly as one of the girls, in the adjoining room, loudly discussed the graphic scene that had confronted her when she'd gone into someone's office unannounced. The comment was heard by everyone waiting. She saw the look that passed between the male applicants and the twitch of the lips indicating they quite clearly enjoyed thinking of the spectacle. She looked at the other three females. Two kept their heads down, the other glanced at Jess and rolled her eyes. She gave her a half smile and concentrated on the portfolio on her knee.

Later, having spent just under an hour in an interview that she'd known wasn't going to get her anywhere, she seriously wondered why she was still in this profession. She'd started her last job full of enthusiasm, and she'd enjoyed it. Had it not been for what had happened, she would still have been there, and would probably have stayed until babies came along. Thinking of babies made her think of Tom, and that was the last thing she wanted to do. His betrayal was something she would never forget.

Sitting in Starbucks with a skinny latte, her mind went over the events of the day, and also the last few weeks. For the first time, she considered a change of career. She'd always wanted to practice law, but somehow the recent insight into what went on in law firms was beginning to make her feel disillusioned. While she was studying, she worked in law offices as a junior assistant during the holidays, to gain experience and an understanding of the procedural side of the law; and that had stood her in good stead. Now she was actually daring to consider taking a step back from being a practising attorney and moving to a more supportive role as a personal assistant. She wasn't sure when the thought first started to work its way into her head, but it was there now, and it probably wasn't such an out-of-the-way idea anyway. At least this would keep her in the legal profession, in case she wanted to return to being a practising lawyer in the future.

She'd been staying with Gemma for just over two months now, and it had been great with just the two of them at first, but now Gemma's relationship with Eric, her boyfriend of almost a year, was about to move into another phase. He was moving into the apartment with her. Gemma was besotted with him, much to Jess's dismay. In her mind, he was a control freak. She'd seen the type before, but Gemma was oblivious to it and ran around after him, seeing to his every need. Jess felt sick at the way he was able to manipulate Gemma without her realising it. She'd made one attempt to point this out to her and had very quickly realised that any criticism of him was likely to cause an argument. So she'd backed down and smoothed over the upset, but in her own mind she could see what he was doing to her cousin.

Gemma was a sweetheart and loved her job as a nurse at the hospital. To all intents and purposes they should have been an ideal couple. Eric was the manager at a local dealership, and according to him the youngest manager within the company. This was where Jess suspected his controlling nature came from. He was probably great at his job, she'd picked that up from a couple of social events she'd attended with Gemma, but when he was at home and they were alone, it was like he was another person. Now that he was moving in, Jess realised that she would have to get some kind of a job quickly, as they wouldn't want her hanging around and being a fifth wheel. A couple of days later, coming home from an unsuccessful eighth interview, she found the entrance to the apartment full of boxes.

"Hi," called Gemma from the lounge. "Sorry about the mess, it's just some of Eric's things. He's decided to move in today rather than wait until the weekend."

Oh great, thought Jess. "It's okay, I can manage. I'll just go and get changed and then I'll give you a hand with things, if you want," she shouted back as she headed off into the guest room.

Walking into the lounge a short while later she found Gemma unpacking boxes. There was no sign of Eric, but then of course he would be at work, she remembered. "So, is Eric definitely moving in today?" she asked, realising that she was seriously going to have to find somewhere else to live now the event was actually happening.

"Yes, oh, it's so exciting to think that we'll be living here together, and sharing a bed every night."

That comment made Jess feel uncomfortable, since she already knew, from the nights he stayed over, what sharing a bed with Eric meant. She hadn't had the heart to tell her cousin that she could hear just how much Gemma enjoyed sharing her bed with him.

It was close to seven when Eric finally arrived, with the last of his things. Helping them both to put things away was the least she could do. Sitting down later, with a pizza and a bottle of wine, she looked across at the couple. Eric was sprawled on the sofa and Gemma was curled up alongside him. He picked up his glass. "Well, ladies, here's to the big move," he said, then downed he contents in one go and dragged Gemma to him, kissing her hard. Jess shuddered. This guy was uncouth. She needed to get out of here, so brought up the subject of looking for a place of her own.

"Look, I know you two will want your own space, so give me a couple of weeks and I'll be out of your hair."

"Oh Jessica, I don't want to push you out, but it…" whatever Gemma was going to say next was drowned out by Eric's voice.

"Oh, no need to worry, Jessica, I'm sure we can all rub along. I might enjoy having two females to wait on me," he said, with a laugh.

In your dreams, she thought, but smilingly told them both that she had no intention of imposing on them any longer than necessary.

By the time the weekend came around, Jess was beginning to think she was paranoid. She was sure than Eric had touched her bottom on two occasions. Once when she bent down to load the dishwasher, and then when she'd been passing a plate to Gemma and he'd been standing behind her. She'd looked at his face after both incidents and it had been devoid of anything that gave a clue that something had just happened, so she put it down to maybe just an accidental brush of his hand, but she couldn't get a niggling doubt out of her head.

By Monday, she was scouring the Internet for jobs, not just as an attorney, but also as a PA in a lawyer's office. She needed to be earning again. She'd been living off her savings and the money she'd got for her engagement ring. She'd put it on eBay with a high reserve, and was astounded when she'd got the asking price. Two-thirds of what it was worth was more than she could have hoped for, so it was a nice sum to add to her savings.

She left Gemma and Eric in the apartment, and was in one of the Internet cafés with her laptop. If she was honest, she was glad to get out. Gemma had taken a few days off work, as Eric had taken a week's holiday, so were both at home. When she left, they were still in bed, and the noises coming from their bedroom had left Jess in no doubt as to what was happening. In fact, she could hear this every night, Eric was very verbal in his lovemaking and she'd taken to pulling the duvet over her head to drown out the sound. She stayed out for most of the day, returning about five to find Gemma upset. Her immediate thought was that she'd had a fight with Eric, and she couldn't help but hope this was the case, but it wasn't.

"Oh, Jess, three people have called in sick at work. I've been re-called and have to go in tonight for a night shift. It's just not fair."

Making sympathetic noises, she persuaded her cousin to look on the bright side. "Look Gem, you and Eric have all the time in the world to be together, what's a few nights apart going to do?"

"Oh, I know what you mean, Jessica, but he... well, he likes, you know... every night."

Don't I know it? she thought, but couldn't say that. "Well, he'll just have to wait until you get home. Then he can spend the day in bed with you."

Once Gemma had left for work, Jess took herself off into her room on the pretext of sending out email applications. Waking early the next morning, she wandered out towards the kitchen. Hearing sounds from the lounge, she hesitated. She had no wish for Eric to see her in her nightdress. Peering through the partly open door, she could see him with his back to her watching the television. She was about to go when the dialogue from the screen caught her attention. Looking at the images, she was shocked. He was watching porn. Not hard-core stuff, but the erotic type, and she could hear groans coming from the chair. Having no desire to be caught, she forgot all about the kitchen and rushed back to her room. She didn't venture out again until she heard Gemma come home.

Disappearing as soon as she'd had breakfast, she could hear the squeals coming from the bedroom as she closed the apartment door. In the elevator she suddenly found herself laughing and wondering if Eric got his ideas from the movies he watched. Oh, she felt sorry for her cousin, but there again maybe she watched them with him. Maybe there was a side to Gemma that she didn't know?

She did the same as the day before and stayed out until late. Coming home she found Gemma there and in the process of sorting out something for dinner. "Not working tonight?" she queried.

"No, but I'm on early tomorrow so I'll have to have an early night."

17

They had dinner and then watched a movie, until Jess decided to leave them together. She'd not been in her room long before she heard their bedroom door close. About to get into bed, she decided to get a drink of juice to have while she read. Going quietly passed their bedroom, she was thankful not to be hearing grunts and groans, but what she did hear was her cousin complaining.

"Oh, no, Eric, I can't, not again. We've been at it nearly all day. I'm worn out and I need to sleep before work. No please, don't do that, I don't want to." The last part was said firmly and Jess wondered for a moment if she should call out and ask if everything was okay, but then decided against it. In fact, she decided against the drink and crept back to her own room.

She was having the weirdest dream, she was being chased by someone, but Tom rescued her. He caught her and told her he was sorry for what had happened, he loved her and would never let her go. He'd taken her back to their apartment and she was now wrapped in his arms. She felt safe. She could feel his body warm against her own and she sighed contentedly. Then she wanted to giggle as she felt him hard against her bottom where her nightdress had ridden up. Still half asleep, she squirmed back into him drawing her legs up and she felt his tip pushing at her entrance, she pushed back opening herself further to him, and she felt his hand hold her hip and pull her back. *Oh this is bliss,* she thought as she felt him push into her a bit further. Then she felt his hand move from her hip to her chest and under her top. Next, her nipple was grabbed in a tight grip that pulled her almost to consciousness. He was rolling her nipple with his fingers, but it was too hard. She felt him pull her body back and at the same time he pushed into her a bit further, then the words came. "Come on, honey, let me get all the way in first, you're so bloody hot. Knew you wanted me."

She froze and was instantly awake. The words were so close to those she'd heard before. Suddenly she realised she'd been dreaming, and none of what she'd thought was happening was true. *Jesus Christ, it wasn't Tom. She was in bed at Gemma's and there was only one person it could be,*

Eric. The thought came rushing into her head as she felt him try to push further in. She slammed her legs down straight, cutting off his entry point. He didn't like that and she heard him curse and he pulled sharply at her nipple causing her to cry out.

"Come on, Jessie, give it up. You know you want it. You've been without it for months now, you must be gagging for it."

"Get off me," she said coldly pulling his hand away from her chest, and arching her body away from him to extract him fully from her entrance. He was still partly touching her and she wanted him gone, she felt sick at the thought of what had nearly happened.

As she pulled away from him, he made a grab for her groin, but she got there first and dug her nails into the back of his hand. That made him yell out.

"Bloody bitch," he cried, yanking his hand back.

"Let me go, you bastard," she shouted as she finally managed to pull away and jumped out of the bed. Pulling the short nightdress down, she grabbed her robe and covered herself. Breathing heavily, she watched as he slowly crawled out of the other side of the bed.

"Don't think I won't tell Gemma about this," she threatened.

"And who do you think she'll believe, when I tell her how you've been coming on to me since I moved in? I can make her believe anything. I know exactly what to do to turn her on, and she won't believe a word against me."

"Go and put some clothes on, you look pathetic," she said, turning away from his naked figure. She kept her eyes averted until he'd left the room, and then she dashed across and turned the lock. Holding the tears at bay, she went into the bathroom and turned on the shower. Standing under it, still in her nightdress, she started to cry. Not only for what had happened, but because, for one second when she realised it wasn't Tom, she'd been tempted to let the incident run its course. To feel a man inside her, making love to her and not thinking of her as inadequate or predictable. Thankfully, the horror of the situation had brought her to her senses and she'd put a stop to it before he'd registered her momentary weakness. This had brought home to her that she couldn't stay here, and she needed to move as soon as possible. In the meantime, she would make sure that she was not alone with him and would keep her door locked.

When Gemma came in from work, Jess had taken herself out. She'd not spoken to Eric, but she hoped the look she'd given him as she'd left would be enough to stop him trying anything like that again. Now, as she was walking along the hallway towards the apartment, she dreaded the reception she might get if Eric had got in first with his lies.

Opening the door cautiously, she heard voices from the lounge. Deciding to play it cool, she made a noise as she approached and entered just in time to see her cousin pulling her top down. Pretending that she'd not noticed anything, she asked how her day had gone. The fact that she wasn't half way out the door by now told her that Eric had kept his mouth shut and, much as she wanted to shake her cousin and tell her what he was really like, she was sensible enough to realise that Gemma wouldn't believe a word she said against him. Deciding to keep her own counsel, she offered to make dinner. After dropping her things in her room, she went back to the kitchen and closed her ears to the noises coming from the other room.

Thankfully, Gemma was on afternoon shift for the next few days, so Jess was long gone from the apartment before she left. Eating out, she made sure that Gemma was home before she got back. Thankful that she'd got through the week, she knew that the approaching weekend would be a problem, as Gemma had already said she was on nights. There was no way she could be in the apartment alone with Eric, so she invented a story. "Oh, that's a shame, Gem. It means Eric will be on his own. I've just heard from friends in Lethbridge that they're coming for a visit, so I'm going to be meeting up with them and staying at their hotel for a couple of nights." She thought she saw a smirk on Eric's face when she made the announcement, but Gemma saw nothing amiss in what she said.

"That's okay, it will give him the chance to watch sports all night."

More likely, porno movies, Jess thought, but didn't say anything.

Packing a small overnight case with enough to last at least a couple of days, she was glad to leave the apartment. Although she was watching her finances, she had no intention of spending the next few nights in a dowdy hotel, and had made a reservation at one of the smart places downtown. At least she would enjoy some luxury for a short time. Also, she was hopeful about a job that she'd applied for, not in the city but in a small town on the outskirts. A single-partner law firm wanted a PA, and the location would at least give her a chance of getting away.

Chapter Three

Walking into reception, wearing one of her work suits, she didn't feel out of place. Pulling her small case, she approached the desk with confidence. She was Jessica Cameron, a successful attorney, and she was to all intents and purposes here on business. Giving her name to the receptionist, she waited and then filled in the appropriate details on the registration form. Taking the wallet with her room card, she followed the directions to the elevator and was soon in her room. Putting away the few things she'd brought, she looked out of the window at the city below. The tenth floor gave her a reasonable view and she pulled a chair up to the window and sat with a book until it became too dark to see properly. She knew she was hiding, but she didn't care. The last thing she wanted was to be alone in the apartment with Eric.

Showering and changing into a pair of smart black pants with a fine green cashmere top and killer heel black shoes, she surveyed herself in the mirror. Yes, she would do, she looked the successful businesswoman. Picking up her purse, she collected her room card and went down to dinner. She'd reserved a table and slipped carefully into the small booth that was both comfortable and partly private. This was just what she wanted, a good meal and to be able to sit back and people-watch without being conspicuous.

Having finished a seafood paella that was the best she'd ever tasted, she turned down dessert but ordered a coffee. Now she was able to sit back and study her fellow diners. The elderly couple in the corner looked as though they were celebrating, and the young couple opposite were lost in each other. Jess couldn't help but smile and remember how she would look at Tom like that. Shaking her head, she pushed the thought away and concentrated on the others in the room, trying to picture why they were here.

Her coffee arrived about the same time as a tall figure came striding in, following the waiter. After what appeared to be some discussion, he was re-directed to one of the booths. Not wanting to appear nosey, she kept her eyes averted as he crossed the room and settled into a booth across from her.

Picking up her book, she had learned never to dine alone without a book by her side, she sat enjoying her coffee. Although she was trying to read, she was distracted by what was going on around her. She could hear a young couple in the booth behind her apparently discussing the décor for their new apartment. The elderly couple were about to leave and she couldn't help but smile as they walked out holding hands. The tall figure in the booth opposite was waiting for his order, but was sipping what appeared to be a scotch. As if sensing her looking, he glanced across and, embarrassed at being caught staring, she lowered her gaze, but then realised that she wasn't doing anything wrong, so looked back up to find him watching her. She felt her cheeks starting to flush and just the faintest twitch of his lips gave away his knowledge of her discomfort. This time she did look away, and stuck her nose firmly back in her book.

She ventured a furtive glance as he was eating. He was quite delectable in a way. He was wearing a pair of smart grey trousers and a white shirt, topped with a grey suede jacket. No tie, so the top couple of buttons on the shirt were undone, and she could see his tanned throat and neck underneath. For all his clothes spoke of money, there was a ruggedness about him that said he spent a lot of time outdoors. The dark hair was cut in a conventional style, not too short, but not too long. As she watched he finished his meal, then lifted his hand and brushed the hair back from his brow. She was about to move her gaze, or was it gawping, she wondered, when he suddenly looked straight into her eyes and raised a quizzical eyebrow. This time she wasn't hanging around, she'd been caught out twice, now, and that was more than enough. Picking up her book, she slid out of the booth and, with her head high, and her eyes looking straight ahead, she walked out and into the lobby. She'd stayed in the restaurant far longer than intended but, for the first time in weeks, she felt at peace with herself.

She was tempted to go straight back to her room but it was still early, and after all she was paying enough to stay here, so she might as well enjoy some of the facilities. Looking cautiously into the cocktail bar she saw it was almost empty. Spotting a table in a quiet corner, she ordered a white wine spritzer and settled back with her book. She was half way through her drink when someone sat down at her table. Glancing up, she saw a stranger, and before she could say anything he was asking her if she wanted another drink. Horrified at this intrusion, and the apparent attempt to pick her up, she declined. But her visitor was not to be put off easily.

"Awe, come on, honey. You can't sit here all alone without another drink. Let me buy you one." She felt her temper rising and was about to refuse again and ask him, not too politely, to leave, when a masculine voice spoke up.

"I think the lady said no, and from where I come from, no means no. So perhaps you would like to leave, before the lady needs to call for assistance."

Her would-be visitor stood up, and for a moment she thought there was going to be trouble. But then, without another word, he shrugged his shoulders and walked away. Jessica was sick with embarrassment but knew she had to thank her rescuer. Looking at him for the first time she saw Tall, Dark and Grey Trousers looking down at her. "Thank you," she managed to get out.

"No problem, enjoy the rest of your night," he said, and with that he was gone.

The intrusion was enough for Jess. She quickly finished her drink and hurried back to her room. *What the hell is wrong with the male population*? she thought, as she put the deadlock on her door. *Can't they think of anything apart from trying to pick someone up?* She'd come here to get away from one pervert, only to attract another potential one. Not that she could even recall what he looked like, she'd been too shocked at the blatant attempt at a pickup, and goodness knows what he thought she was doing, sitting on her own. Tomorrow night she wouldn't make the same mistake.

Surprisingly, she slept well that night and woke the following morning refreshed and ready to spend at least part of the day window-shopping and then perhaps take in one of the parks, since the day looked to be fine. Mid-May could be warm, but then again they could also get snow. As she ate breakfast she looked through the brochures she'd brought down from her room, and noted that she could do both her choices in the same place. The Core Shopping Centre incorporated the Devonian Gardens and a food court. The idea of everything being under the same roof appealed to her. No need to go rushing around from one place to another, she could just take her time and wander as the mood took her.

It hadn't been her intention to buy anything, today was supposed to be window-shopping only, but the scarlet dress on the model in the window had taken her breath away. Simple sleek lines that hugged the figure, and she knew she had the figure to carry it off. The slightly scooped neck and three quarter sleeves gave the dress a modesty that belied the way it skimmed over her bust and hips and ended just on her knee. She looked slimmer than her size eight but this was down to the cut of the style, no belts or tucks, just a straight simple line that needed no embellishment and clung to her body where it should. She had grimaced at the price tag but looking at her reflection in the changing room mirror, she couldn't deny the pleasure she got from wearing it. Anyway, after all she had been through recently, she figured she deserved a treat. But dare she buy it?

Changing back into her clothes, she'd taken out her credit card, quickly paid before she changed her mind, and now she was sitting in the Devonian Gardens with her expensive carrier on the seat next to her. She had been taken aback at the gardens and was amazed to find such a peaceful oasis on the fourth level of the shopping centre. She had expected it to be on the ground floor and tried to imagine what it must have been like to get the plants, trees and shrubs into place, not to mention the water features, but decided that she didn't have

25

the experience or the energy to work it out. All that mattered was that it was peaceful in the corner she'd found, and there was music playing, seemingly from a grand piano. She couldn't see if there was anyone actually playing it, or if it was simply there for effect, but the soothing melodies were just what she needed.

She'd bought some sushi from the food court, but that was long gone and now she was relaxing with a coffee in her hand. All she could hear was the distant noise of people out for the day. Being Saturday, the centre was pretty full but what did she expect? If she'd wanted peace and quiet she should have headed to the mountains, although even there it would be busy on a weekend. She was reluctant to leave her little haven, but knew she must. Heading back to the hotel, she made it just before a heavy shower of rain came down. That was the thing about Calgary, one minute it was sunshine and the next you could have a hailstorm, which made the choice of outdoor clothing interesting at times.

Coming through the doors into the lobby she saw her rescuer of the night before just going into the elevator. Hanging back, she waited until the doors had closed. She had no wish to encounter him again. She'd met him this morning on her way down to breakfast. He'd got into the elevator on the floor below her own and she had no choice but to acknowledge him and thank him again for his intervention the night before. The smile on his face and quick, "you're welcome," did nothing to appease her embarrassment and she was glad when they reached the next floor and an influx of people allowed her to move to the back of the car. Having averted another encounter, she quickly pressed for the elevator and was soon back in her own room.

Showering and washing her hair, she let her mind wander as she dried and styled it. She desperately needed to move out of Gemma's apartment, and had spent some time since coming back from shopping checking her emails. Nothing. She was disappointed. She was pinning her hopes on the PA job in Longville to get her away. Picking her black pants out of the closet, her hand strayed to the red dress. What on earth had possessed her to buy it, and where would she wear it now? It would have been fine for nights out with Tom and clients, but now what use would she have for it? She was tempted to return it to the store, but something stopped her. Putting the black pants back, she lifted the dress down and slipped it off the hanger. Well, she probably couldn't wear it in Longville or anywhere similar, but in a smart hotel in Calgary she could wear it for dinner.

Decision made, she undid the zip and stepped into the dress, pulling it up and slipping her arms into the sleeves. Then it was a case of contorting her hand as she carefully pulled up the zip. Stepping into the black killer heels she'd worn the night before, she took in her reflection. Wow, it certainly drew the eye, but that thought had her almost changing her mind and taking it off. She wanted to be inconspicuous, but this dress would put paid to that. But then again, she was young, not unattractive and a successful attorney, and she needed to boost her confidence after the knock it had taken from Tom, and then the cringing encounter with Eric. Before she could change her mind, she picked up her key card, popped it into her purse, and set off down to the restaurant.

Waiting to be seated, she could see that it was a lot busier than the night before and regretted that she had overlooked making a reservation. Following the waiter across the room she kept her eyes straight ahead, wondering where he was taking her. He stopped in front of a small table set for two right next to the kitchen door. Jess looked at it in dismay. *She was not going to sit here.* Something Tom said to her a long time ago came back into her head, about restaurants often seating single people near the kitchen door because parties of diners would not sit there. He'd told her to always reject such a table if she was ever in that position. Well, he was gone, but his advice stayed with her.

Turning to the waiter she said, quite calmly, "I'm sorry, this table is not suitable." He looked flustered and told her that it was the only table they had, as they were fully booked.

"I can see you're busy," replied Jess, "but I am a guest at

the hotel and my reservation was made several days ago. I had one of the small booths last evening and would like a similar table tonight." She stopped speaking and looked at him expectantly. She trusted he wouldn't check that the reservation she referred to was her hotel reservation, and that she'd not actually made a reservation in the restaurant tonight.

He clearly had no idea what to do, but Jess was not backing down on this. She was entitled to suitable seating and was going to get it. She stood straight and waited for him to speak. She would bluff this out.

"I'm sorry, madam, but there is no alternative table. I can go and fetch the manager and you can speak to him. He may be able to arrange a later sitting for you?"

Jess was considering this option, which would probably bring her slight deception to light, when a voice spoke from behind her. "Sorry to interrupt, but is there a problem?"

The young waiter seized on the intervention and quickly explained about the table. Jessica wanted the ground to open up and swallow her, it was *him* again, rescuing her for the second time. She wasn't sure what she expected him to say but when he spoke, he was clearly on her side.

"Well, of course that table isn't suitable for a young lady on her own."

Before he could say any more, the waiter cut in explaining that there were no other tables available.

"Look," said her rescuer, looking directly at her. "I have one of the small booths and, if you have no objection, I would be happy to share the table with you."

***

Ethan waited, watching the expressions passing over her face. He'd had his eye on her from the moment she'd walked into the restaurant, he and just about all the other males in the room. The dress made a statement and to him it said, aloof and sexy. He wasn't quite sure which category she fitted into, but he would very much like to find out. Last night he'd teased her when he'd caught her watching him, but now he wanted nothing more than to spend some time with her. He'd watched the interaction between her and waiter, and it hadn't take long to realise there was a problem. So he decided to make a move and see if he could solve her problem and, at the same time, satisfy his own curiosity.

***

Jessica hesitated. She didn't want the small table, but she wasn't sure she wanted to share a table with Mr Good-Looking either. Both spelled danger. But she needed to make a decision, both he and the waiter were waiting for her to speak. So which would she pick? The table, over which she didn't want to compromise her principles, or him, because he was too handsome and too sexy, and that was a lethal combination? His eyes were on her as he waited for her reply. Deciding that acceptance of his offer was the better option, she raised her eyes to his and found herself looking into a pair of twinkling grey eyes that told her he found her hesitation amusing.

"Thank you," she said, "that's very kind, as long as you are sure it's no problem."

"I wouldn't have offered if it was," came the amused reply, as he turned and walked back to his booth, expecting her to follow. He stood at the side and waited until she reached him. He couldn't fail to notice the flash of tanned thigh when the dress rode up as she slid into the seat opposite his.

Jessica seated herself with as much dignity as the body-hugging dress would allow, then they waited while the relieved waiter came rushing over and laid out a place setting for her. As soon as the napkin was brought over, the waiter shook it out and placed it over her knees, affording some cover to what she felt were her exposed legs. Taking the offered menu, she quickly ordered fresh salmon in a butter sauce, with new baby potatoes and asparagus. She then ordered a glass of chardonnay along with a club soda.

***

As the waiter was about to leave, Ethan spoke up and asked him to make sure that their orders came out at the same time. He had no intention of eating while she was still waiting for her order. Picking up his wine, he took a sip and a good look at his new dinner companion. She was striking, not in a drop-dead-gorgeous way, but in a way that he had yet to work out. The shoulder-length black hair was sleek and glossy and swung freely as she turned her head. The brown eyes that had looked so intently at him held wariness, but also there was a warmth in them. The light tan on her face he knew extended to her legs, or what he'd seen of them, and he was curious to know if it was an all-over tan. He was intrigued. She had the look of a businesswoman but the dress said she was sexy, and he wondered if she had any idea of what she was presenting to the male population, and in particular to him.

Realising that they couldn't sit across from each other throughout the meal without speaking, he spoke quietly to her. "I guess some introductions would help." The moment he said it he saw the hesitation in her face and a look of something, he wasn't quite sure what, in her eyes. Remembering her encounter the previous evening, and the fact that she appeared to be alone, she probably wouldn't feel comfortable giving her name. "Perhaps that's a bit too forward," he said quickly. "Let's forget about real names and I'll see what name I can pick for you, then you can hide behind a pseudonym for the evening." He couldn't keep the twinkle out of his eyes as he spoke.

She looked quickly up at him and he knew he'd read her thoughts correctly. She hadn't been happy about giving her name to a stranger and this offered her a way out, and he quite liked the idea of her being somewhat of a mystery woman to him. It would give her a façade to hide behind.

"Okay, so what name would you give me?" she asked, joining in with his game.

His eyes swept over her face and the red dress. There was only one name he could give to her. "Red. I'll call you Red, it suits you."

Jess felt her face starting to heat. The reference to red meant the dress, but the comment about it suiting her, well, she wasn't sure if that meant the name or the dress. "So what do I call you?"

"Anything you want, within reason," he added.

She knew she would have to be careful. She couldn't very well call him drop dead gorgeous, which was the first thought that had popped into her head. Staring into his face, she was drawn to his eyes, grey eyes that seemed to search into her own. Okay, if he could call her Red, she would call him Grey.

"I think I'll follow suit and pick a colour."

Before she could continue, he interjected. "Not black, I hope, I'm no black-hearted male preying on single females," he laughed.

She laughed with him. "Not black, but I think... Grey."

"So where do you get the grey from?" he asked, as though he knew full well, but wanted her to admit it.

Jessica chewed on the inside of her lip. He was teasing her, she was sure he knew where it had come from, but he left her with no choice but to tell him. "It's the colour of your eyes."

"Really, I would never have guessed," he said, his lips twitching as he spoke.

She gave in to the laugh that was bubbling in her throat, and he laughed with her. The ice was broken, and he then asked her some general questions; was she from the area, what did she do for a living?

She answered him truthfully. "I'm staying with a friend in the area. I work, or rather worked, in a law office, but I'm between positions at the moment." She saw no reason to say the friend was a relative.

"Redundancy?" He asked the question outright.

She shook her head. "No, I left. Personal reasons." Her tone told him she wasn't going to say any more, and he didn't ask.

As if on cue, their meals arrived and any further conversation was limited to quick comments. She asked similar questions of him, and he told her he was in the city on business and leaving the following morning. Declining a dessert, they both ordered coffee and sat comfortably, talking generally about the city itself. Deciding that she should leave him to enjoy the rest of his evening, she made to get up.

"Do you have any plans for this evening?" he asked.

"No, I did consider going into the cocktail bar but after last night, I think my room may be the better option."

"Look, I have no plans and I was going to have a drink in the bar, but I would rather have some company than sit on my own. So if you would care to join me and save me from a lonely evening, I would be forever in your debt. Call it repayment for the table, if you want," he said, giving her a smile that made her tingle to her toes.

He was dangerous, but if she was honest he was good to talk to, and it was some time since she'd had a proper conversation with anyone. *You're always so bloody predictable and reserved.* Tom's words suddenly came back to her and, before she could change her mind, she accepted his invitation. "Since you put it that way, I'd like that."

Seating her at a small table in a secluded corner of the bar he ordered a bottle of Moet Champagne. "I thought you could help me celebrate," he said by way of explanation.

"Oh, what are you celebrating, or shouldn't I ask?"

"No, no secret. I've just secured a valuable contract today that will mean a lot to my business."

She'd not asked him what business he was in, and she wondered if she should now. "Am I allowed to ask what kind of business you're in?"

"Production, you could say to do with the food industry." He smiled as he spoke. It seemed he had no intention of telling her anything else. This game they were playing with each other was fun. Maybe he liked the idea of keeping their real identities a secret. At least for now. She sensed she intrigued him and he wanted to learn more about her. Well, she wasn't averse to learning more about him.

They waited while the waiter popped the cork and poured for him to taste. He confirmed that it was fine, and she watched as the two glasses were filled. Once they were alone, he spoke. "So tell me, Red, if you are staying with a friend, how come you are in a hotel, or is that a question too far?"

She debated whether to simply say it was, but then, what did it matter if he knew the reason? "My friend's boyfriend moved in a few days ago and, well, let's say he's not quite the gentleman she thinks he is."

His eyebrows lifted. "So he tried it on, and you took flight?"

"I didn't exactly take flight, I just wanted to avoid being alone in the apartment with him while she was at work."

"Like I said, you took flight. Why didn't you tell her what he'd done? Clearly he did try it on because you didn't deny it."

Jessica took another long drink. She didn't like talking about this and had been a fool to mention it. "She wouldn't have believed me, he's manipulating her and he said he would simply say that I'd encouraged him. It wasn't worth the aggro to say anything."

"Must be a really important friend for you to put up with that. What are you going to do when you go back?"

She shook her head. "I don't know. I've not thought that far ahead. I just needed a few days away from the situation and I guess I hoped it would simply go away." She sat back in her seat and crossed one tanned leg over the other, having no idea what she was doing to her companion.

***

She fascinated Ethan. She was a strong businesswoman, he could see that in the way she spoke and held herself, but there was a vulnerability about her, something under the surface had rattled her, and he didn't think it was her friend's boyfriend. Pouring them both another glass, he settled back in his chair and asked her several questions about herself, nothing intrusive, just about the films and music she liked.

The more she spoke, the more relaxed she became, and he had a feeling that this in part was to do with the alcohol she was consuming. The champagne was his favourite and clearly she was enjoying it as well. He couldn't take his eyes off her face as she spoke and although he heard her words, his mind already had her in his room and the red dress, well that was carefully laid over a chair and she was laid on...his mind suddenly snapped back to what she was saying. He was running away with himself. He'd rescued her from a pick-up last night and now he was contemplating the same thing himself. *Bloody hell, I've not come here to pick anyone up. I've come on business, that bit is true, but I've also come to try and sort out my own relationship with Helena. But how the hell can I do that, with another woman in my head?* He should have been annoyed with himself for the way his mind was working, but he wasn't, if he was honest he was more than happy to sit here with her.

He listened to her telling him about the gardens she'd been in earlier in the day. Watching the animation on her face made him smile. She smiled back and it was like a punch in the gut. The smile was open and sincere and he felt a movement in his pants that almost had him back to his earlier thoughts of his room. She excused herself and went to the bathroom and he took the opportunity of ordering another bottle and pouring the last of the first into their glasses. Topping up his own from the new bottle, he sat back and waited. Waited for what he wasn't quite sure, but he was enjoying this evening, he hadn't been this relaxed in a long time.

Ethan was eyeing up Red, and the more he looked the more he liked her. He wanted to take this further, he wasn't sure how much further, but certainly to his room. After that, it would be up to her. Leaning across, he touched her hand and was pleased when she didn't pull back. "Look, this may sound forward, particularly after last night, but shall we take the bottle to my room? I'm not coming on to you...well, actually I am, but I would like to go somewhere a bit more private, where we can talk without other people listening."

***

Their talk had become more daring and teasing, and Jess

34

was long past the reserved and predictable stage. She liked this guy, she enjoyed talking to him and he knew quite a bit about the architecture of downtown. She knew the champagne had gone to her head, but she wasn't drunk, she felt happy and relaxed, and realised that she didn't want the evening to end. But his words had alarm bells ringing in her head. Well, not only ringing but deafening her, yet through all the noise she could still hear *'reserved and predictable'*, and she didn't want to be that any more. She wanted to be spontaneous, and to be with someone who wanted to be with her because of who she was. So she smiled and nodded her head and very quietly said, "Okay." She had surprised herself with the reply. What happened next was up to her. He picked up the bottle and the glasses, then followed her to the elevator. She pressed the button and they stood waiting. She could feel the tension in her shoulders and tried to ignore it. When the doors opened she stepped into the car and asked what floor.

"Nine," he replied, and watched as she pressed the button for that floor.

Swiftly up went the elevator and then came to a silent halt at the ninth floor. He stepped out and turned and waited for her. She was still inside the car and he put his arm up to stop the doors closing. "Red?"

She looked at him and knew he could see the desperation in her eyes. "Sorry, I can't." She shook her head as she spoke.

***

"It's okay," he replied, disappointment flooding through him. He'd expected a knock-back when he'd made the invitation, and her 'okay' had taken him by surprise. He'd risked a lot by asking the question, but it had paid off, or he'd thought it had. This was not how he had envisaged them ending the night. "If you change your mind, it's room 931," he said, then moved his arm, allowing the doors to close. He watched as it went upwards, and stopped at the tenth floor. Turning away, he walked along the corridor to his room. Juggling the glasses and bottle, he slid the card into the door and then pushed the door open with his foot. Putting the bottle in the fridge, he set the glasses down on the table between the beds. He'd hoped to occupy one of the king size beds with her, but now it looked as though he was on his own.

Jess was kicking herself all the short way to the tenth floor. She was half way along the corridor to her room when she realised she had done exactly what Tom said she did. Her reservations at the thought of doing something different, something completely outside her normal comfort zone, had made her flee from the one thing she'd been enthralled with all evening. She'd had a gorgeous guy to herself, and had the promise of perhaps a night with him, and what had she done? She'd run like a scared animal. Oh, she knew she'd been flirty with him, but he had been the same with her, and for some reason she trusted him. Okay, she was certain that the drink had made her lose some of her inhibitions, but she'd been having fun, and now she'd thrown it all away. She stopped and rested her head against the wall. She was an idiot, no wonder Tom had left her, she was too scared to try anything new. Now she'd blown it. Or had she? What room did he say? 931?

Chapter Four

Ethan rolled up the sleeves on his shirt, then poured himself another glass of the champagne. He was about to settle back on the bed when there was a knock on his door. Setting the glass down, he walked to the entrance and looked through the security spyhole. She'd changed her mind and he could see her standing nervously outside. Not wanting to give her a chance to change her mind again, he quickly opened the door and greeted her with a warm smile.

"Hi," she said hesitantly.

"Hi yourself, are you going to come in?" He stepped back as he spoke and waited while she walked past him. He caught the scent of her perfume. Soft, but just slightly musky, he thought as he closed the door and secured the deadlock.

"Sorry about earlier," she rushed the words out.

"Don't worry about it, you're here now," he said filling the other glass and handing it to her. As he did he ran his index finger down her cheek and smiled gently at her. He felt her tremble and took a step back. He didn't want to scare her away, he'd already figured out this was a big deal for her. And if he was honest, it was for him too, he wasn't in the habit of picking up women in hotels; this was totally out of character for him.

She walked across the room and sat on the small sofa. He didn't want to crowd her, so pulled one of the chairs round and sat in front but slightly to the side of her. She was fiddling nervously with her glass and then took a long drink. "You don't need to get drunk," he said. "We can sit and talk, watch television, whatever happens next is down to you. I have no intention of forcing anything on you that you don't want." The words were said softly and sincerely and she looked at him

37

and smiled.

"Do I really look that nervous?"

"Yes," was his simple reply.

"I've not done this before; you know, gone to someone's room with them."

"That makes two of us, except of course it's my room," he said in an attempt to lighten the atmosphere.

"Are you married?" The question was direct.

"No, I swear. I'm not. If I was I wouldn't be doing this."

She smiled, and this time it reached her eyes. He leaned forward and took hold of her free hand and lifted it to his lips. "Red, you don't have to be scared of me. I'm still the same guy you've spent the whole evening with, except now I'm hoping you may spend the night, or at least part of it, with me," he said closing his lips around her middle finger and gently stroking it with his tongue.

***

She trembled so much she almost spilled her drink, and took another long gulp. She couldn't believe she was doing this, but found that she was enjoying the tension, the atmosphere was becoming heavier by the minute. His tongue was doing things to her finger that were reaching down to her groin and she pulled her stomach in, in an attempt to quell the sensation.

His eyes were on her face and he moved smoothly from the chair onto the sofa alongside her. He moved his lips from her finger and retained his hold on her hand and moved forward and gently put his lips on hers. She hesitated, and then surrendered. He deepened the kiss, moving his lips over hers and running his tongue along her bottom lip. She leaned in to him and heard him curse the glasses they were holding. His lips left hers for a moment as he put his glass on the table at the side, and then hers. Turning back, he put a hand behind her head, then moved forward until her lips were but a fraction from his own.

"Are you okay with this, Red? Because if you're not, we

can stop right now."

Her answer was to close the distance between them and put her lips to his. He held her firmly, and then let her take charge of the kiss. She wondered just how far she dared to go. He parted his lips slightly and the tip of her tongue started to explore, and she slipped inside his mouth. Then he found her tongue with his own and circled and danced with it as she plunged deeper into his mouth, until she was hanging onto his shoulder and gasping.

Jessica was totally lost in the sensations raging through her. Nobody had kissed her like this, she felt as though her very soul was being plundered and drawn out of her body. She wasn't sure what she felt, but she could hardly get her breath. One thing she did know; she didn't want him to stop. As he pulled her further to his body, the dress rode up her thighs. Then his hand was on her leg, slowly stroking from her knee to the hem of her dress. When he reached the hem he moved back to her knee, but she didn't want him to do that. She wanted him to go higher, but he didn't, and it was driving her crazy. The whole situation was driving her crazy.

He was giving her so much pleasure, but she wanted to do something for him. She could do the tongue bit, but where did she go from there. What would he like? Should she touch him and, if so, where? For a moment she wavered, this was someone she had only just met. A feeling of inadequacy began to creep over her, but she fought it. Everything that was happening felt so right. He felt so right.

***

Ethan was taking things slowly. He'd seen the look in her eyes, it was the softness he'd been looking for. She was aroused and he didn't want to spoil this for either of them. When she'd slipped into his mouth the jerk in his pants had made him gasp. Caressing her thigh was driving him insane. Her skin was like velvet and the lack of tights meant there was nothing between him and his desire except, he presumed, a pair of briefs. The thought had him hardening by the second.

But this was not the time for him, this was for her and he had every intention of taking it slowly. Taking his lips from hers he moved to her neck and then down to her shoulder. The dress was a hindrance and he wondered if he could ease down the zip that he could feel under his fingers. Slowly he pulled the tab and the back of the dress opened up to him. He eased the material away from her shoulder and proceeded to kiss and nibble the exposed area.

Jessica was shaking in his arms. But then he felt her suddenly tense, as though uncertain. He stopped what he was doing, leaned back, and looked at her.

"What's wrong?"

"Nothing, it's just, I don't know what to do to please you."

The relief showed on his face and he smiled. "Just being here with you like this is pleasing me."

"But there must be something that you would like me to do?"

He couldn't quite believe her, she wanted to please him, was asking what she could do. "Don't worry, you can please me later, right now I want to concentrate on you, and making you feel good about what's happening."

Having said the words, he kissed her gently, easing his tongue inside her mouth and finding hers. His hands started their trail up and down her thigh until he became more adventurous and strayed above the hem. She gasped into his mouth when he did. Ethan knew that the dress, much as he loved it, had to go. Pulling the zip all the way down, he pulled her to her feet. She stood somewhat shakily and kicked off her shoes, then he slipped the dress off her shoulders and peeled it down her body, kissing her as he exposed her skin. When he reached the floor she stepped out of the dress and he carefully draped it over the back of the sofa. Taking her hand, he walked her towards the bed, wondering if this was going to be the moment she stopped him. Standing beside it, he took her head in his hands and looked directly at her. "Are you sure you want this, because we can stop now?"

"I'm sure. I'm sick of being predictable and reserved. I want to enjoy some spontaneity in my life."

The way she said it and the slight glint in her eyes told him that he was right, there was something wrong. Halting his thoughts, he stood back from her, but still held her face, preventing her from turning away.

"Who told you that you were predictable and reserved? And don't say nobody, because I can see it in your eyes. Someone has hurt you with those words."

***

Jessica hated that she'd said that to him. She wanted to forget Tom, and all she wanted was for Grey to carry through what they had started. Now she was scared he was going to stop. Tears began to sting the back of her eyes, but he'd asked her a question and she couldn't lie.

"My so-called fiancé, just after I'd found him screwing another woman in our bed." She said the words coldly, surprised that she didn't feel any hurt.

"Bloody hell," he exclaimed, dropping his hands to her shoulders. "No wonder you want this to happen. Look, Red, you need to do this because you want it, not because some idiot, who didn't know what a good thing he had, lashed out at you. I bet he told you it was your fault he strayed, that you weren't good enough in bed."

She nodded her head wondering how he knew. "How…?"

"Classical response when someone's caught out. Blame the innocent party. Look, you are stunning; you're gorgeous. You have a fantastic figure, your skin is like velvet and your hair is something off a TV commercial. Red, I very much want to continue what we are doing and make love to you, but if you want to stop, you only have to say the word."

The sigh of relief was audible. "I want to continue as well. I want this, not to prove anything, but I want you because you're hot and sexy and, if I'm honest, I like what you're doing, no one's turned me on like this before," she added, with a spark of the old Jessica showing through.

He threw back his head and laughed and then brought his lips down onto hers in a soft kiss. "You know, a woman is like

41

a good wine, she has to be at the right temperature to be enjoyed to the full," he murmured against her lips, before gently laughing and adding, "did I really just say that?"

As they laughed together, she suddenly became conscious of the fact that she was almost naked in front of him, the realisation made her catch her breath and she caught her bottom lip between her teeth. Only a pair of lacy briefs and bra protected her modesty, but there again, modesty was something she was planning on forgetting about, so she moved her hands forward.

Unbuttoning his shirt revealed strong muscular arms with a dark tan that covered the whole of his upper body. And her earlier thought that he worked outdoors was confirmed when he disposed of his pants, as the only part of his body which appeared not to be tanned was that covered by the briefs. Her eyes eagerly took in his body. He had a six-pack that she'd only seen on posters in the gym, and there wasn't a hint of fat on him anywhere. The shirt hung free and she moved her hand and touched his skin, he felt hot and smooth. Well, until she reached the mat of dark hair on his chest, and she curled her fingers through it. Testing her new resolve, she moved up his chest to his shoulders. All the while he stood watching her, not moving.

***

Her hands were causing havoc with Ethan's senses, and her body was even more perfect than he'd imagined. The light tan was all over, well, the parts he could see, and he couldn't wait to uncover the rest. He moved a hand from her shoulder, down her arm and then let his thumb brush lightly over her nipple, he felt and saw her jerk in response. Her eyes lifted to his and, as he held her gaze, he brushed slowly over the tip again. Lowering his lips to hers he whispered against her mouth, "Red, last chance to back out." He felt the shake of her head and looked up and saw what he knew was there beneath the cool reserve, clear to see in her eyes. It was passion. He moved his other hand and brushed the other nipple and then, holding her gaze, he gently kneaded her breasts. The nipples were hardening and he knew that when they were uncovered the breasts would fit perfectly into his hands. He heard the soft moan from her lips and her hands dropped limply to her sides. Leaving one breast for a moment he took hold of one of her hands and moved it down to his briefs and pressed it against his straining erection. "You wanted to know how to please me, this is it," he said, as he gently rubbed her hand over his hardness.

Moving his hand back he took possession of the waiting breast and continued in his exploration. They stood almost naked, with their bodies not touching, not yet. His hands moved slowly down until they rested on her hips. Moving her gently towards him he lowered one hand to her groin, keeping eye contact with her all the time. He needed to be sure she wanted this as much as he did. The look she gave him told him she did and he slid a single finger underneath the lace and found her clitoris.

***

A single touch from him there and she almost exploded. Jessica was beyond being in heaven, this was erotic and sensual. But mostly it was beautiful. His other hand moved to her back and she felt the fastening on her bra give way. It slid down her arms and she moved her hands from him for a moment and allowed it to drop onto the floor. Her breasts were exposed to him now but she kept her gaze fixed on his face, wondering how long it would be before he looked down. He surrendered long before she thought he would and she heard his sharp intake of breath, before his eyes came back to hers. She could see the desire in his face. She'd never had this effect on anyone before and it was overwhelming. Her body was quaking with tension and a need for him that she found irresistible, and frightening.

***

"You're beautiful," he said before moving his hand up to hold her breast. No suntan, this was soft and pink and he couldn't resist lowering his head and flicking his tongue around the tip. He was totally lost and so hard, all he wanted was to make love to her. Moving his finger, he slipped to the edge of the entrance he longed to be at, and gently tested her. She was moist but he wanted her soaking so that the whole journey they were about to take would be one of smoothness with no pain.

***

As soon as he touched her there she had an urge to press down and it was only sheer willpower that stopped her, but her head fell forward, coming to rest on his chest. She moved her hand, finding the opening in his briefs. Her breathing was becoming heavier as she slid her hand inside and felt the hot hardness of him. Taking hold of him she gently moved her hand upwards towards the tip. *He was so big, and so hot, and yet he felt like velvet, would she be able to take him, would she satisfy him?* The thoughts ran through her mind, but not for one moment did she consider calling a halt to what was happening. She wanted this, wanted him more than anything she'd wanted before.

***

When her fingers touched him and held him he felt his size increase. Her hand on him was heaven and hell at the same time. His finger had remained at her entrance and now following her boldness he pushed gently inside. Her head raised as a moan escaped her lips and her eyes met his. He moved his lips from her breast to her mouth and gently parted her lips and sought her tongue with his own. His lips kissed hers as his finger moved further inside and then he felt her press down on him, telling him that he was pushing her too far. He didn't want to have her like this, he wanted this to happen in bed, slowly, seductively and with gentleness. This wasn't a

44

quick fix, he wanted this to last all night, and perhaps what was happening would solve his own dilemma. At this point all he could think of was her. He was consumed by her. Withdrawing his finger, he lifted his head and tilted her chin with his hand and kissed the end of her nose. "Come," he said softly and took her hand and pulled her onto the bed.

She didn't resist, she couldn't have done so even if she'd wanted to, and she didn't. She wanted this as much as he did and she slipped under the covers and into his waiting arms. "Grey," just one word was all she could say as his hands moved over her body.

He removed her last item of clothing and then his own before proceeding to kiss every part of her body, moving down until his mouth closed over that part of her he so desperately needed to be inside. He teased her, stroking her with his tongue until she was arching up underneath his lips, her need for him coming in small sobs from her lips. Then he protected them both, rolling the rubber on quickly, before covering her body with his and slowly and gently he entered her and made love to her in a way he'd never made love to anyone before. He said words to her that he never thought he would say to a woman. Words that came from somewhere he didn't know existed. He'd known her for only a short time, yet she seemed to have a hold on him that no one else ever had. He felt at one with her, as though he'd finally found the missing piece in a puzzle. The piece that made him whole.

***

Jessica was beyond all coherent thought. What was happening was beyond wonderful. She was transported to another world, a world where only the two of them existed. The climax, when it hit her, was like a hurricane and she cried out and clung to him, her fingers digging into his back, then she felt the convulsions that shook his body as he reached his own fulfilment.

***

They lay in the large bed with their arms wrapped around each other. Ethan felt as though he had known her all his life. Jess's head was resting on his chest and he ran his hands absently up and down her spine. Rather than bring some resolution to his own dilemma, this had in fact complicated it. He could hear her gentle breathing which suggested she was asleep, but he didn't want to waste this time so increased the pressure of his hand and let it stray down to her delightful bottom. It wasn't long before he got the attention he wanted as she opened her eyes and smiled up at him.

***

She knew he wanted her again as soon as she looked at him, and if she was honest, she wanted the same thing. Convention and everything else she had stood by was gone, she wanted this man and she was going to have him. Moving her hand, she found the hardened length of him and started to gently rub up and down. Staying her hand, he pulled out protection and slipped this on, then he let her have her way.

Becoming more daring she moved, throwing a leg across his own. When he was hard she took what she wanted and rolled onto his body and sat upright. Keeping her eyes on his face, she lifted and then lowered herself, encasing him as she did. His eyes blazed into hers and she felt the power of him as he pushed upwards. Predictable, reserved Jess was gone and she took her one-night lover and herself into another realm, before collapsing on his chest feeling the saltiness of his skin under her mouth.

She woke suddenly, and it took a few minutes to remember where she was. He was still asleep, his body turned away from her. She looked at the tanned back, and longed to run her hand down it. Slide it around to the front and seek the one thing that she had spent the night dreaming of. One arm was beneath the pillow and the other thrown carelessly to the side. Propping herself up, she looked at the sleeping face and felt an urge to kiss him. But she couldn't, she daren't. Predictable Jessica was returning. She was in bed with a stranger, a stranger called

Grey, and had just had a one-night stand, a night of explosive and mind-blowing sex. But it was more than sex, they had made love and she'd never had that connection, that feeling with anyone else.

Now she didn't know how to deal with the morning after. What was she meant to say? She was embarrassed now, thinking of what she'd done, but she didn't regret it, not one moment of it. She needed to leave before he woke. Slipping carefully out of bed, she collected her undies and put them on. Then stepped into her dress and fastened the zip. Locating her purse, she stopped only to write a short note. *Thank you for a most amazing night. Red x.* She hesitated before putting the 'x' but since they'd done a lot more than kiss last night, she decided that it wasn't out of place. Putting the note on the pillow she then crept quietly out of the room and, using the stairs, went up to the tenth floor.

Chapter Five

Ethan stretched as he started to wake, then remembered and put out his hand to feel for her, but the other side of the bed was cold and empty. He sat up quickly, looking around the room and then called out, thinking she might be in the bathroom. All that met him was silence. Flopping back down, he turned to the side of the bed she'd been in, and that was when he saw the piece of paper. He knew what it would say before he picked it up, *thanks but no thanks,* but he was pleasantly surprised when he read her words. So she'd enjoyed last night as much as he had. Well, that was something, but it didn't get rid of his disappointment that she'd gone. Not only gone, but he didn't know who she really was or how to find her again.

He was using this trip to try and sort out his feelings for Helena and where he really wanted their relationship to go, but Red had now complicated matters. He'd not intended picking anyone up but as soon as he saw her he'd been drawn to her. The episode in the bar and then last night in the restaurant had played into his hands. He'd never thought she would come back after she left him in the elevator, but she did, and what had happened next had now thrown his mind into chaos. What he'd experienced with Red was something he'd never known before.

He wondered if she was still in her room, but then again, he didn't know the number. He thought she was on the tenth floor, which was where the elevator had stopped, but that could have been someone getting in, not Red getting out. He groaned and couldn't believe he'd missed the opportunity to find out her room number. Then groaned even louder when he saw the time and realised that he needed to check out within the next hour if he was going to get to the airport on time. His flight to Edmonton wouldn't wait and he couldn't miss it. He had an appointment with a prospective buyer in the morning and then he was flying to the States for a three-week trip buying new stock. He hated this part of the job, but it was a necessity if he wanted to keep the business thriving the way it was.

In reception, he looked around to see if he could see her as he waited to check out. As luck would have it, when he reached the desk the young man on duty was the same one from the bar the night before. He made small talk with him as he waited for his bill, and then asked the question that was burning on his lips.

"Do you remember me from last night in the bar?"

"I certainly do, sir. You were drinking champagne with the young lady when I came on duty."

"Yes, we were, and excellent champagne it was as well. The young lady and I spent some time together last night but I forgot to ask for her phone number. I was wondering if you had a note of it on her registration details."

"I'm sorry, sir, we're not allowed to give out any personal information about guests."

"I appreciate that, but it's really important that I have some way of contacting her. I suppose a name and address are out of the question?" He knew the answer before he asked.

The young man looked sympathetically at him. "Sorry, sir. Company policy."

"Not half as sorry as I am. I think I've just lost the woman of my dreams."

The young man thought he was joking, until he saw the serious look on Ethan's face. They had made a striking couple last night, he could remember thinking that at the time. Looking across the desk he suddenly felt sorry for him. He knew he couldn't give her name or address, but perhaps he could give him something.

Ethan glanced around the area while he waited for the paperwork. Part of him wanted to stay and try and find her, but the businessman inside him knew he couldn't.

"There you are, sir. If you could just check the total."

The voice brought him back to the present. "Thank you," he said glancing at the paperwork. And then his eyes lighted on the piece of paper stapled to the top, on which was written car details and registration. He glanced up and saw a slight smile on the young man's face. He put the papers in his wallet and then held out his hand. "Thank you, thank you very much."

The young man shook his hand and the hundred-dollar bill slipped unseen from one hand to the other.

In room 1014, Jessica was looking out of the window, a coffee in her hand, reliving the events of the night before. She'd never picked anyone up, or been picked up before, especially in a hotel, and then gone back to the guy's room. She should have been feeling ashamed, but she didn't. In fact, she felt quite wonderful. What had happened last night had felt right. It was as if it had been meant to be. She'd felt disgusted since the encounter with Eric, and the Tom episode had left her doubting her femininity. Last night had given that back to her, and more. She would be ever grateful to Grey for what had happened between them. Just thinking of the way they'd made love made her blush. She'd never been that forward with anyone before. Perhaps Tom had been right in saying she was conservative. Well, not any more. She'd had a taste of what it was like to be with a man, a proper man, and to be made love to. She knew it was a one night only, she didn't expect that she was his usual type, but she envied the woman who was. To have someone like that waiting for you would be every woman's dream. Sadly that woman wouldn't be her. But she wouldn't settle for second best, not after him, and one day she would find someone like Grey, who would want her for herself. Someone she would feel the same connection with that she'd felt with him.

She didn't want to bump into him again for fearing of spoiling the illusion of last night, so remained in her room for most of the morning, ordering room service for breakfast. She remembered him saying at some point during the evening that he had an early start as he had a flight to catch.

Taking a leisurely shower, she ran the sponge over her body and, closing her eyes, could almost feel his hands on her. She took a deep breath and quickly rinsed off and then towelled herself dry, trying not to remember anything else from the night before. Applying body lotion was difficult as every glide of her hand over her skin reminded her of his hands, hands that had been gentle as they'd caressed her, but they were working hands, not the soft hands of an office worker, and that made her wonder about his occupation. The clothes he wore were expensive, as was the champagne they'd shared, but the hands belonged to someone who worked and the body told her that work was outdoors. The only part of his body that wasn't suntanned, was that covered by his briefs. Thinking of his body was not what she'd intended, so she concentrated on what she was doing and tried to put thoughts of him out of her head.

***

Sitting in business class, Ethan had time during the short flight to try and sort out his thoughts. He was kicking himself for not thinking to leave a note at the hotel for her. Why hadn't he thought of that? He couldn't understand why. He was usually on top of his game but this morning his brain didn't seem to be working. Perhaps it was because of what happened last night. One night with Red and he couldn't think clearly. He needed to find her. If only he'd left a note the guy on reception would have given it to her. He groaned at the thought of it. Thank goodness he had her registration number, he could trace her that way once he got back home. He was sure the sheriff would be happy to help, as long as he worked out a plausible reason, like having bumped her car or something like that. The thought satisfied him for now, but he had other things more pressing to worry about. *Helena.*

He and Helena had been together for a couple of years, although not all the time. She lived in Calgary and was often away for weeks on end on modelling contracts, which was where she was now, and why he'd booked into a hotel for a couple of nights rather than stay at her place. He'd wanted to be on neutral ground to work out what to do. Helena wanted to move their relationship onto the next level and move in together, but not before she'd got a ring on her finger, and she'd made it quite clear, by her subtle comments, that the ring she wanted was a wedding band. And that was the stumbling block for him.

He'd enjoyed their relationship in the beginning, but then, who wouldn't enjoy having a tall leggy blonde, with straw-coloured hair that fell down her back to her waist, hanging on your arm, or in your bed? But he didn't think he'd want that for the rest of his life. Did he love her? He'd asked himself that question over and over again. He cared for her and enjoyed being with her, well, most of the time. But there were things she did that didn't appeal to him, and there was a feeling in his gut that told him the relationship wasn't right, something was missing. A connection with her, that special something that made you feel as though you were the other half of that person.

His mother had always said he would know when he met the right person; he would feel it in his soul, and he knew that he didn't feel that with Helena, or anyone else for that matter. Or at least he hadn't until last night, when he'd felt a connection with Red, someone he'd met in a hotel and who could be anyone, even an up-market hooker. He laughed inwardly to himself at the thought of Red being a hooker. One thing he was certain of was that she was not that. Now, having thought of her, his mind went back to last night, holding her in his arms and making love to her, and that was not where his mind needed to be to sort out his present dilemma.

Looking out of the window he saw the ground far below, brown earth and small areas of water dotted here and there. It made him long to be home and not about to leave it for several weeks. Accepting a coffee from the attendant, he turned to when he had first met Helena. Perhaps thinking over the whole relationship would put it in perspective.

He'd been in Calgary at a charity function for injured rodeo riders, and part of that had been a catwalk fashion show.

He'd watched with amused interest at the leering from the elderly gentlemen in the room, and he used that description lightly as far as some of them were concerned. Then Helena had come out, and his disinterest suddenly turned to interest. She was stunning, with legs that seemed to go on forever. He'd barely registered the dress she was wearing, but the hair was like the legs, long and sleek. It was scooped back and fastened in a loose plait that hung down her back. He could remember it clearly, since this was a trademark style for her.

He'd shifted and moved forward and for a moment his eyes had met hers. His first thought had been that the eyes looked cold, but then she smiled and her features softened, and he hadn't been able to stop smiling back at her, before she turned and walked away back along the catwalk. He'd almost put the encounter out of his head, when she'd approached him some time later as he was standing near the bar. He'd bought her a drink and then one of them, he couldn't remember which, had suggested dinner.

He'd been due to travel home the following day, but he'd stayed over another night. They had dinner at her apartment, and he'd not made it to his hotel that night. Thinking back now, he wasn't sure who had seduced whom, but sleeping with her had not been on his agenda when he'd gone for dinner. She was the one who had made the suggestion that it was too late for him to leave and had later produced the condoms they'd used, and he was too much of a gentleman to turn down the lady's offer. The sex had been good, and the body was definitely better unclothed. That had been the start of their relationship.

When she was in Calgary, he would head in for the weekend when work permitted, and most of the time would be spent in bed. He couldn't deny that the sex was good and that she knew exactly how to turn him on, but then again displaying her body was her job, although on the catwalk she was clothed. In her apartment, she wasn't, and took great delight in wandering round naked and dragging him back to bed whenever she could. He'd never felt comfortable with this and there were days when he would almost feel used, and would get annoyed with himself for succumbing to her obvious charms so easily. If he wanted to go out for the day and have dinner out at night, she would complain that she was tired and just wanted to spend time together alone.

Now that he was analysing their relationship, he realised that they had very little in common, apart from the sex. He'd been happy to keep the relationship on its present level but now she wanted more. She'd been to his home a few times but always found fault with the oldness of it. She was ultra-modern, whereas he was old charm and warmth, and what did that say about their relationship? Now, Red. He could see Red in his home and was sure that she wouldn't dislike anything about it, well, not a great deal. Okay, perhaps the kitchen and the bathrooms could do with updating, but that was all. He could just picture Red in his bathroom, her dark hair wet from the shower, walking out towards him, a towel wrapped tightly under her arms. He closed his eyes and he could clearly see her and his fingers itched to pull the towel away.

"Can I get you another coffee, sir?"

The voice startled him and his eyes opened. Smiling, he declined and handed the now-empty cup back to her. *Now where was I?* he thought, and then groaned when he realised that his thoughts had again drifted to his one-night stand. Trying to concentrate on Helena, he felt guilty that he was thinking of someone else, but oddly enough he didn't feel guilty that he'd slept with someone else, and that didn't make sense. Or did it? Securing his tray, he gave up on trying to sort out his head as the pilot announced that they were approaching Edmonton.

Back in the hotel, Jessica had just returned from a leisurely walk downtown and decided to have an early dinner since the restaurant was fairly empty. Requesting a small booth, she was pleased to be shown to one without question. Sitting eating a solitary dinner she couldn't help but remember last night's meal, the one she'd shared with Grey. She was so grateful to him for restoring her faith in herself, but she was even more grateful to him for sharing his body with her. Just thinking of his body made it difficult to swallow and she took a gulp of water to cool her errant thoughts.

She'd only been back in her room a few minutes when her phone rang. Looking at the number she saw it was Gemma. "Hi, cousin, what's up?" Listening to Gemma telling her that she and Eric were going to get engaged made her stomach curl, knowing what she did about him. How could she let her cousin marry the creep? Answering her cousin's question as to when she was returning, she told her the following day and that she would be back mid-afternoon. Ending the call, she sat on the bed. How the hell was she going to get her cousin to see what Eric was really like? The question was still plaguing her when she climbed into bed sometime later.

Arriving back at Gemma's just before four in the afternoon, she was pleased her cousin was at home on her own. After dumping her things in her room she went back through to the lounge, and accepted the glass of wine that was held out to her. Chatting to Gemma, she told her about her weekend with her supposed friends, but not about Grey, he was her secret. Eventually, she broached the question of the forthcoming engagement.

"Are you sure you want to get engaged, Gem? After all you've not know each other very long and look what happened with Tom and me. How quickly it all fell apart? I'd hate for you to be hurt." She'd told her cousin the truth about the breakup and only hoped that this reference to it might make her stop and think.

"Oh no, Jess, Eric is so wonderful, he would never cheat on me. That part of our relationship is amazing and that's how I know he wouldn't cheat, because of the way we are together, and what we do."

Oh God, thought Jess. *I know exactly what you do, I can hear it. Trouble is you don't know what he's like and that he'll take it where he can get it.* Jess knew she couldn't say these things to her cousin, if she did there would be a bust-up and he would probably carry out his threat and say she'd been leading him on, and the last thing she wanted was to fall out with Gem. She had a feeling Gem would need her before too long, as Eric was sure to slip up with someone else. All she could do was smile and tell her that she hoped it would all work out for them.

Going back to her room, she logged on and found, to her great relief, that she had a reply to the job application in Longville. The lawyer wanted her to attend for an interview on Wednesday and gave directions and a time of noon. Replying that she would be there, she was thankful that her stay in Calgary might be coming to an end. Having to congratulate Eric on his pending engagement was almost too much, particularly when he leaned in for a 'family kiss' as he described it. She turned her face so it landed on her cheek, but his whispered, *"there's always room for you in my bed as well,"* made her flesh crawl. Wednesday couldn't come soon enough.

The journey to Longville took just over an hour and she was pleasantly surprised by the town. It was larger than she thought it would be, and she could see several 'To Let' signs as she drove through. Following the directions she'd been given, she was soon pulling up outside a modern-looking single storey building with a sign stating *Francis Slade, Attorney at Law*. Climbing out of the car and locking the doors, she took a deep breath and walked into the building. There was a young girl sitting at an ancient-looking desk on which sat a computer and telephone, together with several other items of totally non-legal appearance. Jessica bit back a smile at the thought of what her old firm would have said to have seen a display like this. Desks were always meant to look professional and tidy.

"Can I help you?" came the enquiry.

"Yes, I have an appointment with Mr. Slade, my name is Jessica Cameron." She waited while the information was digested, and then the phone was picked up and her name was relayed to the person on the other end.

"You can go through. It's over there," said the girl, pointing to a door to the rear of the room. "It's the room on the right, at the end."

Going through, Jessica found herself in a corridor. Walking

along, she passed a door marked *bathroom* and then another unmarked door before coming to the end door with a sign saying *Francis Slade*. Knocking, she pushed the door open at a shout of, "come in," and found herself in a surprisingly light airy room, after the dimness of the corridor, before realising that this came from the glass panels set in the roof.

The interview was short and to the point. He asked her general questions about the law, which she could answer almost without thinking, but then again he didn't know she had a law degree and was probably as well qualified as he was. He asked her about her computing skills and about the other requirements for a personal assistant. She answered them all calmly and clearly without faltering, and he seemed impressed. Then he asked about her previous employer and why she had left. She told him personal reasons, but she had a reference and she produced a copy for him.

She knew he would check it out. She'd already phoned one of her former colleagues and told him that she was taking some time out and was going to do some PA work for a while, but didn't want any prospective employers to know she was qualified. So she had asked him to do the general reference for her and he'd agreed to keep quiet about her law degree when anyone phoned to check. Giving his details to Francis Slade, she was surprised when he asked her to wait while he phoned. Sitting in the waiting room she listened to the young girl chatting on her mobile, presumably to one of her friends. It wasn't long before Francis Slade came through and took her back to his office.

"Well, your references check out. I can't offer a big salary, I'm only a one-man practice, but I need someone who has some knowledge of the law to help me run the place. Young Annie out front is leaving to go to the city, so one of the jobs will be to answer the phone and see to clients when they come in. After that, it will be helping me while we work out what you can and can't do, or at least what I can trust you to do. I need someone quickly and can't be messing about interviewing people day after day. So if you want it, the job's yours. But don't think it will be easy. I may be a one-man

57

show, but I'm busy and out of the office a lot."

Jessica looked at this thirty-something guy, who was clearly showing no interest in her apart from being a replacement for his soon-to-be departing Annie. He wasn't bad looking. His hair was a mousy brown colour, a bit overlong, and the suit was expensive-looking. His face was slightly long with an angular jaw and straight nose. She wasn't sure whether she liked him or not, but she was only going to work for him, and she could probably do the job with one hand tied behind her back.

"Yes, I'm happy to take it. What about salary?" She waited as he went on about costs of running the office, and so on, before he mentioned a figure that was a third of what she'd earned when she first started at her last firm, but then of course she'd been employed as an attorney. This was a real comedown, but then she wouldn't be spending the sort of money that she had in the city, and the rent for a place here would be a lot cheaper.

"I'll need to find a place to rent. What are the rental prices in town?" He gave her a figure that she quickly calculated was well within her means, even on the reduced salary.

"I have a couple of places to rent on my books. So if you want to have a look at them, ask Annie for the keys and go and have a look round now."

"I'll do that," said Jessica getting to her feet. "When do you want me to start?"

"Monday, if you could."

"That's no problem, as long as I have somewhere to live. So I'll go and have a look at the properties now and then come back later, if that's okay?"

Standing in the centre of the lounge of the first property a short time later, Jessica looked around. The small recess near the windows with the window seat was cute, and she could see herself sitting there looking out. There was enough room at the other end for a small table and a couple of chairs. But there was the problem, this property was unfurnished. She would have to buy everything. Common sense told her she didn't want to do that, as she wasn't sure how long she would stay in this job. If she moved on she would have to sell it all, or take it with her and who was to say it would fit into a new place? This house was fine, but she really needed a furnished place. Reluctantly she locked the door and climbed into her car, and drove the short distance to the next house.

Now this looked more promising. It was a cottage, rather than a house, and was clearly older, but in good condition. Unlocking the front door, she went into a small porch area for coats, then through into a small lounge. There was a window at the front and at the far end was an arched opening leading to a kitchen diner. Coming back into the lounge she noticed a door on the right that she'd missed as she walked through. Opening this, she found herself in a small room, which could either be a single bedroom or a study, and going up from this room was a flight of stairs that opened out into a very large modern-looking bedroom. This had clearly been recently decorated and there was a small boxed seat in front of the window that gave a view out across the fields to the rear of the property. There were windows at both ends of the room, the front window simply looking down onto the small garden.

More importantly, this cottage was partly furnished. Well it had the important things, like a sofa and a large armchair. The bedroom had a small wardrobe, dressing table and chest of drawers, but no bed. Well, that was okay because she would prefer to buy a new bed. All the rooms had drapes and the kitchen had a small dining table and a couple of chairs. The white goods were in the kitchen, and although not large they were adequate for her needs. Someone had been through the property with a paintbrush and a tin of white paint and it looked clean and cute, and she liked it. She could live here and, although it was almost on the edge of town, it wasn't too far to walk to the office if she wanted to. Locking the door, she went back to the office and went through the paperwork regarding the rental agreement. That done, she paid a check for the first month's rent, plus a bond. Now all she had to do was to order a bed and sort out bed linen, get some cutlery and so on, and move in.

Before leaving the town, she found a small store that could

order furniture from a catalogue. Looking through the selection, she chose a simple double bed with a pine headboard and a part-sprung, part-memory foam mattress. Waiting while the salesperson checked with the supplier, she was relieved when she found out that it was all in stock and they could deliver on Saturday afternoon as she'd wanted. While there, she also ordered a small oval oak coffee table, and a bookcase. Driving back to Gemma's she called into the shopping mall and went into Sears to buy the bedding, towels and cutlery she would need. The more she shopped, the more excited she became about her move. She was going to create her own little home, just for her, how she wanted it, and with no interference from anyone else.

Arriving back at Gemma's just before six, she unlocked the door and dumped some of her packages in the hallway, and then went back to her car for the rest. Closing the door behind her, she carried the packages in her arms through to her room, and then went back for those she'd left on the floor. She'd just changed into a pair of jogging trousers and a long-sleeved top when she heard the front door close. Thinking it was Gemma, she hurried out, only to come face-to-face with Eric in the lounge. He smiled, or rather leered, when he saw her.

"So, back from the big interview?"

"Yes," she replied not wanting to get into any conversation with him.

"So did you get the job, or are you going to be with us a bit longer?" he smiled as he spoke.

Jessica shuddered at the look on his face. "I got the job. Moving out on Saturday. Where's Gem?" she asked changing the topic.

"Pulled a double shift, won't be back until the morning. You and me can get cosy tonight," he said dropping his jacket on the chair.

"In your dreams," she threw back at him quickly, and turned to go into the kitchen.

"Joke, Jessie, I'm an engaged man now."

She ignored him and opened the fridge and looked through to see what was in. Deciding that she didn't want to cook, she picked up the phone and was about to order a pizza when Eric came through and ask her to order one for him as well. Not feeling able to refuse the request, she placed the order and then took herself off to her room until the delivery arrived.

She'd just finished putting some of her things in her suitcase when there was a knock on her door. "What?" she called out.

"Pizza's here."

Going into the kitchen a few minutes later, she found the table set for two and a bottle of wine in the centre. "It's okay, Jessica. I figured we could at least share a civilised meal."

She was sceptical, but there was nothing in his face that suggested anything other than he'd just said. He turned away and put the pizzas on the waiting plates, and handed hers to her. Sitting down, he didn't look up, as she stood there undecided as to what to do. Okay, she could storm back to her room and eat there, but this guy was going to marry her cousin and he was going to be in her life, whether she wanted him there or not. The alternative was to cut all ties with Gem and she had no wish to do that. Anyway, she had a feeling that Gemma would need her one day. Sitting down, she started to eat and accepted the glass of wine he poured for her. He kept a steady flow of chatter, just about his day and asking about the interview, and she gradually began to relax. Perhaps what had happened previously was him just trying it on, and now he was engaged realised his mistake.

They finished eating and she rinsed the glasses and put them on the drainer, and stacked the dishes in the dishwasher. She went through to the lounge, but he was there lounging in one of the chairs, so she made to go to her room.

"No need to go, Jessica. I'm going to turn in as soon as I've seen the end of this programme."

She hesitated, she didn't really want to be in the same room with him, but it was almost eight-thirty. She wouldn't mind catching up on the news and there was a detective programme she had wanted to watch. She sat down on the sofa and picked up a magazine, and read until he called goodnight and left. Heaving a sigh of relief, she picked up the remote and changed channels. Tucking her feet up she started to watch her programme, but she could feel her eyes getting heavier. She should really go to her room but she was just so comfortable. That was the last coherent thought she had until she was suddenly awoken by her arms being yanked up, as her top was pulled up over her face and the next thing she knew, her bra was undone, and cold air rushed onto her naked breasts.

"Jeez," was the only word she heard, before teeth sank into her breast and she yelled at the pain. Her mind was working fast now. She may have been asleep a few seconds ago but she was wide-awake now, and knew exactly who this was. *The evil deceiving bastard,* was all she could think. She started to struggle, he was on top of her and trying to get her joggers down, which meant he was holding her with one hand. She could feel his skin against hers, which told her he was naked, and then she felt his hard erection on her now bared stomach. If she didn't do something soon he was going to rape her. Oh, he would say she wanted it, but like hell she did.

She thought of Grey, why she didn't know, but she wasn't going to have anyone ruin the memory of what they'd shared. Where she got the strength from she wasn't sure, but she managed to bring her knee up and hit him hard in the balls. In his present state, he couldn't help but feel the immediate pain. He released his hold on her for a split second and that was all she needed. She got her hands free and struck him about the head, and her knee delivered another blow to his now deflating ego. He rolled off the sofa and onto the floor, holding himself between his legs. Jessica was free and she wasn't hanging around, pulling her top down she yanked her joggers up and ran for her room. Once inside she locked the door and put a chair underneath the handle.

Going into the bathroom she peeled off her joggers and briefs with shaking hands, pulled the top over her head and allowed the loose bra to fall at her feet, then stood under the shower and cried. How could she have been so bloody stupid? She thought, as the tears ran down her face. She wished there was someone there to hold her. She wished Grey were there. Why she kept thinking of him, she wasn't sure, but she longed to feel his arms around her, holding her close and telling her everything would be okay.

Sometime later, when she'd managed to pull herself together, she packed the rest of her things. There was no way she was staying here until Saturday. She would check into a hotel for the next three nights and then go straight to Longville on Saturday morning, pick up the keys, and be waiting when the furniture arrived.

She stayed in her room with the door locked until Gemma knocked the following morning. Moving the chair and unlocking the door she pinned a smile on her face as she greeted her cousin. She was surprised, Gemma was in her nightdress, and commented that she must be tired. "Yes I am, but I'd hardly got in the door before Eric was wanting… well, you know what, and it was easier to pull this on than get dressed again."

Jessica felt sick at the thought of the way he used her cousin's body for his own pleasure, and knew he would use her own if he could. "Don't you get tired of doing it all the time? Particularly when you're just off a double shift." She ventured to ask the question and waited for the reply.

"Yeah, sometimes, but he knows which buttons to push, what to do, where to touch, and before I know what's happening, it's happening."

"So where is he now?"

"Just gone off to work. He says you're leaving on Saturday and that you got the job?"

"Yes, I did but I'm actually leaving today. There's quite a bit to sort out with the property I'm renting. I'm sorry to be leaving so quickly, but I really do appreciate you putting up with me these last few months. You have no idea how grateful I am." She longed to tell her to break with Eric, but knew this was the wrong time. She was going to have to let her find out what he was like for herself, and only hoped that the wedding wasn't going to happen quickly.

"Don't let him get you pregnant, Gemma," she wasn't sure where the words came from but the shocked look on her cousin's face told her that she'd probably said too much.

"Sorry, that came out wrong. What I meant was, don't start a family too soon, enjoy being together and getting to know each other first." She watched her cousin's face and hoped that the hastily-added comment would smooth things over. It did, as Gemma's face broke into a smile.

"Don't worry, Jess, Eric's in no rush for kids and while I love them, I'd like to wait a while. After all, I work with them every day in my job on the children's ward," she said. "Look," said Jessica, "Let me cook us brunch before you get off to bed. That way we can have a really good catch-up, before I leave."

Chapter Six

Jessica had been working for Frank, as he liked to be called, for over two weeks now and was beginning to get the hang of the way he did things. Not that she was happy with all that he did. Coming in a few days ago with a Will that should have been witnessed as it was signed, and asking her and Annie to do it afterwards, had caused her considerable concern. She'd raised those concerns but he'd just waved them away.

"George is always changing his Will and there's never anyone around to witness the damn things, so it's usually done back here. Isn't that right, Annie?"

Annie, who was in her last week before leaving, had readily backed up his statement. Without getting into a detailed legal argument and quoting rules and regulations, which she shouldn't have a great deal of knowledge about, there was little Jessica could do. She just hoped it was a one-off, but she did make a note of the client's name and details of the signing in her own notebook, just in case there were any problems at a later date.

She was now settled into the cottage. She'd taken a six month let, with an option for a further six months, and she was happy. She'd been sorry to leave Gemma, but there was no way she could have stayed at her place any longer. She'd spent a few nights in a hotel, thinking a lot about Grey, and getting back the confidence she'd gained from their time together. Despite her concerns about the way Frank worked, she was quite enjoying the job. Finishing work at five and having the evening to herself, instead of working late and then taking files home to work on as well, was a refreshing change but it often left her with spare time, particularly on a weekend. She'd tidied up the small garden and had planted a few flowers to brighten the border. Being outside had given her a chance to meet her neighbours, an elderly couple who kept pretty much to themselves, but they did make conversation with her when they saw her.

With another weekend approaching, she decided to investigate the local livery stable that she'd spotted advertised in the local hardware store window. It was years since she'd ridden, but this was the ideal place to start up again. Rising early on Saturday morning, she made her way to the stables and introduced herself to the middle-aged man who appeared to be in charge. Explaining her riding ability, she waited while he brought out a bay gelding.

"This one will do you fine. Rory, he's called and he's steady and gentle. He'll take you where you want to go and back, without a problem."

Watching as he saddled up the horse, she stood at its head talking softly to him. Having been given instructions as to the best places to ride, away from any traffic, she set off at walking pace, which soon changed into a gentle trot. Two hours later, she was back at the stables wondering why she had ever given up riding. She'd had the most amazing time, and booked Rory for the following morning as well.

Monday seemed to come round quickly and, apart from a bit of stiffness, she had to concede that she'd had the best weekend in a long time. The week seemed to pass quickly, and now that Annie had gone she was busier, answering the phone as well as dealing with the paperwork Frank passed over to her. He had quickly realised her competency and was loading more and more onto her. Not that she was worried, she was more than capable of dealing with it. He left to her to compile general letters to clients, and simply read them through before signing. She'd told him she used to compile letters in her previous position, which was true except she would dictate them and her assistant would type them. Once he knew she could do that, he was more than happy to pass the job over to her.

By Thursday, she was looking forward to the weekend. She glanced at the clock. It was just after two, and Frank wasn't long back from lunch. She'd eaten at her desk, as she wanted to finish off the work on one of the files she had. She was busy looking for an account she needed to do with the file, when Frank came through wanting a file from one of the cabinets. Asking him if he'd seen the account she needed, he told her it was probably in the tray on his desk, or if not, it would be in the pile of papers at the front of his desk.

Leaving him looking through the cabinet for the file, she went through to his office. It wasn't in the tray, so it must be in the papers stacked on his desk. Sighing, she started to go through them one by one. She was so engrossed in what she was doing, she only faintly registered footsteps coming along the passage, and stopping. What she did register was that no one had actually come into the room. Then a voice she'd thought she would never hear again spoke.

***

Ethan hated having to deal with his cousin, Frank, over anything to do with the ranch, but there was no way of avoiding it, thanks to his kind-hearted but misguided mother. Coming into the office he'd found Frank in the reception area, and was told none too politely to go through, and that he'd be there in a moment. Now, standing in the doorway to Frank's office, he was looking at the very person who'd been disturbing his sleep for the last few weeks. Well, he wasn't actually looking at her face, but he could see her rear view and he knew without a doubt that it was Red. Resting against the doorframe, he looked her up and down. The tailored suit, with the skirt that stopped at the knee, the shapely legs that went down to a pair of heels, not killer heels like she'd worn with the red dress, but still high enough. He couldn't stop the smile that curved his lips. Nor could he miss the recognition twitching in his jeans.

"Well, of all the towns in all the provinces, you walk into mine." He couldn't help the movie reference, and waited for her reaction.

***

Jessica straightened up and slowly turned. Even before she was face to face with him, she could feel her cheeks flaming. When she finally looked over at him, she bit down the gasp that sprang to her lips. He was lounging against the doorframe dressed in a pair of faded jeans, a denim shirt with the sleeves rolled up, and his thumbs were hooked into a broad leather belt. The stetson was pushed back and the look on his face was one of pure pleasure. He was exuding testosterone and she could feel it across the space between them. Every part of her body was aware of him and she had an urge to pull her jacket closed, but then that would make no sense since he'd seen her in fewer clothes than she had on now. In truth, he'd seen her naked, had made love to her. *God, he's been inside me, loved me and we did all that stuff together.* She was stunned, speechless.

"Cat got your tongue, Red?" his mouth twitched before breaking into a smile.

Jessica could only shake her head. "What are you doing here?"

"What, here in this office, or here in this town?"

"Both."

"Well, I live in this town, or rather just outside, and as to being here, Frank is my cousin and I'm here to see him on business."

She didn't have time to reply as Frank could be heard coming along the passage and, as soon as he entered the room, he looked from one to the other. "Oh, sorry, I forgot you were in here. Jessica, this is my cousin, Ethan Slade. Ethan, my assistant, Jessica Cameron."

"Pleased to meet you, Jessica Cameron," he said drawing out her name and holding out his hand, leaving her no option but to shake it.

"Mr Slade," she replied, still shell-shocked.

"Oh, call me Ethan, everyone does. Unless you want to call me something else?"

Jessica felt her face go red and quickly mumbled, "Ethan

will do fine."

Frank looked from one to the other, before asking Jessica if she'd found what she was looking for. Shaking her head, she said no but she'd come back later. Telling her to wait, he quickly went through the papers and found the account she needed. Standing in front of Frank's desk, she was aware of Ethan standing right behind her, and was even more aware when he moved slightly forward, so his body was almost touching hers. She could feel the heat from him and a tremor ran through her. She knew he'd seen her reaction, knew he was aware of her, just as she was of him. There was a hardness pressed against her back and it took her mind back to a certain hotel room. Was he thinking the same? Then his hand moved slightly forward until it just touched hers and she trembled again. Poor Frank had no idea what was going on in front of him.

Jessica was shaking as she took the account from Frank and then, turning quickly, found herself looking into Ethan's shirt. She had no intention of looking up at him. She needed to get out quickly. "Excuse me," she said sidestepping him and disappearing out of the door, which she closed firmly behind her.

He remained in Frank's office for almost an hour, and Jessica could hear raised voices. Whatever was being discussed was not going well. But the longer he was in there, the more chance she had of getting her emotions under control. She'd just finished working on her file when she heard Frank's door open.

"I don't give a damn what you think, Frank. It's what's needed to be done and since I have the majority share it's up to me. You're only in the loop because of Mother, so don't kid yourself you have any real power."

The words were spoken as Ethan strode along the passage and back into reception. He stopped when he saw Jessica. The scowl on his face disappeared and he flashed her a completely and utterly devastating smile. If she hadn't been sitting down she would have fallen. They both heard the slam of Frank's door.

"So, Red? Or is it Jessica?" he asked as he walked to her desk and hitched a seat on the corner.

"It's Jessica."

"I know, but I still like Red. In fact, I like Red a lot…" He was about to say more, but the outside door opened and Frank's four o'clock appointment walked in. "See you," he whispered, as he stood up and walked out.

After the encounter she'd just had, she was glad to get home. She parked the car outside her cottage and opened the door. Locking it behind her, she went upstairs and changed into a pair of joggers and sleeveless top. Wandering back down and through to the kitchen, she switched on the coffee machine then got a bottle of water from the fridge. Walking back into the lounge she stopped dead, when she saw Ethan sitting in the armchair.

"How the hell did you get in?" she almost spat the words at him through shock.

"Sorry, I thought you would be expecting me. Landlord's inspection," he said, swinging a set of keys from his fingers. "Just checking you're keeping the place up to scratch."

"What, you're my landlord?"

"The very same. Look, I'm sorry, Jessica, I couldn't help it. When Frank said you'd leased the cottage I just wanted to have a bit of fun with you. You have to admit it was a bit of a shock seeing each other again like that."

By now she'd recovered her composure somewhat. "So what do you want to inspect, the whole of the property?"

"Now there's an interesting thought. We could start with the bedroom, the pretty one upstairs."

Jessica looked at him and could see the glint in his eyes, which told her he was teasing her. Or at least she thought he was. The idea of them going upstairs to her bedroom was something she didn't want to think about. "I don't think so. In fact, I do believe you have to give me several days' notice of a landlord's inspection, so if you don't mind I've got things to do."

Ethan laughed at her reply, making it quite clear that he would have loved to have gone up to her bedroom, and she

70

had no doubt that his mind was already way ahead of him. The look on his face told her he was, remembering the pleasures they had already shared and could enjoy again.

Standing, he took as step towards her. "Touché, Red."

She turned and walked towards the door and put out her hand to open it. His hand got there first and he held the handle and trapped her between his body and the door. Keeping his eyes firmly on her face, he lowered his head until his lips touched hers and he gently kissed her. He didn't push her, but waited until the first stirrings of response swept through her, and then he pulled away. "Until next time, Red."

Jessica had been determined to hold out against his kiss. He was playing a game with her, a game that he appeared to be enjoying. But slowly the sensations had taken over and she felt herself weaken and start to respond, and that's when he'd pulled back and left her wanting more. She watched his retreating back as he walked down the short path and took the greatest pleasure in slamming the door shut. It was barely a minute later when the landline rang. Answering it she heard, "Damaging the property could result in forfeiting your bond, Miss Cameron," then a laugh, before the line went dead. She fumed that he was mocking her and was annoyed at her own lack of restraint.

Friday, fortunately, was an uneventful day, apart from her visit to the local hardware store where she bought a sturdy bolt and spent Friday evening securing this to the front door. That will stop any more sudden landlord's inspections, she thought, as she tested the bolt and found it ideal to keep out unwanted and unexpected visitors.

Saturday morning, she was up and at the stables by nine. Riding out across the range on Rory, she was completely at ease. It was a glorious morning and she could smell the grass and the pure air. Kicking Rory on, she cantered slowly up the small hill and stopped at the top. Below her the land stretched out as far as the eye could see. Away in the distance, she could see a cloud of dust that was probably cattle being moved. She wished she'd brought some binoculars so she could have seen clearly what it was, and made a mental note to bring a pair next time.

Riding along the ridge, she eventually stopped and dismounted. Ground-tying Rory, she sat on a boulder and took out one of the trail bars from her pocket. Washing this down with water from the small pack fastened to her saddle, she settled back on the boulder and closed her eyes. She could hear nothing, apart from the occasional snort from Rory and the jangling of his tack. This was heaven and she could almost fall asleep, but that wasn't what this was about. She was here to enjoy the countryside, not sleep.

It was the sound of horse's hooves and the welcoming snickering from Rory that started to pull her from sleep. By the time she was fully awake, she was in the shadow of a horse and rider towering above her.

"You know, you look so inviting when you're asleep."

The lazy drawl pushed away any remaining sleepiness and she sat upright, shielding her face with her hand as she looked upwards. With the sun behind him, she couldn't see his features.

***

Ethan had seen the lone rider whilst working with the men on the herd. He'd pulled out his binoculars but couldn't see who it was. Leaving the men, he'd ridden over until he was close enough to see the intruder. He didn't want trespassers on his land, but when he recognised the intruder, he decided that this one was more than welcome and he would go over and personally extend that welcome.

She'd looked delectable, laid out across the boulder, and he would have loved to have taken her there and then. Where the hell these thoughts were coming from he didn't know, or at least he wasn't prepared to explore their origin yet. Dismounting, he led his horse to one side and ground-tied him, and then walked back to his intruder. Sitting down alongside, he pushed the stetson back on his head and waited until she spoke. She didn't, so they sat there for an extremely long time with neither of them speaking. "Are you mad at me?" he

72

finally asked.

"Why would I be mad?"

"Well, last night springs to mind."

"Why, what happened last night?"

"I think it was a case of what didn't happen last night," he replied with a chuckle as he removed the stetson and put it on the ground.

"I don't know what you mean. Nothing was going to happen last night."

"Okay, have it your way, Red, but we both know that something is happening, even if only one of us will admit it." He watched as the blush spread across her cheeks. Putting up his hand he ran a finger down the side of her face. "Don't keep me waiting too long. I still remember Calgary."

He mentioned Calgary to make her remember all they'd done. But he could tell he wasn't going to get a repeat performance, by the way she turned angrily to him. He took the opportunity to capture her lips before she had time to deny what was between them. This time the kiss wasn't light, it was passionate and he pushed her back, keeping his hands under her shoulders, while his thumbs lightly caressed the side of her neck. He could feel her slowly surrendering to him, even though she was trying to remain stiff in his arms. But the kiss wasn't rejected and from the softness of her lips he knew it was something she was enjoying.

Ethan wanted her. It would be so easy, even though her body was denying she wanted him too, but he would let her have this triumph. He was in this for the long game and she was the trophy he intended to have. This thought settled his dilemma. Jessica was everything he wanted, and more. Easing back from her, he sat up, pulling her with him. Drawing breath into his lungs, he knew he had to behave, or he would lose what he wanted. Looking at her, he smiled. "That was sneaky, I know, but I just can't help it, you have such a kissable mouth."

She snorted, "And that's about as corny as a woman having to be at the right temperature, like a good wine."

He roared with laughter. "So you do remember Calgary."

73

"Of course I do."

"Well, you did say it was the most amazing night, and you left a kiss for me."

This time she laughed openly. "Okay, yes, it was amazing, but I'm not saying anything more on the subject."

"Okay, we'll keep it our little secret. I can promise you other nights as good as, if not better than that, but only if you want them too, Jessica," he said standing up. Putting on his Stetson, he collected his horse, then mounted and rode away.

Riding back to the men, he thought on the fact that he'd just sorted out his dilemma without really trying. What he was feeling towards Jessica was way more than he had ever felt for Helena, and he was quickly realising that he would now have to extradite himself from a relationship that had run its course, without causing too much pain. The forthcoming weekend was going to be difficult, but he needed to end it.

Jessica watched as he rode away. What had just happened had caught her off guard, but she couldn't deny that she had been drowning in his masculinity and the heat in her body had been heading south when he'd broken the kiss. The urge to press into him had been great but she'd resisted. She wouldn't give him that satisfaction. But she did give him the kiss, she wanted it as well, in fact she'd wanted more, but she couldn't let him know that. She had thought they were a one-night stand, but now she wasn't sure.

Chapter Seven

It was a hard week for Ethan. He tried to push Jessica out of his thoughts, but that proved almost impossible. Suddenly it was Friday morning, and he was supposed to be going to Calgary tonight. He'd thought about inventing an excuse not to go, but he knew this needed to be sorted without delay. At least going to Helena's meant that he could leave when he'd made the break. That afforded him some relief but then, just before he left the house, the phone had rung. It was Helena, and for some reason she'd decided that she wanted to come to him. Now it was late afternoon and he was heading back to the house for a quick shower before she arrived. She hated him smelling of the land and horses, whilst he thought it was one of the most normal smells there was.

He was just about finished in the shower when the door slid open and a pair of arms came around his waist. He froze. This was not what he wanted, but how the hell was he going to get out of this predicament? He grabbed the hands before they reached their intended goal and turned round. The face that greeted him was smiling and he hadn't the heart to say anything, so he did the only safe thing he could do and kissed her. Not a long, lingering kiss, but just long enough to keep her happy. Then he somehow managed to slip past her and out of the shower, calling back that he thought they could go out for dinner and then call in at the Community Hall, as there was a dance on. He really needed to keep out of the house, later tonight was going to be difficult enough, and keeping to a public place would give him time to think. Before she had time to comment, he grabbed a towel and headed for the bedroom.

By the time she came out of the shower he was dressed, smart brown chinos with a checked shirt, and a leather belt with silver buckle. Slipping his feet into brown loafers he said he would go and pour them a drink while she got ready.

***

Watching his retreating back, Helena was smarting at the rebuff. She could tell a refusal when it was staring her in the face, and he'd just turned her down. She was going to have to up her game, she'd invested two years in this relationship. She'd been attracted to him when she first saw him and he smiled at her. Then she'd found out what an eligible bachelor he was, and more importantly how much he was worth, and that had considerably increased her interest.

She disliked being on the ranch, but figured that once they were married she could persuade him to spend more of his time in the city. She could give up her apartment and they could buy a penthouse, so she could spend time there when he had to come back to the ranch. Now he seemed to be going cold on her, and that was definitely not in her plans. Modelling was unpredictable, unless you were right at the top, which she wasn't. Although she did earn a reasonable living, she needed security for the future, and a rich husband was an ideal choice. The fact that Ethan was young and good looking was an advantage.

Knowing how conservative people were here, she dressed in a pair of tight white jeans with a plain white vest top, and a floating green long-sleeved over shirt that she turned back to reveal slender wrists. Clasping a chunky gold bangle on her wrist, she secured gold hoops through her ears, before fastening a heavy gold chain around her neck. Sliding her feet into a pair of high heeled green shoes, she picked up her purse and went downstairs, pinning her most seductive smile on her face.

Jessica was enjoying the dance and had been able to socialise with a few of the people she'd already met. But now she was thinking of going home, as she intended to be up and at the stables early. She knew when he came into the hall, how she wasn't sure, but perhaps it was the tingle in the back of her neck. Turning, she saw him talking to a middle-aged couple and then, as he went to move away, he looked in her direction and pinned her gaze with his. She swallowed hard at the intensity of it and knew that she needed to leave. Before she could move, a tall blonde creature walked up to him, draped herself around his neck and pulled him onto the dance floor. His arms went around her as they started to sway to the music. Curious and suspicious, she spoke to the elderly lady standing next to her. "Who's the blonde? Can't recall seeing her before. She's quite stunning and the clothes look like designer labels, not something she'd picked up from the local store." She laughed and hoped the reference to the clothes would disguise her interest in the girl.

"Oh, that's Helena Turner, Ethan's girlfriend. She's a model, hence the clothes."

She felt sick. *Girlfriend.* The two timing bastard, she thought, finding herself using a word she hated again. In fact she was using that word more and more recently, and she didn't like it. She turned back and began talking again to the lady next to her, and tried to avoid watching them, which was extremely difficult as the blonde was certainly making a spectacle of them with her moves. Jessica could feel his eyes on her, but she was damned if she was going to look at him. Finally, she'd had enough and started to make her way through the crowd, intending to go home.

She'd almost reached the door when Frank collared her. Much as she was enjoying her job, the last thing she wanted was to spend time socially with her boss, but that proved difficult as Frank started to talk about work and left her no alternative but to answer his questions. Finally, she managed to break away and get outside but couldn't resist taking one backward glance. Ethan was still wrapped in the blonde's arms and he swung her round so he was facing the door and he looked directly at her, holding her in mid-step with his stare. She shook her head to break the bond and quickly turned and hurried away.

***

Frank was watching Ethan as he danced with Helena. *Lucky sod,* he thought, but then he saw the look on his cousin's face as he began searching around the room. He saw the interaction between Ethan and Jessica, just for a fleeting second. *Oh, got some interest there, cousin, have you?* He kept Jessica talking as she tried to leave, while he watched Ethan's eyes on them both, and he could see that he was more interested in Jessica than the woman in his arms. *Interesting,* he thought. *Wonder what Helena would make of this apparent development?*

He waited until there was a break in the dancing before moving close to Helena as she stood near to the bar and struck up a conversation with her and Ethan. Just general talk, at first and then, when Ethan left to go to the bathroom, he broached the subject that was burning in his head. "So how are things with you and Mr Moneybags?" He didn't wait for her to reply, but continued, "Seems to me like he's losing interest, although I can't understand why."

"What are you talking about, Frank? Everything's fine with us." Her tone was off-hand, but he could tell his words were ringing a warning bell, making her wonder if something was wrong. It was quite clear she wasn't going to let him see she was bothered.

Frank laughed softly. "Didn't look like it earlier. He couldn't take his eyes off someone else."

Helena turned to face him. "Who?"

He watched her face. She was trying to appear unconcerned, but both the turn and the question were a little too quick. "Ah, so things aren't all lovey-dovey then. Didn't think so, and as to the whom, well that's my secret for the time being. She's gone now so you needn't worry, but he's certainly got an interest in her. Call into the office tomorrow if you want to have a chat about it. Ethan's a fool to let you go." With that he left, telling her to say goodnight to his cousin. He kept the invitation to talk casual, but hoped that she would take it up. If Ethan wasn't interested, he certainly was. She was just the kind of woman he liked, eye-candy that attracted interest. But apart from that, he'd been lusting after her ever since she'd first come on the scene.

***

Damnation, thought Ethan. He'd spotted Jessica just before Helena had wrapped herself around him and dragged him onto the floor. He tried to catch her eye, to give her some signal that what she was seeing was not what it appeared to be, but she kept evading his eyes. Finally, he trapped her with his gaze as she was leaving, but the look on her face told him exactly what she thought, that he was flirting with her while going out with someone else. It looked as though he was doing exactly what her former fiancé had done and there was no way he could put her straight, because if he was honest that was exactly what he had been doing. He was involved with Helena but he was chasing Jessica. And it was the latter that he wanted.

Ethan had used the bathroom as an excuse to get away from Helena for a short time. He'd seen the look on Jessica's face when she'd seen Helena in his arms. He needed to talk to Jessica, to put her straight. He'd rushed outside, jumped into his car and driven out onto the highway. It was only a few minutes before he was pulling up outside the cottage. She was home, her car was outside and the light was on, although the drapes were closed. He opened the gate, walked up the path and knocked softly on the door, so as not to disturb the neighbours. He waited, no response. Leaning against the door he called quietly, "Jessica, it's me, let me in, I can explain."

Still no response, but then the downstairs light went out and a few seconds later the bedroom light came on. He stepped back and looked up at the window. The drapes were open but then she appeared. She glanced down at him and then pulled them closed, leaving him in no doubt that she wasn't going to listen to him.

"Damn, damn, damn," he muttered under his breath. This night was turning into a disaster, and he still had to avoid the inevitable bedroom scene with Helena. He walked slowly back to his car and took a last look up at the window. He could have sworn he saw the drapes move, but that could have been wishful thinking on his part.

Parking the car back outside the community centre, he wandered in and involved himself in a conversation about cattle with a few of the other ranchers. He was still there when Helena, having got sick of waiting at the bar for him, finally tracked him down. Apologising for keeping her waiting, he bade the others goodnight and suggested that they leave.

Once back at the ranch, he offered her a drink and poured himself a whisky. Helena took the glass of chardonnay and sat in the corner of the large sofa, waiting for him to join her. He didn't, he stood in front of the fire, resting one hand on the oak surround and swirling the whisky round in his glass with the other. "Sorry, I guess you didn't really enjoy tonight. I keep forgetting that country ways are not really your thing." He'd finally found something to say.

"Oh no, darling, it's okay. I know you like to mix in with folk," she answered sweetly before taking a large drink from the glass. "Did you enjoy it?"

Ethan turned to look at her. That was a question he was not used to hearing from her. "Yeah, I guess I did. Got a bit quiet though, towards the end."

"Yes, I thought that. In fact, I thought you'd deserted me. I couldn't find you anywhere and no one seemed to have seen you."

"Oh, I went outside for a bit of air and got talking to a couple who were leaving. I guess I lost track of time." He couldn't believe how easily the lie slipped off his tongue.

He watched her face as she digested the information and he felt a moment of regret that their relationship was dying. It had been good in the beginning, but they were like chalk and cheese. She liked the bright lights and the city, whereas he was content with the countryside and the ranch. At first, he'd thought they might be able to find some compromise, but then as things progressed it became clearer and clearer that what they had just wasn't enough. Not enough for a lifetime of happiness. It was this dilemma that had sent him to stay in the hotel in Calgary, rather than at her flat. And it was there that he found the thing that was missing from his relationship with Helena. An instant attraction, a feeling of belonging with someone. Now he'd probably blown that, by not being upfront with Jessica about his relationship with Helena. Tossing the remains of the whisky down his throat he poured another, and then refilled Helena's glass.

Helena seemed to be watching him from beneath lowered lashes. Perhaps she sensed there was something wrong. There was a tension in the air. He waited, he didn't want this to get out of hand, but there was a calculating look on her face. Suddenly she smiled as though she'd come to a decision, and was damned if she was giving up without a fight. Finishing off the wine, she set the glass down on the table and held out her hand. "Come to bed, darling."

He smiled. "You go up; I won't be long."

She paused, and the smile faltered, making him wonder if she was hurt. But then, for a fleeting second, he saw anger surge through her, before she seemed to master herself and just said sweetly, "Okay, but don't be long. I need you."

He nodded his head and kept the smile on his face until she'd disappeared. Heaving a long sigh, he sat down on the sofa and held the glass between his hands, watching the fire reflecting in the golden liquid. Downing the drink, he pulled the bottle across and poured another. Perhaps if he got drunk he could perform just one more time. After a fourth drink he realised that getting drunk wasn't going to solve anything and going upstairs was going to be one hell of a mistake. He couldn't make love to someone when he didn't want to. And he didn't want to. That was the reality of the situation. There was only one person he wanted to make love to, and at the moment she wasn't speaking to him. He groaned as he laid his head back on the cushions and closed his eyes.

He knew Helena had crept down some time later, and he'd pretended to be asleep on the sofa.

She was in the shower when he came up, so he quickly pulled out clean clothes for the day and went into the guest bedroom to use the shower in there. By the time he came back

81

into the master bedroom, she was out of the shower and wandering round in the bedroom with a towel wrapped round her body. He smiled. "Hi. Sorry about last night. I guess I was more tired than I thought and I must've crashed on the sofa."

"Oh, you poor thing. You should have said you were tired. We could have stayed in last night," she said sympathetically. Reaching for a flimsy thong, she dropped the towel, exposing her creamy body to him. Stepping one foot and then the other into the garment she pulled this up and then, picking up a very brief matching bra, she leant forward and eased her breasts into the cups and then walked towards him. "Fasten this for me will you, darling," she purred, as she presented her back and the open bra fastening to him.

His hands shook slightly as he fastened the catch and then dropped a kiss on her shoulder. He knew what she was doing. He was only human and he could have taken what was so clearly being offered, but that would have been insulting to both of them. He didn't want to use her for sex, for a quickie because the sight of her body was having some effect. Any man worth his salt would have been moved. Giving her a playful slap on the rear, he said he would see her downstairs and he made a very quick escape before he made things worse.

Down in the town, Jessica was awakening from a disturbed sleep. She still couldn't believe that he had been two-timing his apparent long-term girlfriend, and cheating with her. She'd been in the position of the wronged fiancée, and she had no wish or intention of becoming the other woman. She'd thought better of him and couldn't relate this side of him to the person she spent the night with in Calgary.

When he had turned up at the cottage last night, it had taken all her willpower not to let him in and give him both barrels of her anger. But she was not prepared to risk him trying to seduce her. More worrying was that she didn't trust herself not to respond. Throwing back the covers, she showered and then dressed ready for riding. A long session in the saddle would chase away the blues, and she couldn't wait to get outside.

Left on her own while Ethan rode out with the men, Helena phoned Frank and arranged to meet with him at his office at noon. When she'd found him asleep on the sofa it had been tempting to wake him and scream at him, but she intended to find out what was going on. She needed to get things back on track. She had no intention of letting a rich potential husband slip through her fingers.

She arrived at Frank's five minutes early and found him already waiting for her. Locking the door behind them, he took her through to his office. "Want a drink, coffee, or something stronger?"

"Something stronger," she replied without hesitation. After the morning she'd had, she needed a good stiff drink. Taking the glass from him she tasted it, whisky, not her favourite drink but it would do. "Okay, so what were you on about last night?" she asked, coming straight out with the question.

"Oh, I didn't know you were really interested."

"Yes, well, I am."

"What's wrong, didn't Mr Moneybags come through last night?"

Helena turned her head away and studied the picture on the wall. She had no intention of admitting anything to him.

Frank chuckled. "Oh, I see he didn't."

She turned back to face him, her eyes flashing. "I didn't say that."

"You don't have to, honey. It's written all over your face. So I was right, he does have an interest somewhere else."

"Just because he's tired one night," she said, deliberately forgetting that he'd shunned her earlier in the day as well, "Doesn't mean he's losing interest in me."

"Oh, I think it does, Helena. If a man can turn you down, then he's either gay or looking for it elsewhere. Or perhaps he's already getting it elsewhere." He watched, as her face paled at his last comment.

"Well, he's not walking away from me without a fight," she said, the words relaying her anger.

"What is it you're scared of losing, Helena, the man or the money?" asked Frank keeping his eyes on her face.

"Well, both. I've put a lot into this relationship. Once we are married, I can persuade him to spend more time in the city and leave the ranch to others."

Frank put back his head and roared with laughter. "You certainly don't know Ethan if you think that. There is no way in hell that he'll live in the city. The ranch is his life. If you marry him, he'll expect you to be the perfect rancher's wife, you know, baking, helping out, oh, and of course babies. He'll want lots of babies to inherit the business."

Helena swallowed hard at his words. She didn't want babies, didn't even like them, but she needed a plan for her future. Already, one of her modelling contracts had not been renewed because the firm wanted someone younger. She was only twenty-eight, but in her world that was old. Now her back-up plan seemed to be falling apart.

***

Frank watched the range of emotions passing over her face. He'd got her thinking, which was exactly what he wanted. In fact, what he wanted was her, had done for some time. "You know, perhaps you're with the wrong cousin?" He waited as his words sank in.

"Frank, you can't be serious. You might be easy on the eye but you have nowhere near the money that Ethan does, and quite frankly, if you'll excuse the pun, I can't see myself as a lawyer's wife."

"Who said anything about a lawyer's wife?"

"You did, well, in a way you did. You're a lawyer and if we got together that would make me a lawyer's wife, or whatever…" she trailed off, seeming to realise that he'd never mentioned marriage.

"Ah, yes but what if the lawyer suddenly came into money? A lot of money, and was able to move to the city and spend a lot of time and money on his wife?"

This time, Helena laughed. It appeared he was thinking of marriage. "Yeah, and where would the lawyer get this money from?"

"Ethan." The one word that was spoken lay heavily in the air.

"How the hell would you get Ethan's money?"

"Not quite figured that out yet, but I bet between us we could come up with a plan. Unless, of course, you just want to hang around until you get dumped. Anyway, think about it and see if a rich lawyer would fit into your future plans."

Helena looked at him as though unsure whether he was kidding or not, as his face wasn't giving anything away. "You're serious about this?"

"Never more so. But I need a prize to go with the money and I've had my eye on the prize I want for some time."

He saw the gleam come into her eyes when she realised he was talking about her. He wanted her, which was apparently more than Ethan did at the moment, but he knew her and doubted she was ready to burn her bridges just yet. He could wait. She would come to him. He was right about this other woman.

"I need time to think about it," she said, standing up.

"Of course you do. You need to find out for certain whether Ethan has another woman, before you take up my offer. Don't worry, I'm not offended, as long as you make the wait worth it when you do come to me," he said suggestively.

Helena studied him. He knew he was good looking, about a couple of inches shorter than Ethan, but he dressed smartly and he was charming. His hair was lighter than his cousin's and cut more conservatively. He knew she wasn't averse to him, in fact she'd flirted with him on occasions, even while Ethan was around. But now, if Ethan wasn't going to be there for her, he was offering her another chance. He could see her calculating. Smiling, she answered him. "It will definitely be worth the wait. That is, if I decide to help you."

"Oh, I think you will. Ethan's definitely about to play away from home, if he hasn't already done so." He walked to the door, held it open for her, and smiled as she brushed her body against him as she passed.

"So who do you think Ethan has his eye on?" she finally asked the question that had clearly been burning in her head.

"Jessica, my assistant." He made the statement quite calmly.

"What, the girl who works in the office? That little blonde thing?"

"No, that was Annie. She's left. Jessica is a trained personal assistant. Only been here a short time. She's renting one of Ethan's properties on the edge of town," he told her, giving details as to where it was. "And you know what, he has keys to the place, and possibly even has landlord's rights, if you get my drift." He watched her face harden at his words. "Don't worry, Helena, I'll be here when it all falls apart, and I'll make it up to you."

Ethan arrived back at the ranch late to take Helena out to dinner. She was already changed and waiting to go. Telling her that he wouldn't be long, he took a quick shower and dressed. He'd reserved a table at Benny's, one of the two decent restaurants in town, knowing it would please her. He still hadn't worked out how to break off their relationship, despite hours of turmoil. He wasn't cruel and wanted to do this as gently as he could.

The meal was good and he kept up the conversation throughout, but even he could tell it was stilted. She held his hand as they left the restaurant and he let her. It would have been un-gentlemanly to pull away. Dropping her at the front of the house, he drove the car into the garage and then walked slowly back. This was the part he was dreading. How does one avoid sleeping with the woman you've just spent the evening with, and the last two years? Well, part of the last two years, when work permitted. He didn't believe in miracles but he thought one had just happened, when his foreman came hurrying across the yard towards him.

"Thank God you're back. That prize heifer is having a hard time calving and we could lose them both. We may need to call the vet."

"Okay, Jim, give me five minutes to change and I'll be down. I'll make a decision about the vet when I've seen her."

Running up the steps into the house he called out to Helena, telling her what had happened.

"Can't the men deal with it?"

She sounded annoyed, and he knew why. "Not this time. The heifer's too valuable," he called back as he made his way upstairs.

He was back down, changed and dashing out of the door a few minutes later, leaving her on her own. His, 'don't wait up for me,' was bound to do nothing for her mood. Little did he know, but she did wait, until one in the morning, then gave up and went to bed, eventually falling into a restless sleep.

It was almost eight next morning when he finally felt able to return to the house. It had been touch and go at times during the night. He'd admitted defeat and called the vet out in the early hours, and between them they finally managed to save the heifer and deliver the calf, a young bull. With the breeding stock from both parents, he would be worth a quite a few thousand dollars in the years to come.

Now exhausted and bloodied from the birth, he walked across to the house. It was quiet, so he presumed Helena must still be in bed. Going silently into the guest bedroom, he slipped the lock on the bathroom door and stood under the shower, letting the water wash the fatigue away. Wrapping a towel around his waist, he unlocked the door and went along the passage to the main bedroom. He could see Helena still under the covers, so he quietly collected clean clothes and took them back to the guest room.

He was preparing eggs and bacon when she appeared. A thin robe covered her body and he knew from experience that there would be nothing underneath. He flipped the eggs and then poured a coffee for her, and put the mug down on the table.

"Sorry about last night. Things got a bit heavy out there and I've only just got in."

"Well, you've had time to shower, I see," she said sweetly. "You should have woken me and we could have showered together."

"Didn't like to wake you. You looked sound asleep, so I thought it best to let you enjoy it." He knew it was a lie and only hoped that she didn't. "Do you want eggs and bacon, or just toast?"

"Oh, just toast I think. I can do it," she replied sliding past him and popped a couple of slices in the toaster. Coming back, she slid her arms round his waist and pressed her body against his back. "Why don't you come back to bed for a while?"

He tensed. "Afraid I can't. The boys are heading up to the north pasture this morning and I need to go with them. Doubt we'll be back till late." The men had always been going, but he had just decided to join them. "So I can't keep them waiting." That, at least, was the truth. He turned to face her. "Sorry I have to cut and run."

She was suspicious. "So, what would have happened if you'd been in Calgary? You couldn't have gone with them."

"They would have called me back." The explanation was straight and to the point. And a downright lie. He hated this, he wanted it over, but he was going to have to put it back until next weekend. Ethan knew he was being a coward, by avoiding the issue, but at the moment he'd had enough drama over the last twelve hours and a hysterical woman was something he didn't want to have to deal with now. He glanced at her. She looked pensive and he was sure she wasn't convinced, but there was little she could do about it.

"Okay, rancher's life and all, but I'll be gone when you get back," she said reaching up and kissing him.

He wanted to pull away but didn't, and she pressed against him. But that was as far as she got as he broke away, saying the bacon was burning. God, he felt such a coward.

Thirty minutes later he was gone, and Helena was left on her own to gather her things together ready for the drive back to Calgary. She had a lot of thinking to do, and a lot of planning. She had a back-up plan with Frank, but she would rather go with the intended plan. But whatever happened, she had no intention of losing out altogether.

Chapter Eight

Jessica kept a low profile the following week. Riding out, she made sure she avoided Ethan's land. Although that was difficult since he seemed to own most of the land around the town. She hadn't realised how wealthy he seemed to be, but every time she queried some point of interest or building, it seemed that he owned it, or at least part of it.

She managed to fit in a couple of evening rides, but now it was Friday and she was looking forward to tomorrow. She'd hired Rory for much of the day, ten till four. Now, as she finished off the last of the letters, she collected the enclosures, picked up the envelope and took everything through to Frank for signing.

"All done, Jessica?" he enquired as she walked in.

"Yes. This is the last of them. The rest can wait until Monday, unless you want me to stay and finish them?"

"No, there's nothing that can't wait. So what are you planning for the weekend?"

"Oh, nothing drastic. I'm planning on riding out tomorrow for most of the day and perhaps again on Sunday. I hadn't realised how much I would enjoy getting back in the saddle."

"So you've ridden before?"

"Yes, but years ago. I'd not thought of getting involved again but the district here is so lovely it's a shame just to travel by car to see it."

"You should ask Ethan if you can ride on his land. He's got some fantastic riding areas."

Frank was watching her face as he made the suggestion and he couldn't fail to see the tightening of her lips, or the slight flush on her cheeks. So he wasn't wrong. There was something going on between them.

"Oh, I don't need to do that. I can find lots of places to ride without troubling him." The reply was offhand and, bidding him goodnight, she took the signed post. She would drop it in at the post office on her way home.

As she drew up outside the cottage, she saw the pick-up waiting. She had no intention of getting into a conversation with Ethan, so she quickly got out and started to walk up the path to the front door. She heard the slam of a door and then footsteps behind her.

"Jessica, for God's sake stop."

"No." She answered him without turning round but then her arm was caught, and she found herself swung around to face him.

"Jessica, please listen to me. It's not what you think."

"Oh, I believe it's very much what I think. In fact, it's what most of the town thinks. You have a girlfriend, or perhaps I should say partner. For all I know, you could be living together." She couldn't keep the distaste out of her voice.

He pulled her towards him, his voice low. "I admit I have a girlfriend but she is not my partner and we do not live together."

"Maybe not, but you sleep with her."

"Yes, I do, or rather I did. I've not slept with anyone since Calgary."

"Oh yeah, you expect me to believe that a gorgeous blonde stays at yours and you sleep in separate rooms."

"Actually I do. I wouldn't lie to you. But I will correct one thing. We didn't sleep in separate rooms, I slept on the sofa. Damned uncomfortable it was. And I can also tell you that she wasn't pleased at being turned down. But how could I sleep with her, when I wanted to be with you?"

Jessica kept her eyes on his face as he was speaking. He seemed genuine, but then again everything Tom had said to her had seemed genuine at the time. "So she knows we've slept together?"

He shook his head. "No. I'm not that cruel. I'm trying to break things off as gently as I can without upsetting her too much."

Jessica could feel herself wavering. She could also feel the firmness of his arm holding her and the heat from his body, which was far too close. She had to bring this to an end. "Well it would appear that you have a problem. I don't enjoy being the other woman. Nor do I enjoy being made a fool of. So if you'll let me go, I have things to do."

He looked intently at her as he spoke. "So if I was free you wouldn't be averse to being with me?"

She bit her lips together before answering. "I didn't say that. In fact, I don't recall saying anything about being with you." As she spoke she pulled her arm free and continued walking towards the door. She expected him to follow, but he didn't.

"I'll not give up, Red." The words reached her as she closed the door. She was mad with him but couldn't deny she was also attracted to him. She hoped he didn't give up, but she wasn't getting involved with him while he was with someone else.

Helena had just found the road the cottage was on when she saw the car pull up outside. She also recognised Ethan's truck waiting. She could feel her anger beginning to boil. He was supposed to be coming to Calgary tomorrow, but she had decided to surprise him by coming to him today. Curiosity had got the better of her and she wanted to check out where the threat to her plans was living. What she didn't expect was to see the woman herself, and then see Ethan approach her. It was quite clear that what was being said was intense. The body language told her that as he pulled the woman close to him. She just wished she could hear what was being said. She put her car into reverse and backed out of sight.

Ethan had just reached home when he saw Helena's car coming into the yard. This was the last thing he needed. He was about to phone her and invent a reason why he couldn't go to Calgary this weekend, but now that plan was scuppered. Pinning a smile on his face he walked over to greet her. "I thought I was coming to you?"

"I figured I'd surprise you. Last weekend was a bit of a disaster so I thought we could make up for it this week."

91

He carried her bag inside and then up to the bedroom. She followed him and closed the door behind her. Slipping off her jacket, she then proceeded to remove her shoes, then her blouse, followed closely by her pants. Standing provocatively in front of him in a thong and bra she waited for his reaction. "Well, Ethan, don't you want to unwrap the rest of the package?" Helena was taking a risk, forcing him to make love, or prove Frank's words to be true.

His eyes darted around the room looking for anything to light on, other than the partly clothed body in front of him. This was something he'd really tried to avoid. It was one thing telling her face to face that he wanted to end things, but to do it while she was almost naked and vulnerable was not what he intended at all. Finally realising that he had no option he faced her. "I'm sorry, Helena, I can't."

"What, can't get it up generally, or don't want to with me?"

He could hear the anger in her voice and he should be honest. "It's just not working for me any more. It's not you, it's me. I've changed. I know that sounds like a cliché. You're gorgeous, anyone in their right mind would want you, but just not me anymore." Having said the words he'd been trying to say for a long time, he went to move past her, and leave her to get dressed. He had no wish to prolong the encounter.

He knew Helena would be furious. To be rejected in this way was totally humiliating and would be alien to her.

The slap caught him off guard as he walked past her. It wasn't a tentative slap, he felt it and his head snapped back with the force. He bit down his reaction. He should have expected that, he deserved it, so he would allow her the satisfaction. "Sorry, Helena," he said as he opened the door and left.

He saw her car going down the track a short time later and felt sad, and more than a little guilty that it had ended like this. But mostly he felt relief. She was the dilemma that had sent him to Calgary and that in turn had led him to Red. He'd known for some time that it was wrong between them and her reaction now had just confirmed it. He was free, but would the person he wanted still be interested in him?

Helena didn't drive far before she pulled over. She was damned if Ethan was going to get away with this, but she was going to be clever and bide her time. Picking up her Blackberry, she called Frank and twenty minutes later she was sitting in his house, with a glass of wine in her hand.

"So he's dumped you?" The question slipped off Frank's lips.

"I didn't say that."

"You didn't need to. It's written all over your face."

"Okay, so you were right. And there is something going on between him and that girl. Not quite sure what, but I saw them when I first arrived."

"I'm never wrong, Helena. And I'll tell you this for nothing, you will be far better off with me than you would have been with Ethan. I'll give you the life you want. Penthouse, travel, clothes, anything you desire will be yours. All we have to do is work out how to get control of Ethan's money."

Helena looked at him from beneath her lashes. Well, she'd struck out with Ethan but here was another man apparently desperate to take her on. Crossing her long legs, she wished she'd worn a skirt to tease him. Anyway, she wasn't going to come across as easily as that. Holding out the glass for a refill, she thought carefully about this new opportunity.

It was too late for her to drive back to the city, and anyway she'd had too much to drink. It had been surprising to find Frank could actually cook, and he'd whipped up a meal for them in no time. Now she was relaxing with a cognac and listening as he explained that if they could discredit Ethan, perhaps even have him sent to prison, then Frank, as part shareholder, and family, would be able to find a way to take over control of the company and the money.

"Well, you'd have to get him sent down for a hell of a long time to be able to take over the running of his company." She took a sip of cognac as she waited for his reply.

"I know. I'm still working on that. I have a plan but it's a bit sketchy. If it works, Ethan will rot in prison and we'll enjoy the good life."

"Why do you hate him so much?"

"Easy. Half of what he has should be mine. His father inherited everything from his parents. They cut my father out of their Wills, just because he'd been a bit wild in his young days. So Ethan's dad got everything, and built up even more. My dad got nothing and he and my mother had to lead a very modest life. I only have a ten per cent share of the company because Ethan's mother felt sorry for me. And that's what annoys Ethan. He hates it that I have even a part of his empire. Not that I can do anything, but I do get a small income from it. If he wasn't around, I could take control and then utilise the money how I want. Within reason of course, but I can put in a manager to run the ranch. There are oil drilling rights in one section. That's what bugs me the most. There's a fortune under the ground but he won't touch it. Says it's an environmental matter to him and the area is one he won't touch."

Helena's ears pricked up at the sound of this. "So how much do you reckon the oil would be worth?"

"Probably millions, but I would have to play carefully with him to get him to hand control over to me. It would mean sucking up to him but I could do that. Particularly if he's stuck in prison and the prize is big enough." His voice lowered as he smiled seductively at her. Leaving her in no doubt that she was part of the prize.

"So what if he won't hand over control to you?"

"Then I'll apply to the courts as a shareholder and next of kin. Oh, it may be a battle, but I'm confident of winning, particularly if he's facing life behind bars."

"Sounds like you've got it all worked out."

"Not quite, but as I said, I'm working on it."

"So what is your plan?"

"Can't say yet. Not until I've got some more information. Anyway, I think we've discussed my cousin for long enough." He moved across to the sofa as he spoke and sat next to her, draping his arm along the back.

His hand dropped casually onto her shoulder. She would let him get away with that. She wasn't prepared to jump straight from Ethan's bed to Frank's. Except she hadn't been in Ethan's bed for some time, as there had always been something to prevent it. Either her work schedule or his, but now she was beginning to see that his work had probably just been an excuse. However, she had cared for Ethan and in time she may have come to love him, whatever that was. She didn't really know, most of her life she'd used men to get where she was now. And Ethan was the last part of her plan, the one that would keep her in the style she wanted for the rest of her life. Now she was looking at a new plan.

She'd got into her present modelling agency by giving the Director a blow job during her interview. She'd known from the moment she walked in the door that he was almost salivating. By parading her body, it hadn't taken long to give him a hard on, and after that it was plain sailing. One blow job equalled one contract. Then, after the first day's full shoot, he'd held her back. She knew what he wanted and she was only too happy to keep him on side. They'd made full use of the sofa in his office, which conveniently converted into a bed, and she'd given him the ride of his life before he went home to his wife.

After that, it had been easy keeping him satisfied and her contract had been renewed for the past six years. But the models were getting younger and his attention had turned to a newer version. She was fearful that her present contract wouldn't be renewed at the end of the year and the fact that she'd just lost one client wasn't going to help her cause. She couldn't even use the threat of telling his wife as he'd just divorced her, because he'd found out she was playing away with her tennis coach. So much for marriage and fidelity, but then again in her eyes infidelity was part of marriage.

Frank's fingers stroking across her shoulder brought her back to the present. She turned and smiled. "I think I'm about ready to turn in." She saw the flare of excitement in his eyes and bit back the laugh that threatened. She knew what he expected, but he was in for a disappointment. Well, tonight anyway.

"Sure, I'll just put the glasses away," he said rising.

She waited until he'd gone through to the kitchen before

asking where the guest bedroom was. She looked towards the door as he reappeared, disappointment clearly showing on his face.

This time, she did laugh. "Oh Frank, you really didn't think I was going to give in that easily, did you?"

"Well, a guy can hope. Top of the stairs, turn right and it's the door on the left. Or, if you change your mind, it's the door on the right."

"I won't, Frank. Well, not tonight," she said picking up her bag.

He rushed forward. "Here, I'll get that," and he took the bag from her and led the way upstairs.

The room was quite charming, old fashioned but at least it had an en-suite. She wouldn't have liked to queue for the bathroom, particularly with Frank in his present state. But there again, she didn't want to push him away. Having showered, she slipped on a negligee. She could hear him downstairs still. So she sat in the wicker chair and waited until she heard him come up. Just as he was about to open his door, she opened hers. "Frank."

He swung round and stared. *Bloody hell,* he choked the words back, as he took in the blonde apparition standing in the doorway. He almost came to attention on the first look. "Yeah?" was all he could manage.

"Just wanted to say goodnight, and thanks for the bed." She spoke the words softly and with a smile. Then she moved slightly forward, and placed a kiss on his lips. Before he could respond she was gone and the door closed. Leaning against the door, she was pleased with the reaction she'd got. She'd seen the straining in his pants and, if she was honest, for a moment she'd been tempted to relieve him of the discomfort. But taking him to her bed right now was not in her overall plan. If he was going to be rich, she wanted to be certain that she was going to be at his side to spend the money.

Frank almost staggered into his bedroom. All he could see was the tall blonde figure in a negligee that was almost transparent. Her breasts were hardly covered by the material and his eyes had been glued to them as she spoke. Now he was so bloody hard it hurt. He couldn't go to bed like this, but nor could he go out to one of the ladies in the town who would have eased his pain. God, he wanted her so badly, and that thought wasn't helping. There was only one way he was going to be able to sleep and that was to relieve himself. Opening one of the drawers, he reached under the clothes, pulled out one of his special magazines, and went through to the bathroom. It took five minutes standing over the toilet, before the first spurt of semen shot out. After that it was easy and he shook as his hand worked its magic until he was empty. He'd not done that for years and he had no intention of doing it again. Next time she got him worked up like that he would take what she was teasing him with. He wasn't quite the gentleman she thought.

Going into work on the Monday, Frank was hardly able to keep the smile off his face. He'd persuaded Helena to stay until the Sunday evening, not that he'd got past first base. Oh, she'd let him kiss her and things had got a bit steamy, but she had slept alone and, despite his vow, he'd had to adjourn to the bathroom again.

Jessica was already at her desk when he arrived and she couldn't help but notice he looked pleased with himself. "Good weekend, Frank?" she enquired.

"Exceptionally good," he replied, as he went through to his office.

The week was uneventful for Jessica. When she rode out she kept off Ethan's land as best she could, but she'd not seen him since the encounter outside her cottage. She didn't know whether she was pleased or disappointed. Part of her was furious with him for deceiving her. But part of her remembered Calgary and what they had had, and the teasing she'd enjoyed with him, before she found out he had a girlfriend. She was totally confused by her feelings and decided the best thing to do was to keep well out of his way. At least until one of them was able to sort out what was happening, and she wasn't sure that would be her.

Frank went early on the Friday and left her to lock up. After dropping off the post she drove the short distance to the

97

cottage and parked up. She planned on doing some laundry tonight so she could spend most of tomorrow out on Rory. Opening the door, she threw her jacket on the chair and walked through to the kitchen. She stopped dead in her tracks. Ethan was lounging against the unit top with his arms folded.

"How the hell did you get in?" she yelled the words at him. Partly because he'd scared her half to death, and partly because she was scared to be alone with him. Turning, she marched back into the lounge. "Get out." She didn't get chance to say anything else as he grabbed her arm and swung her round to him. Holding both her arms with his, he stopped her where she stood.

"Jessica, for goodness sake, will you just listen to me?"

"Why should I? You've just broken into my home and I want you out."

"I haven't broken in, as you very well know. And anyway, it was the only way I could see to get you on your own and make you to listen to me."

She glared defiantly at him and he broke into laughter. "God, you look wonderful when you're mad." Without hesitating he took her lips with his, deepening the kiss and moving his hands round to her back, pulling her close.

She couldn't do anything to stop him. Her hands were trapped between their bodies and she could feel her resolve slipping as the seconds ticked by. There was only one thing for her to do, trickery. Groaning she parted her lips and surrendered to him. His grip loosened and she was able to free her hands, moving them around his waist.

He murmured against her mouth, "Let's get more comfortable?"

She nodded her head in agreement and held her breath as he eased away from her. Raising her head, she looked up at him. She hated what she saw, but she loved it at the same time. He was totally focussed on her. His hands came up and held her face. "Jess?" The question hung in the air between them.

Oh God, no, she thought. *I really don't want to stop this, but I have to. I won't be used.* "Get out," the words were low and clear.

Ethan stepped back, unable to believe what he was hearing. He frowned and made to hold her but her hand came up to make contact with his face. It would have done so, had he not realised what was about to happen and pulled back. He grabbed her raised hand and then the other and just held her as he looked in amazement, at the woman who'd gone from kissing him to trying to batter him. "What was that for?"

"You know perfectly well what it was for."

"What, for kissing you? You seemed to be enjoying it."

"Well I wasn't. I only gave in so I could get away."

He smiled. "Believe what you want, Red. Your lips say one thing, but your eyes and your body are telling me another. But if you want me to, I'll go and I won't break in again. Unless you ask me to, that is." He dropped her hands as he spoke.

"That won't happen," she said holding out her hand. "Keys."

He reached into his pocket and lifted out the keys and dangled them from his finger. Looking at her set face it was clear he wasn't going to win this round. He wasn't worried as he was more concerned with winning the war. Smiling, he held out the keys to her.

She took the keys quickly before he changed his mind and walked to the door. Holding it open she stood silently waiting for him to go.

He walked slowly towards the door then stopped in front of her. "You're only kidding yourself, Red. You'll come to me next time, and I won't turn you away."

"You're mistaken. I won't come to you."

"You will. Calgary told me you will."

She was about to close the door when he called back, "I do have another set of keys." She slammed the door before he said anything else and pushed the bolt home.

Leaning against the wood she was angry with herself and with him. He was right, she was only kidding herself. She wasn't sure what was going on between them, and she wasn't sure she wanted to know. But when he held her she could feel her body surrendering to him, even when she didn't want it to. She wanted to feel his hands on her, to feel him stripping her

99

clothes away and then to sink deep into her body. She shook her head to chase the thoughts away. She needed to concentrate on laundry and that should ground her. Tomorrow she would be out on Rory and there would be no time to think about Ethan Slade.

Chapter Nine

It didn't take Frank long to find Helena's apartment, which was located in a tall elegant block downtown. He'd brought an overnight bag in the hope that he would be staying. She'd phoned him on the Tuesday and thanked him again for letting her stay. That was when he suggested he took her out to dinner tonight, and he'd been more than delighted when she accepted, and made the reservation at a restaurant she'd recommended. Leaving his bag in the car, he parked in the visitors' parking area and took the elevator. She let him in when he buzzed up.

Now standing with a drink in his hand, he was looking out of the window onto the city below. "Nice apartment," he commented.

"Yes, but I would really like to go upmarket."

"Well, I told you we could have a penthouse. Will that be upmarket enough for you?"

"Could be." She wasn't going to say more than that until she found out what he was planning. He'd already hinted that he had found a way to solve their problems, and she was eager to hear what he had to say.

They kept the conversation general while they ate dinner, since he said he didn't want to discuss the other matter until they were back in the apartment. Once there, she opened a bottle of wine and poured two glasses. Handing one to him she sat on the sofa next to him. "Okay, Frank, so what is your great plan?"

"Well, as I said it still needs some working on, but if it comes off Ethan will be out of the picture for a long time, probably life."

"Life?" she said warily. "You're surely not going to kill him?"

"Good God, no. What do you take me for?"

She heaved a sigh of relief. "I don't know. It was just what you said."

"No, what I have planned, or hope to plan, is for Ethan Slade to spend the rest of his natural behind bars. But I want to know if this is what you want too and, if you do, then we do it together."

"I don't want to go to prison." She sat upright, scared at the thought.

"Neither of us is going to prison. We are just going to help the person who is going to send Ethan to prison."

"Oh, and who might that be?"

"I'll tell you that in a minute. Right now, I need to know if you want this. And if you do, I come with it. I've watched you with Ethan and I've been out of my mind with jealousy. Now not only can I get what's due to me, I can have you as well."

"What, as eye candy until you get fed up and want someone else?"

"No. I'm offering what you wanted from Ethan. The whole thing, marriage, money. Kids, if you want them?"

"Oh, God no, not kids."

"Fine. I'm not into kids either. But I do want you in my bed and performing, if you know what I mean. So do we have a deal, or should I say, partnership?"

She had listened to Frank as he spoke. She wanted security and he was now offering her that. She wasn't averse to marrying him. They'd flirted and had a couple of fumbling kisses at parties in the past. And if his reaction to her when she stayed at his home was anything to go by, he'd keep her satisfied in bed. If not, she could get that elsewhere as and when she needed it. He was waiting for her reply.

"Okay." Just one word and that settled her future.

Frank smiled and poured them another glass. "You realise I won't be able to drive home. I'll probably have to crash in your guest bedroom." He knew it was corny and a leading comment, but he felt he was entitled to a down payment for what he was planning.

She knew it as well. "I don't have a guest bedroom, Frank.

There's just the one bedroom. So I guess you'll have to sleep on the sofa." He was smiling, but her comment wiped the smile away.

"After what I've just offered you? No bloody way. I'm in your bed tonight, or the whole thing is off. And I don't just mean in your bed, I'm having you. I've waited long enough."

Helena sat back, listening to what he was saying. She liked this aggressive side to him. So he was going to have her tonight, was he? Well perhaps they'd better get started. At least she could judge tonight's performance and decide whether the risk was worth it. Although the offer of marriage was. Rising, she held out her hand. "Better not waste any time then."

He almost dropped his glass in his haste to put it on the table. Following her into the bedroom, his gaze was fixed on the large round bed. He couldn't picture his cousin in it, but he could picture himself there. She went into the bathroom and he could hear the shower running. He was unsure what to do, so he waited. She came out a few minutes later wrapped in a robe.

"Waiting for me, Frank? You could have joined me. But perhaps you should have a solitary shower now. Just to wash off the day's events."

He didn't need asking twice and rushed off. It was the quickest shower he'd ever had and he wrapped a towel around his waist and came back into the bedroom. Helena was sitting on the edge of the bed and rose as he came in.

"That's better, Frank. Nothing like a quick shower to waken one up. Don't want you falling asleep on me." She wasn't going to let on that she was as eager as him. It was weeks since she'd had it and she was over-ready. As she spoke, she moved towards him and pulled the towel away, leaving him fully exposed to her eyes. "Nice," was all she said as she stared at his erection and handed him a condom. She watched as he pulled it on. Then, before he could say anything, she pulled the belt on her robe and it fell to her feet.

His gasp was loud. "Oh my God." He just stared at her. Everything about her had his insides doing somersaults. From the long legs to the smooth area between them, up to the full breasts and the hair that fell about her body to her waist. She looked like a goddess to him and he couldn't believe that he was about to do what he wanted to her.

"What's wrong, Frank, cat got your tongue?" Her tone was sultry.

He didn't reply as her hands started to run up and down his chest. Then he made his move. His hands hauled her to him and his lips came down onto hers. He forced her lips apart and his tongue thrust in seeking her own. Pushing her backwards they part fell onto the bed and both scrambled towards the centre, not taking their lips from each other. His hands were everywhere. Kneading her breasts and then in her hair. They were both like a pair of drunks who had found a bottle of whisky and couldn't wait until they reached the final drop.

He pulled his lips from hers and travelled down to her breasts. Taking one in his mouth he started to suck. Gently at first and then harder, pulling at her and scraping the nipple with his teeth. One hand went to the other breast and rolled the nipple between his fingers. Not gentle but hard, as hard as he was getting by the second. The other hand was making its way down across her stomach, over the smooth groin and buried itself between her legs. He found her clitoris and rubbed it gently. This was one area he didn't want to be rough with. Her body was rising with his onslaught and he put a leg across hers to hold her down. He could hear her crying for him. "What do you want, Helena?" He savoured asking the question.

"You, you Frank." She cried between gasps. She was desperate for this.

He thrilled to hear her say it. He'd wanted her for so long. But he remembered that she'd been with his cousin, so he wasn't going to make this easy. Also, he needed her to know that he was in charge, not only of this, but of their relationship. He might have appeared weak to her but that was a good cover, and had worked on many a female in the past. Pushing a finger inside her wet entrance, he was almost beside himself when she gripped him hard. Moving further in he whispered in her ear. "You want me to love you like he did?"

"No, not like him. Like you, like you will love me."

"Oh, I'll love you. But not like him. I'll fuck you till you don't know what day of the week it is. Then I'll come back and give you some more."

The words registered in her head despite the turmoil inside her. *So he liked to talk dirty, did he? Well, she could do that.*

"So you wanna fuck me, Frank. Well, you'd better do it hard."

She'd hardly got the words out when he was on top of her, his finger was replaced and he was inside her. Neither of them was intending to make this gentle so she parted her legs and thrust up to meet him. He pushed into her hard and felt her open up to him. Then her legs were up around his waist and he was banging into her like there was no tomorrow.

This was everything Frank had wanted for the last two years. He'd come close to having a feel on a couple of occasions but now, he wasn't just feeling, he was screwing, and loving every moment of it. All the pent up jealousy he'd felt was being exorcised with every thrust. He came before her but he stayed with her until she climaxed. He had no intention of denying her anything. He just wanted her to know he was in control, but the truth was he loved her and he would take care of her. But love wasn't a word he intended to use, just yet. This needed to be a business arrangement until he figured the time was right and then he would tell her.

***

He woke her again in the night and she denied him nothing. She was thankful to have her future secured and the sex with Frank was the most surprising thing of all. He was hard but tender and he made sure she was taken care of. Not that Ethan hadn't been good in bed, but he'd never had that hardness like Frank and sometimes she liked it hard. And she liked the dirty talk. That was something Ethan would never do.

By the time she woke the next morning she knew she was right in trusting Frank. He stayed until Sunday and they made love several times and in several places in the apartment. By the time he left she was sore but content, although she hadn't learned a great deal more about his plan. He was going to work that out this coming week and would be back in Calgary next weekend. It was too early for her to be seen with him in Longville, he said, so he would come to her. She had a full schedule for the coming week so was happy to go with his plan.

Monday morning found Jessica at her desk long before Frank arrived. She'd had a tense weekend after her visit from Ethan on the Friday. Riding out on the Saturday she'd deliberately gone in the opposite direction to his ranch and headed towards the foothills. It had been a fine sunny day when she set out, but by mid-afternoon the sky had clouded over and it was just beginning to rain by the time she arrived back at the stables. Once home, she'd secured the door with the new bolt. She didn't think he'd noticed it last night since he'd made no comment. That night she tried to relax and watched television before going to bed, and thankfully slept somewhat better than she had the night before.

Sunday was dry and cloudy but she wasn't put off. Collecting Rory, she rode out for a couple of hours before coming home and having a long soak in the bath. After that, it was the same as the night before, a meal in front of the television and then bed, ready for the week ahead. For a short time, she wondered what it would have been like to spend a day with Ethan. Would she have got home? Or would she have ended up in his bed, where he clearly wanted her?

The week passed uneventfully. There seemed to be a lull in the work, and Jessica was able to take things a bit easier. But that caused its own problems, as it gave her time to think about Ethan and the situation between them.

Tuesday evening she'd just settled down with a coffee when her phone went. Picking it up, it took a moment for her to recognise her former secretary, Anna's voice. After greeting each other Anna asked about her new job, and then told her how she missed her and didn't seem to have the same relationship with the new lawyer that she now worker with. Although she told Anna about her job she didn't say it was as an assistant. She didn't want Tom to find out that she'd downgraded and have him think it was because of what he'd done. Anna hesitated for a moment and Jessica sensed that there was something coming that she was not going to like.

"Look, Jessica, I don't really know how to say this, but I feel as though you should know."

"Know what?" she asked, a sick feeling coming over her.

"It's about Tom. He's got engaged."

Jessica was surprised that she almost felt relieved at the news. "Don't tell me, to Christina Delaney?"

Now it was Anna's turn to be surprised. "You know?"

"Not until now. It hasn't taken him long, though."

"Sorry, Jessica, you've lost me. Did you know he was seeing her after you left?"

"I guessed he would be, since he was screwing her while we were together." She didn't hold back on this information.

"Oh my God." Suddenly the broken engagement made sense to Anna. "He was cheating on you and you found out, and that's why you broke it off. How on earth did you find out? Or is that none of my business?"

"It's no secret, well, not between the three of us. I caught them screwing in the apartment when I went home sick one day. He came clean and told me about it and that was the end of us."

"Oh God, Jessica. How awful for you. I would never have thought he was like that.""No, that's the trouble, you don't always know what people are like, even when you think you know them." She was thinking of Ethan as she spoke. "But hey, I'm fine. I'm over it and moving on. I just couldn't stay with the old firm knowing they would get together. Didn't want the sympathy, because I don't need it. I reckon I've had a lucky escape. If he cheated on me, he'll probably cheat on her eventually."

They talked some more before promising to keep in touch. Once the call had ended Jessica tried to analyse her feelings. To her surprise she found she wasn't upset or angry. Tom had got the corporate wife he wanted and she had, well she wasn't sure what she had, other than the experience of a night in a hotel in Calgary. But whatever it was, she was happy at this moment in time, and whatever the future might hold, she had yet to discover.

She spent the rest of the week arranging appointments for Frank with a couple of new clients. She still wasn't totally happy with the way he did things, but she was watching and keeping notes. The last thing she needed was to be caught up in anything dodgy that would affect her own career. A career that Frank had no knowledge of, at present. Maybe if she felt more comfortable, in time, she might tell him she had a law degree and see about a partnership. But that would depend on the work, whether there was enough to sustain two partners, and whether what he was doing was above board. It would also mean settling here, near Ethan, and she wasn't sure if she wanted that.

By the end of the week, she was itching to get out riding again. The weather had been wet at the start of the week but, by Friday, it was warm and the weekend forecast was for it to be hot. She spent Friday night doing laundry and sorting out some paperwork of her own. She hated doing these things on a weekend when she could be out and about doing other things.

Saturday morning was really hot and Jessica wondered if she'd done the right thing in taking Rory out. Weekends were the only time she got to have a long ride and to forgo one wasn't something she wanted to do. She'd made sure she had plenty of water with her when she set out. Now, she was at least a couple of hours into her ride and, having ground-hitched Rory, she was sitting on a large boulder surveying the land around her. She could see the Rockies way off in the distance, too far for her to ever reach on horseback. But she would like to drive over there some day.

Reaching into her pocket, she pulled out a trail bar and started to eat. There was little sound and the silence almost felt unnatural. It was Rory's snort and then soft whinny as he raised his head that alerted her. Swinging her head round she saw the cloud of dust in the distance. At first she thought it was a vehicle, but then realised that there were no roads, so it must be a rider. She stood up and pulled the pair of small binoculars from her saddlebag. She'd started carrying them with her, as there were so many things of interest not always visible to the naked eye. Turning to the rider, she focused in. Ethan Slade, and he was riding at such a speed, he would have been with her before she could move, had it not been for Rory. Putting the water back in her bag, she mounted and turned Rory away from the oncoming rider and set him into a gallop. *If you think you are going to ambush me, Ethan Slade you can think again,* she thought, as Rory's hooves flew over the ground.

Rory was going faster than he had in a long time and with the bit between his teeth he was thundering across the ground. She let him go. The more distance between her and Ethan the better, so they galloped on. She didn't see the tree stump in front of her until Rory jumped it. But his back leg caught and he stumbled. As he righted himself, she lost her stirrup and began unceremoniously sliding, in what seemed to be slow motion, out of the saddle. Kicking her other foot free she braced herself. Her hands went up automatically to protect her face so they took the force of the fall. She hit the ground with a thud that knocked the breath out of her, and then she rolled and felt her head hit something hard, then blackness.

Rory, sensing all was not well, came to an abrupt halt and turned and walked slowly back to her before stopping and gently nudging her with his nose. He wasn't the wisest head in the stable but even he knew this wasn't good. Pawing the ground near to her back, he nudged her again, but no response. Whinnying softly, he nuzzled her face, his nose moving through the blood that was seeping from the cut on her forehead. Lifting his head, he looked around but could see nothing. He looked back at the still figure on the ground and did the only thing he could. He turned and headed for home. *They would know what to do.*

Ethan had thought he could cover the distance between himself and the figure sitting on the rock before she realised he was there. That was a misjudgement on his part. He saw her jump up and mount and the next minute she was galloping away from him. Well, he knew better than to chase her, so he pulled his horse, Kohana, to a walk and then turned back. "Looks like the lady's not up for company again," he spoke softly to the gelding as they headed back to join the men. Would he ever manage to pin her down long enough to have a proper conversation with her? At this rate he doubted it, but he wasn't one to give up. Particularly when he was chasing something he really wanted.

It was early evening when he and the men rode into the yard. It wasn't usual for the men to be here on a weekend, unless they were moving a herd, which they'd just done. Maggie, his housekeeper, had offered to come in and cook a meal for when they got back and he saw her standing at the top of the steps leading to the house. He raised his hand in greeting and was surprised when she came hurrying towards him.

"Oh, thank goodness you're back. Bob from the livery stables has just rung. That young girl, you know, the one that works for Frank? Well, she took one of the horses out and the horse is back, but on its own. Not only that, but there was blood on its nose, but not from the horse. So he reckons she's taken a tumble and could be injured. He's going to try and get some people rounded up from town to look for her, but he says she often heads out this way and wondered if you could help search."

Shouting to the men not to dismount, he told them to let the horses have a drink as they were going to have to head back out. "Maggie, phone Bob back and tell him that I saw her earlier and she was over in the south section, up near the ridge. I'll head back there with the boys and see if we can spot her." He spoke calmly, but inside he was a mess. This was his fault; he was sure of it. He'd sent her galloping off and now she was probably lying somewhere injured, all because of him. He watched Maggie's retreating back and then turned and went across to the men and explained what had happened.

Chapter Ten

Jessica opened her eyes and the first thing she saw, when she managed to focus clearly, was an ant right near to the end of her nose. She tried to sit up and felt dizzy, but knew she had to move. Where there was one ant there were probably a hell of a lot more. Struggling to her feet, she saw her hands were scrubbed and bleeding, her jeans were torn and there was blood seeping through from her knee. Looking down, she saw a small rock and then the blood on it. Putting a hand up to her head she felt a sticky wetness, and then saw the blood on her fingers. Feeling in her pocket for a tissue she gently wiped her head and then tried to feel how bad the cut was. It didn't feel deep but she couldn't be sure.

Looking around, she couldn't see Rory. Calling to him, she waited, but he didn't come. She hoped he was alright. She could remember him jumping and then a stumble. Then she was slipping and whatever happened next was a blur. But Rory wasn't here, so that must mean he was okay and had probably gone back to his stable. She hoped so, because that would mean someone would come looking for her. But now her main concern was how the hell was she going to get back? And apart from that, where was she? Limping, she set off walking in, hopefully, the direction she'd come from. The dizziness came in waves as she set off, but gradually it eased.

Thankfully it was June and it was still light, so she could at least see where she was walking. Tramping over uneven terrain was bad enough when you were fit but with an aching and bloody leg it was no picnic. She had to keep stopping as every part of her body ached. She cursed Ethan for chasing her, and she cursed herself more for running. If she'd only stayed none of this would have happened. But then if she'd stayed something else probably would have happened. She couldn't trust herself with him, and she trusted him even less. Being angry for putting herself in this predicament took her mind off the aches and pains she was feeling.

She had no idea what time it was. She'd looked at her watch but she'd obviously broken it in the fall as the time had stopped at five-thirty. She was due back at the stables about six, so they would know she was missing. How long she'd been unconscious she didn't know but, looking at the low sun, she figured it must be about seven or eight. She wasn't sure. In fact, she wasn't sure if she was even walking in the right direction. She seemed closer to the foothills than she had been before and feared that she was walking diagonally. She needed to be going away from them and altered her track.

It was starting to get darker, and she was scared. There were no snakes around, she knew, but dusk would bring out predators, bear or cougar, and she was injured so they would smell the blood. Bears could smell from a distance of about twenty miles away, so she knew they would have no trouble in sensing her, and her distress. The only thing that stopped her from panicking about a bear was that they usually avoided humans. But the cougar, or mountain lion, that was another thing entirely. It would possibly attack, particularly if it thought she was injured and weak. Oh Christ, now she was scared. She could feel tears of panic welling up and swallowed hard and told herself not to be stupid. There was no indication there were any bears or cougars in the area. She just had to keep on walking and she would soon be back in town and then home in her cottage. She concentrated on thinking about her cottage. How welcoming it would feel when she got there. A hot shower, or perhaps a bath, would ease her aches and she would need to see to her hands and knee.

She stumbled on over the rough grass and then stopped. Her senses were on alert. She'd heard something. She could feel her heart thumping in her chest. Then she heard it again, *'coooeeee.'* Was it an animal? Then, *'J...e...s...s...i...c...a.'* She couldn't mistake that for an animal. Someone was calling her name. "Here. Over here," she yelled back as loud as she could and kept calling. Then she heard a noise and someone call her name again "Jess, is that you?"

Oh shit, she thought as she recognised the voice. Even in this predicament she knew it was him. Then she heard the thundering of hooves and Ethan appeared.

His horse hadn't even stopped before he was on the ground and running towards her. She wanted to run to him. To have him hold her and make her feel safe. She could feel the tears running down her face. But she couldn't move so just stood and stared at him. He was the last and the only person she wanted to see.

He was talking to her, asking questions. It was only when he asked what had happened that her mind cleared. *What happened?* She asked herself the same question and didn't have an answer. The concern in his voice and the obvious worry on his face, which she could just make out in the fading light, took her back to Calgary. To the man she met there and the feelings he evoked in her. She had an urge to reach out her hand and touch his face, to wipe the lines of worry away, but she held back and the moment was lost.

***

He'd been going out of his mind with worry about her. Hearing her answer their calls had been a huge relief. His first instinct had been to grab her and hold her in his arms to convince himself she was okay. His second instinct was to hold back or he would be in real trouble. Seeing her standing there, bloodied but okay, brought him to a stop in front of her. "Jesus, Jessica. What the hell has happened? Are you hurt?" The question seemed stupid even to his ears. "Of course you are, you're bleeding," he said. By this time, he was inspecting her head and then her hands and the blood-stained jeans. Lifting his eyes to her face, his voice was strained. "Is this my fault?"

She shook her head. "No. I lost concentration for a moment, then a stirrup, and that was it. But I seem to have misplaced Rory. I can't find him anywhere."

113

"No, you haven't lost him," he called to her, as he walked back to his horse. "He's fine. He made his way home and that raised the alarm." He came back with a canteen of water. Taking a clean handkerchief out of his pocket he poured water onto it and gently wiped her forehead. She winced as he did. Then he poured water over her hands to wash away the dirt and carefully wiped them. Looking at her knee in the fading light he knew he couldn't do a great deal with that unless she took her jeans off, and he couldn't do that here. In fact, they couldn't do anything here.

"Look, you need to be cleaned up properly. You'll have to come back to the ranch so I can see to these injuries."

"No way," she replied.

He sighed. "They need to be properly cleaned or you'll get an infection. The Lazy B is closest and I have all that we need." He lowered his voice to avoid arousing his men's curiosity. "If you're worried about being alone, don't be, my housekeeper will still be there." He saw her hesitating. "Look, Jess, I'm not going to argue. You're hurt and your injuries need to be cleaned. So you're coming back with me if I have to haul you over my saddle and take you there. But I would much rather you rode in front of me…upright."

He was waiting for a reply from her. "Come on, Jessica. I'm more concerned with treating your injuries than making advances to you. Surely an unexpected visit to my home isn't all that difficult to accept."

"Okay, if you insist."

"I do. You have no idea what you can pick up from the dirt if it's not cleaned out properly." He turned and spoke to the men who were patiently waiting, and told them to go back to the ranch and tell Maggie what had happened and call off the search. Once they'd done that, he told them to ask Doc Hadley if he could come to the ranch to check Jess over. He was concerned that she'd been unconscious and had no doubt that she would refuse to go to the doctors or to the hospital. Facing her with a *fait accompli* seemed to be the better option.

"Can you mount?" He asked the question and waited for her reply.

"Of course I can." The answer was short and abrupt.

Ethan brought his mount close to her and held Kohana steady as she put her foot in the stirrup and hauled herself, none too gracefully, into the saddle. What would usually be easy proved much more difficult with her injuries. But he knew she wasn't going to accept any help.

He watched her mount, and couldn't help but admire her tenacity in handling the situation. Mounting behind her he swung the gelding around. "Come on, Kohana, let's head for home."

Riding with her in front, and effectively in his arms, was his idea of heaven. He eased forward putting his body against her back. He knew she would be cold and the heat from him would warm her. But apart from that, he simply wanted to feel her body against his. He thought she would move away but she didn't, and that told him she was cold. In fact, the atmosphere between them was cold. You wouldn't think he'd just rescued her. But then again, she probably blamed him for what had happened, despite what she'd said earlier. No doubt he'd get it in the neck at some point, but for now he was content just being close to her and knowing she was safe.

He waited for some time before eventually speaking. "Do you plan on ignoring me all the way home? He whispered in her ear. "Or can we be civilised and talk?" He noticed the stiffening of her spine and knew he'd hit home with his remark. "Well?"

**

They were going at a walking pace, for which she was thankful. She was aching in places she didn't know existed, not to mention her painful head and a knee that was stinging like crazy. Watching him as he'd cleaned her hands had been frustrating. If she hadn't tried to run away from him she wouldn't be in this predicament now, and to make matters worse he was about to take her to his home. That was the last place she wanted to be, but at least there would be someone else there. The gentle movement of the horse and the feel of his warm body close behind her was almost lulling her into a sense of false security. She could smell the sweat on him, but it wasn't unpleasant. He smelled of the land. But she had no intention of letting him know any of this, or indeed of starting a conversation that would probably end up in a row, or something else that she didn't want to dwell on.

His words broke her out of her daydream. She didn't want to talk, she just wanted to keep her thoughts to herself, because if she started she would let him have both barrels. She had no idea why she felt so belligerent, apart from the fact that she'd just looked a fool in front of the one person she didn't want to lose face with. Falling off was bad enough, but then to get lost, that was too much to take. The final straw had been her own reaction when he appeared. She wanted nothing more than to be held in his arms and that had annoyed her, but she wasn't prepared to work out why. But being petty wasn't really her thing. "I guess we can talk."

"Good," he said. "So perhaps you'd like to explain why you were riding like somebody crazy earlier. I presume that's what led to your obvious fall, despite what you said?"

Jessica was in no mood to have a lecture. "Perhaps you can tell me why you were chasing after me?"

"I wasn't intending to chase after you. I just wanted to talk to you. It seems turning up at your place doesn't work, so I thought out in the open you might be a bit more receptive to what I wanted to say. But I soon realised it wasn't when you took off, so I backed away and left you. That seems to have been my mistake. If I'd kept after you I'd have been able to prevent you from hours of wandering around looking like animal fodder."

"I don't really want to hear what you've got to say on any subject. And anyway I'm sure whatever it is wouldn't be of any interest to me."

"So if I were to say that I'm now officially single, with no girlfriend, that would be of no interest to you?" He whispered the words in her ear.

"Absolutely not."

"Come on, Red. You can do better than that," he said

116

starting to laugh. "After what we've shared you seriously expect me to believe that you aren't interested?"

She had no intention of answering him and kept her eyes looking straight ahead. But her insides were doing cartwheels. *He was unattached!! How was she going to handle that?*

"Okay, have it your way. But your silence tells me more than any words could. You're interested, but you're scared. I misled you and you're afraid to trust me, and I deeply regret that. You trusted me once before and I didn't fail you. Did I? So trust me again, Jessica. Let me show you how it can be between us."

She kept her eyes forward. She couldn't look at him, if she did she would be lost. His words and reference to Calgary hit a nerve.

Realising that he wasn't going to get a reply he muttered, "Seems like the lady won't answer us, Kohana."

Jessica felt her lips curve into a smile at the comment. "What does it mean?"

"What, the fact that you won't talk to us?"

"No, your horse's name."

"Ah, Kohana. It's Sioux for 'swift.' He can run as swift as an arrow if you let him have his head. At least that's what one of our old hands, who was part Sioux, declared when he was a few weeks old. And yes, I could have given him another name but I liked Kohana. It seems to suit him and I like the sound of it. Just as I like the sound of Jessica, or even more so, Jess. And I certainly like Red."

Now, despite herself she was intrigued. "Why Jess? Nobody calls me that."

"All the more reason for me to. It makes it special between us and it sounds much more intimate than Jessica."

"I have no wish for there to be anything intimate, or otherwise, between us." The conversation was getting into risky waters again and she wanted out of it.

"Ah, but Jess, you see there is intimacy between us. Or rather, there has been, and if I recall it was a most enlightening experience, for both of us."

That comment was most definitely not getting a reply, but

117

she did turn her head and give him a look that told him in no uncertain terms that the conversation was over. That he couldn't see it in the fading light didn't matter. He'd know she'd just glared at him. He started laughing when he saw her turn and that did nothing to appease her.

They rode on in silence for some time before the ranch buildings came into sight. Kohana, seeing home, started to prance and Ethan held him back. "See how eager he is to reach my home. One day you'll feel the same, Jess. I promise you will."

She ignored the comment. He dismounted and helped her down. This time she didn't refuse his help. She followed him up the steps into the large house. A middle-aged woman came hurrying to them in the hall.

"Thank goodness you found her."

"Yes, fortunately for her. Any later and we would have lost the light, and goodness knows what harm she could have come to out there on her own. But she does need some medical care." As he was speaking, he took hold of Jessica's elbow and pulled her forward.

"Jessica, this is Mrs Green, or Maggie, as everyone calls her. Maggie, this is Jessica Cameron, Frank's assistant."

The two women nodded and said hello. "I'll fetch a bowl of warm water for those cuts," said Maggie looking at Ethan. "Doc Hadley's in the lounge."

"No, it's okay, Maggie. If you just leave the bowl and the antiseptic on the kitchen top I can see to them, once the doc has finished. Don't want to delay you, I know you have a busy night planned."

As they were talking Jessica had been looking around the entrance hall. The house was solid wood and although it didn't look new, it looked strong and sturdy. There was a long bench just inside the door, along one of the walls, and above it a rack for coats. There were several doors leading off the hall and a wooden staircase leading up to another level. It was the words, *Doc Hadley,* and then, *don't want to delay you,* that got her attention. There was a doctor here and the housekeeper was leaving. That wasn't what he'd indicated. He said she would be there and there was no need to worry. She glanced from Maggie to Ethan but all she could see was concern on both their faces. Maybe she was getting paranoid, but then who could blame her? Everywhere she went he seemed to be there. Well, perhaps not everywhere but often enough for it not to be a coincidence.

She let him show her through to one of the rooms that turned out to be a lounge. The doctor was waiting and gave her head a good examination and checked out her other injuries. He was concerned that she shouldn't be left on her own for a few hours in case of other symptoms occurring. Before she had chance to speak, Ethan told him there was no problem with that and she would stay with him until he felt she would be okay on her own. They were talking about her as though she wasn't there and that irked her. Although she wanted to speak out, she was simply too tired. Apart from that, this was the first time she'd met the doctor and didn't want to appear ungrateful.

Once the doctor had finished he left. Ethan went out with him but was soon back with a bowl of warm water and a bottle of something that Jessica was sure was going to sting. He disappeared for a moment and then returned with two mugs of coffee that he set down on a nearby table. What she expected now, she wasn't sure, but he was concentrating purely on seeing to her hands.

Rolling up her sleeves, Ethan gently bathed both hands in the warm water, wiping the dirt away. Then, using a pair of tweezers, he picked out bits of embedded grit. She could see him grimacing as though trying to close his ears to her pain. She felt it sharply, and sucked in her breath every time he pulled out a piece of grit. Now he carefully dried the hands, but she knew this was going to be the worst bit. Telling her to grit her teeth, he soaked a clean cloth in the antiseptic and held it over her hands. She tried to pull away but he held her firmly and looked into her eyes. The tears welled up and she could see he hated what he was doing, but knew it was better than the alternative.

The first tear escaped and ran down her cheek. He lifted a

119

hand and wiped it away, giving her a sympathetic smile as he did. She smiled back, or perhaps it was a grimace. Then he picked up the bottle and gently poured some more antiseptic over the cloth. This time she yelled. "Sorry Jessica. It has to be done."

She nodded her head. "Get on with it."

Having checked her hands, he was finally satisfied that he could see no more grit in the cuts. "I'll put a dressing on both hands shortly. But for now that's the hands dealt with. Now the knee." The words were said dispassionately. They had to be, because the only way he could treat her knee was for her to remove her jeans. He clearly had a feeling that he was about to face a battle.

Jessica looked at him. *Her knee.* She looked at the torn jeans with her knee sticking through, looking bloody and no doubt full of grit, the same at her hands. *Oh shit,* she thought. *How the hell is he going to do this? More to the point, if he doesn't, how can I, with both hands out of action?* She looked down at her knee again. "How do you plan on cleaning it?"

"Same as with the hands, I'm afraid."

"Okay, you'd better get started." She had no intention of making any suggestion as to how he should do this.

He ran his hand through his hair. "Jess, you're going to have to take your jeans off."

"No way. You can cut the leg off my jeans, it doesn't matter."

"Yes, I could do that, but I need to make sure that there are no other cuts on you that could become infected."

She stared at him. She knew he was making sense, but the thought of being half naked and alone with him was more than she could handle. *Yes, but you've already been fully naked and alone with him,* said a voice in her head. *Yes, but that was different,* she told it.

He was watching her. He wasn't stupid. He would see the emotions running across her face, telling him she was having one hell of a battle with herself. While she knew he'd find the thought of having her semi-naked in his home delightful, it did seem that all he wanted to do at the moment was to make sure that her injuries were treated. Could she trust him not to take advantage of the situation? But then, did she have any choice?

"Come on, Jessica," he said, deliberately using her full name to avoid any suggestion of intimacy.

She stood up and tried to undo the button on her jeans but couldn't. Looking at him she didn't need to say anything. His hands came forward and he undid the button, slid down the zip, and then carefully eased the jeans down her legs, taking extra care over her knee. He was kneeling down as he reached her ankles, he could probably smell the perfume from her body. She briefly closed her eyes, wondering if he was remembering Calgary. Stop it, she told herself and looked down. He lifted his head and his eyes travelled the length of her legs. He would see the shadow of dark hair through the silky briefs, and she stifled a groan. Then saw him take a deep breath as though to steady himself, before his gaze finally met hers. She knew what was going through his mind.

"Don't even think it," she said, scowling at him.

He couldn't help the grin as he asked her to lift one leg, then the other as he removed the jeans. Telling her to sit back down, he disappeared and returned shortly with fresh water and a fleece blanket that he suggested she cover herself with. She was grateful and thanked him, and then waited for the pain to hit as he started to bathe her knee.

***

If anyone had told him that holding a slim suntanned leg without being able to run his hand the length of it would have been so difficult, he doubted he would have believed them. Despite the circumstances, his fingers itched to reach up, to travel to her thigh and then beyond. He carefully cleaned the blood and dirt away and then started the painstaking job of holding her leg close to his face so he could see any grit that needed removing. She winced every time he removed another piece. Her pain should have cooled his ardour, but it didn't, and he was ashamed of himself for having such thoughts while she was hurting so much. Eventually the wound was clean, and now all he had to do was apply the antiseptic. This time she swore at him, and he lifted his head and raised an eyebrow at her. "Language, Jessica."

"I think you're enjoying this, Ethan Slade," she flung back at him as she brushed the tears away with the back of her hand.

"I'm certainly not enjoying causing you pain. Although I have to admit the job does have some very attractive benefits."

Satisfied that it was thoroughly clean, he then told her to stand up. And was surprised when she did as he asked. Pulling the blanket away, he turned her around checking her for any other cuts, but found none. Finally turning her to face him he found himself looking at her groin. It was too much of a temptation and he leaned forward and kissed it. She pulled back and he was sure she would have hit him if she'd had an uninjured hand.

"Sorry, Jess, that was wrong of me. You're a guest in my home and I shouldn't abuse that. Anyway, right now I need to see to your forehead. Fortunately, it's not as dirty as your knee and hands. I'll just get some clean water."

He was back shortly and found her sitting on the sofa with the rug across her thighs. Kneeling in front, he proceeded to clean the cut on her forehead. Luckily, it didn't need any stitches. He wasn't sure how she would have reacted if he'd had to stitch her head. Wiping the wound clean, he then applied the antiseptic. This time he winced with her as she yelled. The injuries weren't serious but they would be painful for quite a few days.

"Sorry about the kiss earlier." He stood up as he was speaking until he was looking down at her. "But you can't really blame me, can you? You're driving me crazy. We spent the most amazing night together and made love but now you won't even talk to me, let alone go out with me."

Jessica's anger seemed to die in an instant as she looked at him. He was so frustrated he was sure it must show on his face. There was something between them that she couldn't go on denying. He watched her weigh things up. If he was now single, was there really anything wrong in seeing where things went? Or was she going to be afraid to step outside her comfort zone again? What if she'd not done that in Calgary? What if she'd gone to her room and stayed there? They would never have seen each other again, never have experienced what happened between them that night. Was she brave enough to take another step outside her normal limits? He waited. Finally, she took a deep breath. "I wasn't aware that you'd asked me out."

Hope flared in his eyes. "Okay, so I'm asking you now. Will you stay and have dinner, here with me tonight? Look, let's do this properly. Up to now we've done everything the wrong way round. Miss Jessica Cameron, I'm very pleased to meet you. I'm Ethan Slade, single, aged thirty-two, a rancher and owner of the Lazy B Ranch. I would shake your hand but in the circumstances I don't think that's possible."

She laughed at the sudden seriousness. For he was sincere, she must see it in his face. Then he relaxed as she joined in with his game. "Pleased to meet you, Mr Slade. I'm Jessica Ann Cameron, single, aged 26, I work in the law and I'm tenant of one of your properties." She held back that she was in fact a lawyer. She didn't want to have to explain that to him, not now.

His eyes twinkled and his mouth curved into a smile. "So will you stay, now we've been formally introduced?"

"Sorry, I can't. I need to get back."

"For what. To try and cook a meal with your hands like that?"

He was right and she knew he was. "Not only that but I need to have a shower. It may have escaped your notice but I am rather filthy." The twinkle in his eye told her she'd used the wrong terminology.

"I might like you filthy, Jess."

She was exasperated. "You know what I mean. I need to clean up."

"You can do that here. I have a perfectly good bathroom. You could shower before I dress your hands and knee."

She looked at his face. It was straight and no hint of humour. Could she trust him? It would be wonderful to have a

123

shower, even better to soak in a bath and let the aches and pains subside.

"Oh no, I couldn't. I can wait until I get home, or in the morning," she said knowing she had no intention of going to bed without showering.

"Look, Jessica, you are tired and I have no doubt that every part of your body aches. You also need to eat. If I take you home now you will have to manage on your own and then try and sort out a meal. It makes more sense to shower here, while I start to prepare a meal. That way, when I take you home, you can go straight to bed. And anyway, the doc said you shouldn't be on your own for a few hours, so you either spend the time here with me or we both go to your place."

So she was caught by her own words, by saying she needed to clean up, and had no reason to put forward by way of argument. "I can hardly stay to dinner dressed like this," she said, indicating the state of her clothes.

"No, true. Much as I would love to sit down with you part naked and wearing those delightful briefs, I think I can probably find something for you to wear, although they may be a bit on the large side. Look, let's go upstairs; I'll find something for you to wear. Then, while you have a shower, I can start on dinner."

It all sounded so simple. Probably too simple, to her, but the thought of someone taking care of her for a short time was clearly tempting. She was beginning to look weepy. No doubt the shock of all that had happened was finally hitting home. He wanted to reassure her, but didn't want to add pressure, so he waited until she came to the only decision that made any sense. When she did reply she couldn't even answer him, and just nodded her head.

"Good," he said holding out his hand to her. "Come on, I'll show you where things are."

He guided her into the guest bedroom and through to the bathroom. He couldn't take her into his room, much as he wanted to. When he took her there for the first time he wanted it to be special. He wanted to lead her in by the hand and then spent the night making love to her. This was definitely not the right time, nor was it the right time to be having these thoughts.

She'd wrapped the blanket around her as she followed him and was now stood looking at the cream and blue bathroom. There was a walk-in shower, but much more appealing was a large corner bathtub. He remained in the doorway, while she looked around. The she turned to him. "Could I use the bathtub rather than the shower?"

"Of course. Probably a good idea, as a soak will help to ease the pain. Here, let me turn the taps on. You can use the jets if you want; the controls are just on the side. There's some bath salts in the cupboard," he said, reaching in and offering her pine or lavender. "I prefer lavender, if that's any help," he said with a mischievous grin.

She scowled at him. "I'll have pine then," she replied and then appeared to bite back a further comment as he deliberately poured lavender into the bath.

"Lavender is good for healing. Pine would probably aggravate. I'll get you some towels and then leave you in peace."

He was back in a short time with two large blue towels and put them on the rail to warm. She was waiting for him to go so she could get into the ever-so-inviting water that was now waiting for her.

"Do you need a hand with anything before I go?" The question was serious with no hint of any undercurrent.

She looked at him and he had the feeling she was about to say no when she realised that she probably could do with some help. Turning her back to him she asked him to unfasten her bra. She shook as his fingers brushed against her skin, and released the strap. He was thinking back to Calgary. To when he'd undone her bra there. Was she remembering the same? He could hear her breathing becoming unsteady. Unable to stop himself he dropped a kiss on her shoulder. The reaction was instant as a tremor shot through her body.

Ethan couldn't resist the kiss. He'd been so much of a gentleman up to now but her naked back was too much. He expected a reaction but not the violent shudder that he saw. So he knew she was feeling the same as him. They were both back in another room and about to do something wonderful. Except this time, they weren't. He was going to behave, much as it pained him to do so. He moved his hands to her shoulders and whispered, "Enjoy your bath. Next time I'll join you." He'd almost reached the door when he remembered she needed something to wear. "I'll leave some clothes on the bed for you. Take your time, there's no rush."

***

She heard the door close and then turned around. The bathroom was empty. Dropping the towel and bra she removed her briefs and then stepped into the warm water. If she'd had a tie she would have fastened her hair up. But she didn't so the ends would get wet, but she didn't care. This was bliss and she rested her head back against the rim.

When she finally emerged into the bedroom she found a pair of cargo pants on the bed together with an over large T-shirt. She put her undies back on, managing to fasten her bra at the front before twisting it round. Then she pulled the T-shirt over her head and was about to step into the pants when there was a knock at the door. She froze, thankful that the T-shirt covered enough of her modesty.

***

He didn't wait for any response but walked straight in. Seeing her state of dress, he couldn't hold back the grin as his eyes roamed over the tanned legs. How he wished things were different, that she wasn't injured. This night would have a far better ending. As she attempted to get her leg into the pants he stepped forward to help, holding her steady as she stepped into them. Then as she pulled them up, he moved in front of her. "Here, let's see what we can do with them." Rolling up the bottoms for her he pulled out a length of cord and tied it around her waist to hold them up. Pulling the T-shirt down he grinned. "You look quite delectable, Miss Cameron." She would have been delectable in anything, he decided. He'd just spent an agonising time downstairs imagining her in the bath and now, seeing her in her impromptu dress with her hair hanging damp on her shoulders, was almost his undoing. To him she had never looked more adorable, but he had no intention of telling her that. Well, not just yet.

Sitting her in the lounge, he dressed her hands and then rolled the pants up and saw to her knee. Once that was done, he applied a small plaster to her forehead. Then they sat down to dinner and ate his perfectly cooked steaks with salad and managed a civilised, but decidedly teasing on his part, conversation as they did. He interpreted her every need and had even had the forethought to cut up her steak. Once he had loaded up the dishes he drove her home. Up to now he'd behaved perfectly, well almost, and he had no wish to blot his copybook. As he pulled up outside her cottage he turned towards her. "So, since this is a date, do I get to be invited in for coffee?

***

She'd been quite moved by his thoughtfulness all evening, but knew he would try something like this and she had no idea what she was going to say. He'd behaved all night, well, apart from the two small kisses on parts of her anatomy that she didn't wish to remember, but neither wished to forget. Could she trust him if he came in? "Well, I guess I could repay some of your hospitality. Although you'll probably end up having to make the coffee yourself," she said holding up her hands.

"No problem. It'll be a pleasure." He couldn't keep the grin off his face.

"One condition. No funny business."

He held up his hands. "Okay, no funny business."

He let them into the cottage and it wasn't long before she was settled into the armchair holding a mug of coffee, as best she could, in her hands. He kept up a steady flow of conversation until he realised that she was falling asleep.

Standing up, he took the empty mugs through to the

127

kitchen. "I should go; you need to sleep. But I can help you undress before I leave. But only if you want me to," he added mischievously. The look she gave him told him quite clearly that any help would not be welcome, and then laughed when he threw up his hands. "Can't blame a guy for trying." Reaching the door, he turned back to face her. "You know you can only be scared of yourself for so long, Jess."

"I don't know what you mean. And don't call me, Jess."

"Okay, Jessica. Have it your way." He made to go through the open door but turned back and very quickly kissed her on the lips. "Night Jess...ica."

She couldn't hold back the laugh and closed the door on him before he took advantage of her again. She wasn't quite sure how she'd gone from running away from him to ending up having dinner and then coffee with him. He seemed to be able to turn her decisions upside down. And she wasn't sure whether that was a good thing or not. But now, all she wanted to do was to sleep.

Climbing the stairs, she felt every muscle screaming out and was glad when she was able to collapse on the side of the bed. But that was the start of the next dilemma. The pants were okay to get off, as was the top and the briefs, but the bra proved difficult. Now she wished he was here. *No, she didn't*, she argued with herself. If he was here she wouldn't be spending the night alone in her bed, and she was in no state to engage in any kind of lovemaking. Managing to get her arms out of the straps she slowly inched the back round to the front and then managed to undo the clasp. Pulling a nightdress out from the drawer she pulled it over her head and then fell exhausted into bed.

Chapter Eleven

By Monday morning her hands were still sore and she wore a pair of smart pants to work with a matching jacket, to cover the dressing on her knee.

Frank was late in, which was unusual but when he did arrive he seemed in high spirits. He'd asked what had happened to her hands and she made light of it. By lunchtime she had cleared the work he wanted her to do, so he told her to take a long lunch. He gave her work he needed doing that afternoon but said there was no need to be back before two. She wasn't going to argue, so set off towards the local diner. It was unusually quiet, so she finished eating in record time. Walking back along the sidewalk, she saw it was only one o'clock and that meant that she probably had another hour to kill. Deciding that it didn't matter about a long lunch, she headed back to the office. She would rather be back at work and tackling the files she had for the afternoon, particularly as she was working more slowly because of her hands.

The office was locked so she let herself in. Kicking off her shoes, which had begun to pinch, she picked up the top file. She'd only been working for a few minutes when she realised that she needed some old papers that were in the storeroom next to Frank's office. Going along the passage, she thought she heard voices from Frank's office and figured that perhaps he was in and on the phone. Opening the storeroom door, she went inside. She knew roughly where the papers she needed were and bent down to the lower shelf. Suddenly she heard voices, loud and clear. At first she couldn't figure out where they were coming from, but then she carefully moved some files and saw the air vent and realised that she was hearing the conversation in Frank's office. She tried to figure out where the vent was. She couldn't remember seeing one in his office. Then she realised that it must be behind the cabinets and that's why she'd never seen it. She was about to stand up and go, but there was something about the tone of the conversation that kept her crouching down and listening.

"You said you wanted to get away from here and start a new life with Joey. Well I'm going to offer you the chance to do that, but in exchange you will have to do something for me. Something that will involve you going to court."

"I don't want no trouble with the law, Mr Frank," said a female voice.

"No, you won't be in trouble, Lacey, but someone else will be because they will have done something really bad to you."

"Why would I let someone do something bad? Anyway, Joey wouldn't let them, he'd protect me."

Jessica heard Frank laugh. "Nobody will have really done anything bad to you, but you will say they have. And if Joey helps a bit, I'll give you some extra money so you can both set yourselves up in the city."

"How much money?"

"Twenty-five thousand dollars," said Frank. "That's if Joey helps."

Jessica was astounded by what she was hearing and sat down on one of the deed boxes and listened intently to the rest of the conversation, keeping as quiet as she could.

"Twenty-five thousand. What do I have to do for that, and what's Joey got to do?"

There was a creak as Frank settled back in his chair. "Well, what you have to do is pretend that someone has raped you. And what Joey has to do is to have rough sex, and I mean rough sex, with you just beforehand, to make the allegation look realistic. And it would help if he knocked you about a bit."

"Joey aint gonna be happy about knocking me about."

"Well if he doesn't want to, the price drops down to twenty thousand. So a few cuts and bruises are worth five grand. Ask Joey about it and I'm sure he'll be able to make an exception."

***

Inside the office, Lacey looked at Frank. She wanted the money. She desperately wanted to get away from her family and this place. She was fed up with looking after her younger brothers and sisters while their mom was out drinking. Joey was the best thing that had happened to her, but he wouldn't hang around for long if they couldn't get away. He worked with cars and would be able to get a job in the city, and she wanted to go to beauty school and this money would mean they could do that. "Thirty thousand," she said, "if you want me roughing up."

Frank laughed. "Tell you what. Twenty-five thousand, but a bonus of another five if any appeal fails and he stays in prison." Frank knew there would be an appeal and he needed to be sure that she kept up her story right to the end. He could see Lacey thinking over the offer.

"I don't know. I don't want to get into any bother with the police."

"Lacey, I've saved you from bother with the police before. Now what would Joey think, if he knew how you used to earn some extra dollars? He wouldn't want to know how many men had enjoyed your favours before he turned up, would he?"

"No, but I was always careful who I picked. You should know that, you've paid me enough in the past."

"Your word against mine, Lacey. But I don't want to tell Joey, all I want to do is to get this plan to work out so we both benefit. Think what you'll be able to do with all that money. Nice apartment and a new start." He waited, while Lacey thought over what he'd said. She knew he could make things difficult for her and the last thing she would want was for Joey to find out what she used to do. What he was offering them was a way out, but would she think it worth the risk?

"Okay. So who is supposed to be raping me?"

"I'll tell you that nearer the time. There'll be someone to give us some help and they will give him a light drug and get him into bed. Then you will go to his house and get into bed with him. Nothing will happen because he'll be out of it, but

131

you can work on a man and make him…you know, hard. And you should be rough in handling him since he's supposed to have forced you. Then, when he starts to leak, you get some on your fingers and smear it inside you. That way his DNA will be in you and he won't be able to get away with denying it. But you'll need to get it all out of him, empty him. I'm sure you can do that."

"So where does Joey come into it?"

"Before you go to his house, you and Joey need to have really rough sex, but you need to use protection. Don't want Joey's DNA inside you. Then he needs to slap you about a bit, and bruise you. You know, between your legs and grip your wrists, so they bruise. That way any tests will show you have had sex and it most probably wasn't consensual. When they find this person's sperm inside you, they will accept your story that he raped you."

Inside the storeroom Jessica couldn't believe what she was hearing. He had it all planned. She wasn't a criminal lawyer but she knew enough, and clearly so did he, to be sure that this evidence would most likely convict the person.

"So what would I say about why I was there?"

"Say you were walking home and he offered you a lift. Then he suggested that you went to his place for a drink. You could say you'd had a row with Joey, so you went just to spite him. When you got there he gave you alcohol and then he started to kiss you but you got scared. Then he dragged you to the bedroom and threw you on the bed. He was too strong for you but you fought him. You can scratch him so you have some of his skin under your nails. Then he ripped off your clothes and raped you. After he'd done that, he took something. That will account for any traces of a drug in his system. Then he fell asleep or passed out. That was when you made your escape to the other room and called 911."

"That's brilliant," said Lacey. "That's all I have to do. Have rough sex with my own boyfriend. Get into bed with an unconscious man, smear his semen on me…"

Frank interrupted. "Not only on you but it must be inside you for when they take a swab."

132

"Yeah, yeah, I know. Then I call 911 and collect twenty-five thousand dollars."

"Not quite," said Frank. "You'll get ten thousand on the night after it's happened. Then a further fifteen thousand when he's convicted. He'll appeal, and when you've given evidence at the appeal, and if he's still inside, you'll get a further five grand. Maybe if I'm feeling generous I might even increase the bonus, but no promises."

Lacey looked at him suspiciously. "Why'd you want to do this? What's this guy got on you?"

"That's my business, save to say that he has money that's owing to me, that should be mine."

"And you want to get your hands on his money, so you can get what's due to you?"

"Yes, you could put it like that," said Frank with a sickly laugh. "So are you going to do it?"

"I guess so. But I want the ten thousand before I do anything," said Lacey. She had no intention of taking any part in this without some of the money in a bank account.

Frank, seeing he had no choice in the matter if he wanted his plan to succeed, agreed. "Ten thousand in a bank account in your name, in the city, five days before this all happens. But if you double cross me, or don't do it, I'll say you stole that money."

"Yeah, yeah. If I say I'm doing it, I will." said Lacey. "So how's it going to happen and when is it supposed to take place?"

"Soon. I'll let you know when. I just have a few more details to sort out. I'll be in touch."

Jessica felt sick. She'd never heard such a debased plot before in her life. She wished she'd had her phone. She could have recorded this, but it was in her purse in the front office. She'd heard enough and crept out of the storeroom and back to the front office. Putting on her shoes she grabbed her purse and went quietly outside. She needed fresh air after what she'd heard. Not only that, she needed to figure out who Frank had been talking about and what she was going to do about what she'd overheard.

133

Over the next week, she looked through as many of Frank's files as she could to see whom he had a Power of Attorney for. She could only think that this was the way he was going to get hold of this person's money. She was still reeling from what she had heard, but she had nobody she could speak to about it. She couldn't go to the police and tell them, she had no proof. Frank would just deny everything, and that would be the end of her job.

The one person she might have been able to mention it to was Ethan, since there was acrimony between him and Frank, but he was conspicuous by his absence. She hadn't seen him since the night he brought her home, although he had phoned the following day to see how she was. He was probably playing games with her, staying away in the hope that she would go looking for him. Well he was going to be disappointed. Although she still had his clothes and they would need to be returned sometime, but she was in no rush to do that. At the moment she had more pressing things on her mind.

By the start of the following week her hands were almost as good as new. She had shortened the list of clients who Frank might be trying to frame. There were three men for whom he held Power of Attorney. One was already in a care home so she was able to discount him. The other two were more likely, although one was married and that would make getting control of any monies difficult. The other was elderly, in his sixties, and lived alone. He was the most likely, but why would Frank pick on him? In fact, why would Frank be willing to do this to anyone?

On Tuesday night she phoned Dan, one of her former colleagues who had some knowledge of criminal law, and asked a few hypothetical questions relating to Frank's plan. She was dismayed to find that the plan could very well work, despite the intended victim denying it. Her colleague had expressed concern at her enquiry and she told him it was just something she thought she'd overheard. That she might be mistaken but just wanted to check out whether it was feasible. His *'yes'* had shocked her. What shocked her even more was discovering that if Frank could get control of the person's money, then he would have pretty much a free hand in what he did, within reason, if there were nobody to keep track of him. What she still couldn't figure out was why Frank wanted the money, and why he would go to these lengths. She needed proof.

Thursday was uneventful, until a lanky young chap came into the office asking to see Frank. When he gave his name as Joey, she was instantly alert. Waiting until he'd gone through to Frank's office, she quietly followed him and slipped into the storeroom. This time she took her cell phone with her and also a file as cover for her being there. Crouching down she listened to the conversation and switched on record on her Blackberry.

"Look, Joey, it's not a big deal. Nobody is going to hurt Lacey, well, no one apart from you and I know you'll be as gentle as you can." Frank's voice came loud and clear.

"Well I don't like the idea of her being in bed with some bloke. What if he jumps her?"

Frank laughed. "How the hell can he jump her? He'll be out for the count."

"How can you be sure of that? And I don't want Lacey near him until he's out of it."

"She won't be. There'll be someone else there, someone who will slip the drug to him. Then, when he's unconscious, she'll tell Lacey, and then she'll go there."

"Who's this other someone? I don't want any bloke near my girl."

"It's not a bloke, it's a woman."

Jessica could feel her legs going numb with crouching, but there was no way she was moving. This was even worse than she thought.

"So do I really have to knock Lacey about?"

"Yes, that's one thing you have to get right. Bruises on her inner thighs and on her wrists. If you can get some on her neck that would be even better. And you will need to make the sex rough."

"Yeah, well I've got that covered. Gotta new condom that's

really good. Got these raised tips on them. I reckon that doing it hard with that on will make it look really rough."

Frank held up his hand. "Okay, okay. I don't need all the details."

"So if I do all of that, you give us the extra five thousand dollars."

"Yes, that's what I agreed with Lacey. Twenty-five thousand, as long as you were on board with it."

"Yeah, then another five later."

"Yes, well, that's a bit down the line. But if it all works out, yes, there's an extra bonus."

"So this five thousand for me being on board. I want that up front."

"No," said Frank. "That's not what was agreed."

"Yeah, well if I have to rough up my girl, I want to have the money in my hand for doing it."

Frank thought for a moment. This was not what he wanted, them laying down the terms. "Look, tell you what. Once you've done your bit, I'll give you the five thousand in cash. But not before you've done what's needed, and I want photos to prove it. You can take them on your phone."

Joey hesitated. This was easier than he thought. He wasn't stupid and he wanted his money up front. "Okay, it's a deal," he said sticking out his hand. "But as soon as I've done it, I'm coming for my money. If I don't get it then Lacey won't do nothing."

"Okay, okay," said Frank and shook the outstretched hand, sealing the deal. "So where do you want to meet to get the money?"

Jessica had heard enough for now and stood up and turned off her phone recorder. Holding the file firmly in her hand she slipped the phone into her pocket and quietly opened the door and crept back to the front office. She was shaking. Not only that, she was scared by what she'd heard. If Frank knew she'd overheard the conversation, goodness knows what he would do.

Putting her phone into her purse, she tried to concentrate on the work in front of her. She smiled weakly at Joey as he left shortly afterwards and then tried to act as calmly as she could when Frank eventually came through. To her relief, he said he was leaving early and wouldn't be in the following day. Within a few minutes he was gone.

She stayed until the normal office closing time and then quickly made her way home. Once she was changed she set up her laptop. She listened to the conversation on her phone and then connected it to the laptop, inserted a memory stick and copied it, then made a backup copy that she intended to send to her former colleague, Dan, for safe keeping. Now she had hard evidence of what she'd heard. She also copied it to the hard disk on her laptop. Once that was done she put one of the memory sticks in a case and took it upstairs and hid it. Now she had the copies, she deleted the conversation from her phone. There was no way she wanted anyone else to discover it. All she had to do now was to figure out what to do next. She thought she knew who the supposed victim in this was, but she wasn't one hundred per cent certain. And Frank could always make something up to account for the conversation, although that could prove difficult. But she would put nothing past him.

Friday nights were spent in sorting out laundry, so she could spend the next day with Rory. Tonight was no different, except her mind was elsewhere. But she wasn't starting anything until she phoned Dan in Lethbridge about the package she was going to send to him. Tomorrow would be the first time she'd ridden out since her fall. Not that she'd abandoned Rory, she'd been to see him several times. The owner was thankful she'd not been seriously hurt and she assured him that what had happened was simply an accident and in no way Rory's fault. But she still held Ethan to blame for setting off the whole sequence of events. That he'd not been around was probably best for both of them. They'd had dinner together, and she had to admit that she'd enjoyed herself, but she was still wary of him, and he was making no secret of his intentions. And that was the problem, because she was even more wary of herself. The effect he had on her was becoming difficult to control, and his intentions were starting to look very appealing to her.

***

Frank was in Calgary in record time. He knew Helena was finishing her modelling job at lunchtime and he intended spending as much of the weekend with her as possible. Taking a day off was not something he normally did, but the prospect of the day in bed with her was too powerful to resist. She was the one who'd suggested it and he'd been only too eager to agree.

Helena had just finished showering when the buzzer went and she let him up. Tying the belt of her robe she opened the door to him. "Hi. Good journey?" she asked as she secured the door.

"Yes, and I like the greeting even more." He pulled her to him and kissed her hard.

"Well, if you want to have a shower and get comfortable, I can make the greeting even better." He disappeared off to the shower and she set about lifting wine out of the fridge and then took this and two glasses through to the bedroom. She was lounging on the bed when he came out. "Like the towel, Frank," she joked.

"Yeah, but I don't really need it, do I?" he said dropping it on the floor.

She slowly uncoiled her body, stood up and took off the robe. "No darling, you don't. Would you like to pour some wine while I order in some food? Chinese okay?"

He nodded and watched as she walked naked from the room back into the lounge. He went to the door and watched her as she made the order. The she turned and glided across the floor back to him. Into his arms and then into bed. They made love gently and he exploded inside her just as she climaxed. They lay naked talking, drinking and making plans. Then the food arrived and she put on her robe while she answered the door. Coming back with the food, she held out her hand and led him to the small table. They sat and ate, both as naked as the day they were born. For Frank, this was all of his birthdays and Christmases come together. Once they'd eaten they adjourned back to the bedroom and she took control. During the next few

138

hours he discovered positions he never knew and ones he wanted to try again in the future.

The following morning when they woke, she slid out of bed, showered and then spent the morning walking around naked. She persuaded him to do the same. He felt awkward at first, but then when he saw that this was clearly something she enjoyed, he decided to embrace it. After a while he began to like the sensation. No clothes, nothing to restrict movement. He was in a permanent state of semi-arousal and found touching her and penetrating her just a little, when she wasn't expecting it, teased them both. "Did you do this with him?" He couldn't help but ask the question.

She stroked his arm and let her other hand move to his erection. She began to stroke him gently. "No. He wouldn't do it and he didn't really like me to."

"Well, I enjoy it. And I really like you being naked. So this can be our world here, where we can do what we want. When we want," he said pushing her to the floor and taking her without any foreplay. She responded instantly and they both exploded at the same time. He felt drunk with what was happening. When he thought of what they would have, when he got his hands on Ethan's money, he was ready to explode again.

By the following morning, he'd given up on condoms. He told her if she wanted them both naked all the time then she was going to have to face the consequences. "I've no intention of pulling on rubbers every five minutes, unless of course we're doing anal. You're on the pill, and as far as I'm concerned that is all the protection we need."

She wasn't happy with what he was saying. "Look, Frank, it's okay for you, but what if you get me pregnant? I don't want kids and there's no way I would keep it. So if you're thinking that's the way to a quick family, then you can think again."

"I don't want kids. I only want you. You and this, what we're doing, a smart apartment and plenty of money to share with you. All I want is to keep us both satisfied. If you do fall pregnant, we'll deal with it."

Jessica was at the stables early on the Saturday. Rory's ears pricked up as soon as he heard her voice. He waited impatiently while they saddled him up, but it wasn't long before she was mounted and they were riding out and away from the town. Rory was in good spirits. He liked these rides with this gentle rider. Not like some of them that used spurs that hurt his sides. He'd been worried when she'd fallen and wouldn't move, but he'd not been in any trouble. In fact, she'd come to see him with treats and he was feeling quite important with all the attention. Now he would have to be careful. He didn't want a repeat of what happened last time. So he would make sure that he kept an eye on where he was going. No more sudden obstacles and catching his back foot. That had been stupid. He'd not done that since he was a colt and had almost gone head over hooves.

Jessica wanted to ride in a different direction. And if she was honest she was rather hoping to bump into Ethan. Not that she would have admitted that to anyone. Swinging round, she headed back in the direction she thought his ranch was. The Lazy B, he'd called it and she wished she found out exactly where it was before she set off.

It was some time later when she saw the outline of farm buildings. But she couldn't be sure it was his place. It had been dark when she was there. Halting Rory, she slid down and ground-tied him. Checking the grass for anthills, she sat down on the green turf. It was a lovely day. She could smell the grass and the heat of the sun. Hugging her knees, she sat and watched the tiny figures she could see moving. She presumed they were cattle, but she couldn't see any men. She sat there for some time before accepting that he wasn't going to show. But then again, this could be somebody else's ranch.

Mounting, she turned Rory back the way they came and let him have a short gallop. It was late afternoon when she took him back. She'd kept an eye on the time, not wanting to worry the owner. This time she'd brought her phone with her too. Okay, she might not get reception everywhere, but at least it was a possibility if she had any further problems. If she'd had it with her last time, she might have been able to call for help.

She was driving back through town when she decided to call in at the ice cream parlour. She'd not been in there before but had heard about it. An ice cream sundae seemed just the thing for a hot day. Finding a parking spot, she wandered in and found a table. She was studying the menu when the young waitress came across. Giving her order, she checked her messages while she waited. Putting the Blackberry down on the table as she saw her sundae coming towards her, she noticed it was a different waitress. A pretty blonde girl this time.

"Can I get you anything else?" she asked.

Jessica kept the smile on her face. "No, I'm good thanks." She recognised the voice. Not only that, the name badge clearly said 'Lacey.' Watching her retreating back, Jessica let her breath out slowly. So this was Lacey, the person who was plotting with Frank. Suddenly the sundae wasn't so appetising but she wanted to watch this Lacey, so picked up the spoon and started to eat. Now she had a face to go with the name and the voice.

Chapter Twelve

By the time Frank left Calgary on the Monday morning, he was firmly settled in Helena's bed. She had no complaints about his prowess and had told him that if she'd known how well he would perform and how good he was to her, she would have taken him on long before. That thought kept him smiling most of the way to Longville. He couldn't wait to get out of the town and move to Calgary and start spending Ethan's money. He'd planned on returning the night before, but the thought of another night with Helena had kept him at her apartment.

Going straight to the office, he greeted Jessica. He was more than happy that she'd come to work for him. If she hadn't, then Ethan wouldn't have become interested and dumped Helena. And he wouldn't have just spent the weekend screwing her senseless. Just thinking of it made him twitch in his pants, so he hurried through to his office.

Jessica saw no real difference in Frank's behaviour, except he seemed happier. Was that because he was going to fleece one of his elderly clients? She'd been doing some digging into the finances of the one client she thought it was going to be, Henry North, who was in his early sixties. He'd owned a large property that had been sold for a couple of million and now resided in a modest house on the edge of the town. He had income from his investments and he'd given Frank Power of Attorney three years ago since he had no other relatives. His wife was apparently dead and they had no children. He was the only person Jessica believed could be the intended victim. But why go to these lengths, why not just discreetly steal from the fund and cover it up?

It was now over three weeks since her last encounter with

142

Ethan Slade and, if she was honest, she was quite put out that he hadn't been making a nuisance of himself. She'd got quite used to their little spats and was actually missing them. And, if she was honest, she was missing him, too, not that she was prepared to admit that. By Wednesday she'd decided that he'd been lying to her about being single and was back with his girlfriend. Probably off together, getting things back on track. The thought depressed her. She didn't want to think of him with anyone else. She was sitting in the local café with a coffee in front of her when those thoughts hit her. Take an early lunch, Frank had said, and she'd been only too happy to do so. Now she was plagued with thoughts of the one person she'd spent weeks trying to avoid. If she concentrated really hard she could almost remember the smell of the land on him and the way his body had felt against her own as they'd ridden home that night on Kohana. Then when he'd driven her home, he'd smelled of musky pine and it had been intoxicating.

She was so wrapped up in her thoughts that she almost didn't see Lacey walk past the window, but the bright pink jacket caught her attention. She watched as she went along the sidewalk and then disappeared. There was only one place she could have gone into along there, the office. Finishing her coffee, she left the money on the table and went outside as quickly as she could. No sign of her. That convinced Jessica that she had gone into Frank's.

Hurrying along the street, she found the office door locked. Using her key, she quietly opened it and re-locked it. Pulling her phone out of her purse, she crept along the passageway and into the storeroom. She heard the voices as soon as she entered. Crouching down, she turned on the recorder.

"Don't know why you couldn't tell me over the phone."

"Simple, Lacey. I didn't want anyone else overhearing what I have to say. So just listen. That little job you are going to do for me, well, it's probably going to happen next weekend. Not sure of the day yet, but possibly Saturday."

"Okay, so you need to put that money in the bank account I've opened in the city. I've got the details here. And I'm not doing anything, nor is Joey, until the bank tell me the money's there."

"What's wrong, Lacey? Don't you trust me?

"Don't trust any man, except Joey. Learned that lesson a long time ago, when my step-dad told me it was okay for him to stick his cock in me."

Frank felt a bit guilty when she said that. He'd prosecuted the guy for abuse when Lacey's mom had found out what he was doing. Now he was taking advantage of her. But this was different. She wasn't being abused, or even raped. And she was getting well paid for it. A new start away from here was what she wanted, and he was able to help her get it.

"Yeah, yeah. I know, Lacey. What he did was bad, but I'm not doing anything bad to you. In fact, I'm doing something good, something that will get you and Joey a new life. I'll get the money sent to the bank today."

"Okay, but I will check. So are you going to tell me who this man is, that you want me to say raped me?"

"Yes, I think I can tell you now. But you've not got to breathe a word of this to anyone, or you'll be in big trouble."

"I know. So who is it?"

"Ethan. Ethan Slade."

"Ethan Slade," repeated Lacey. "Him with all the money. But he's your cousin or something."

"Yes, well there's always been bad blood between us. He's got what I should have had and I want it back. And you, Lacey, are going to help me get it."

Jessica almost cried out with shock when she heard, and clasped her hand over her mouth to stifle the cry. She'd been on completely the wrong track with Henry North. They were intending to do this to her Grey. The man who had so gently made love to her in Calgary. Granted, he'd been a pain in the butt recently, but that didn't stop her from having feelings for him. In fact, he was only a pain in the butt because she wouldn't accept that she had feelings for him. She felt sick and glanced down at the phone in her hand to make sure it was still recording. It was. She could hear Frank still talking to Lacey.

"Like I said, this will most likely happen next weekend. Depends when my friend is able to get here. She'll go to the ranch and will get the drug into him. Then I'll phone you on your cell phone and ask you to call to see me on Monday. That's the signal for you and Joey to have rough sex. And Joey needs to wear a condom, although I gather he's got that planned. Once that's done, you need to get out to Ethan's place and then do what I told you. Just make sure you get his semen inside you."

"What if I can't?"

"Hell, he's a good-looking guy, use your imagination. I'm not bothered how you get it inside you. Just do it. If you've got to fuck him, do it. Nobody will know but you. When you've done that, you need to call the police and then be all weepy when they turn up. Might be an idea to lock yourself in the bathroom or somewhere to make it convincing that you're scared. Then when the police arrive they will take charge and you just do as they say. Let them do all the checks and tests, and all you have to do then is wait for the money to fall into your account when he's convicted."

They continued talking, but it was about the bank transfer. Jessica figured she had heard enough of this conversation. Once back in the front office she let herself out and went round the corner to her car. She needed somewhere to sit down and be alone. She was shaking. She thought what she'd heard during the first conversation was bad enough, but this? He was practically telling Lacey to rape Ethan. The thought of someone doing that to him had her fighting back tears. This was scary and she really didn't know what to do. Did she have enough evidence to go to the police, or would Frank come up with some explanation for the conversations? She took a deep breath to pull herself together and put her legal mind to what excuse Frank could come up with. She couldn't think of one. And who was this other person who was going to drug Ethan? She spent thirty minutes sitting in her car before she was able to go back to the office. The first thing she did was apologise for being late back.

As soon as she got home, she copied the conversation as she had done last time. She talked to Dan that night and told him what had happened. He was concerned, but more about

145

her being found out. He was as shocked as she was at what was being proposed but said that the involved parties could still say it was all just talk and they had no intention of doing anything. Although the money paid into the bank account would show intent. He told her that it would be preferable if she could find out exactly when it was going to happen and then forewarn the intended victim. They ended the conversation with Dan warning her to be careful. She posted the second flash drive off to him on her way to work the next day. She really needed to find out where Ethan was.

Friday was uneventful, apart from Jessica hardly being able to look at Frank. It took all her willpower to appear normal. When he did comment and ask if she was okay, she told him she was fine, just had a headache. When he asked if she was riding out over the weekend she said yes, and hoped that she didn't bump into his cousin, in the hope that Frank would say something about Ethan's whereabouts. The comment paid off and she found out that Ethan had in fact been out of town and in America for the past three weeks on business. *So that's why he's not been in touch,* she thought. And was pleasantly relieved to know he'd not just been avoiding her, or been with his old girlfriend.

"So I guess he's glad to be back home," she commented trying to appear disinterested.

"Don't know about that, he's not back yet. Not until the end of next week."

"I guess that means I won't have a disturbed ride, then, if I dare to venture onto his land," she said with a slight laugh.

"No, I guess not."

It was a relief when he took himself back to his office. This somewhat stilted conversation with him was tiring. But at least she'd found out why Ethan hadn't been around, and the fact that he wasn't going to be back until next week meant that she couldn't speak to him about what she'd found out. That was frustrating. One thing she could do was to find out exactly where his ranch was. Then, when he was back, she would drive out there and tell him all she knew. She couldn't leave him in ignorance, not when it was something so serious. Not when her own feelings for him were so confused.

Having changed when she got home, she logged onto Google Earth and put in the address she'd managed to find out from some papers in the office. Checking out the route, while eating a hastily prepared meal, she realised that it was about thirty kilometres to the house itself from the town. She printed out the route and then decided to do a trial run. The last thing she wanted was to get lost on his land when he was around. At least this way she could be certain of how to get there when he was back. Putting the empty dishes in the dishwasher she picked up her keys and set off.

At first she thought she'd missed the turning, and was about to retrace her route when she saw the wooden arched entrance ahead. The Lazy B sign was hung from the top section, so she knew this was the right place. She stopped the car. Should she turn around now or should she drive a bit further? Curiosity got the better of her and she put the car into drive and moved forward. It was another fifteen minutes before she saw the ranch buildings ahead. Slowing, she came to a stop. This was as far as she wanted to go.

She could see the main house and presumed the other buildings were barns for the animals, and she recalled the housekeeper referring to a cookhouse. She had no idea how large the ranch was. She'd been tempted to find out but had resisted, telling herself that his home was of no interest to her. That thought was now blown away. Both he and his home were definitely of interest to her, more so him. But she wasn't ready to concede that yet. Turning the car around she headed back to town. At least she now knew how to reach him.

***

Frank was delighted that his plan was taking shape. He was just coming into the outskirts of Calgary. Hitting the button on the hands-free he called Helena to tell her he wouldn't be long. He'd stopped letting her take the lead in this relationship. He'd been happy to do that to start with, but now he was in control.

She answered on the third ring. "Hi, honey."

147

The silky sultry voice sent a shiver down his spine. "Hi, I'll be there in about twenty, traffic permitting. Do you want to go out to eat?" He listened to the response and then told her to make a reservation for eight. That done, he settled back to concentrate on the traffic.

As soon as he'd rung off, Helena made the reservation and booked a cab. She had no intention of either of them driving. That done, she wandered through to the bedroom. Standing in front of the mirror she looked at her figure. She could still turn heads. Turning slowly she took a critical view of herself, but she couldn't really see any faults. Her legs were long and smooth. She'd just had a Brazilian wax so her groin was silky-smooth. Her stomach was flat and the small implants she'd had in her breasts gave them extra uplift, without being obvious. She was happy with her figure and knew that Frank was. When she thought of how Ethan had rejected her, she felt angry. But now she and Frank were going to get their revenge.

The front door opened. She'd given Frank his own key and password so he could come and go as he pleased. Going quickly through to the lounge she melted into his arms and let his lips take control of hers. While he was playing with her tongue she was playing with buttons and zips. Soon they were both naked and she pulled him towards the bedroom, teasing him with her body. They sank onto the round bed and he let his primeval instincts take over and sank firmly and deeply inside her. Then he rode her like one would ride a prime mare until she bucked and kicked under him as she hit her climax. He let her come and then he thrust one more time, taking his own pleasure, and poured into her while she groaned beneath him, murmuring his name. He loved this. Loved the feeling that he was getting one over on Ethan. He had the woman who'd shared his cousin's bed for two years. The woman whom he'd lusted after himself. And now she was his. His to take and enjoy whenever he wanted, because she hadn't wanted to be alone. But it was even better now because she actually wanted him.

They dressed ready for dinner. This was something else he loved. Walking into a restaurant with her on his arm and

148

seeing the other guys drooling. Now and again she was recognised and that made him almost combust with pride. They were seated in a small-secluded booth and her hand was resting on his thigh. They gave their order and then waited until the wine had been poured. Once they were alone he put his hand on her leg and raised the hem on her dress. Slipping his hand underneath he felt the smooth groin and grinned. "See you did as I asked."

"Of course I did, Frank. I'll always do what you want, to please you. As long as it's something I want as well. What do you want to do now?" He smiled and dropped a kiss on her cheek. "Nothing yet. I just like knowing that your cute little ass is uncovered, but no one here knows that."

They ate their meal completely at ease with each other. The drive home was done in virtual silence. Once inside the apartment he undid his zip, told her to bend over the table, pushed up her dress and took her without another word. He gripped her hip with one hand, holding her firmly to him, while the other hand held her down on the table top. He was in absolute total control of this and left her in no doubt about it. All the fantasies he'd had about her over the years were now coming to fruition and he wasn't going to waste one of them. This had been on his mind all night and he'd been eager to get home and do the deed.

***

With her face pressed against the table Helena began to wonder what she taken on with Frank. He was gentle when he wanted to be but other times, like now, he could be ruthless. Her breasts were forced into the table and she could feel the edge against her groin. But he was oblivious to this. She knew that from the language coming from his mouth. Dirty talk, he liked doing that, and tonight he was relentless. She knew he was using her now. But later he would make love to her gently, and then tomorrow he would take her out and buy her something nice. She could put up with this. In fact, most of the time she enjoyed it, even like tonight. She should have known

149

he would be like this. Telling her to leave her thong off when they went out was his way of exciting himself and working himself up to this point.

She felt him come and the warm liquid ran down her leg. There was no way she could climax in this position, and told him so when he asked if she was okay. Pulling her upright he took her through to the bedroom. She wasn't sure what he was intending. He was no use to her. She could see his deflated penis hanging from the open front of his trousers. Pulling down the zip on her dress, he threw it onto the chair, followed by her bra. She stepped out of her shoes and rolled down the hold-up stockings. He liked her to wear these. Telling her to lie on the bed and close her eyes, she did as he asked. She could hear movement so knew he was undressing. Her legs were parted, a finger tested her for wetness and then she felt an object being pushed into her. It was hard but smooth, and then a buzzing started, and she recognised the motion of a vibrator. He moved it forward and back as he lay at her side, biting her breasts until the tips were upright. Then he flicked his tongue around them. She could feel herself building and started to groan, her body arching with the sensations running through her. The vibration increased and she screamed, then his tongue was on her clitoris and within seconds she exploded.

As soon as she came, the vibrator stopped and was pulled out. Then his mouth closed over her entrance and his tongue sank deep inside. She knew what he was doing. Tasting her, drinking her and most likely taking himself into another erection.

She was still shaking from the climax and his tongue, when she felt him push into her. *Oh God, not again,* she thought. Not that she didn't want it, she just wasn't sure she could come again. Sometimes she thought he was depraved, the things he wanted to do. But she wanted them as well, so perhaps they were both depraved, and up to now he'd not asked her to do anything she wasn't comfortable with. When he did, she would call a halt and pull things back in line. Now she was concentrating on her future. He'd promised her a ring as soon as the Ethan situation was over. Until then, they had to keep their relationship under wraps. When they were out together, every touch was done discreetly, which was why he liked playing games like tonight. Pulling her thoughts back she tightened and gripped him, released and gripped him again. He pushed against her, took her lips with his, and rode them both to climax. They came together this time, and afterwards lay wrapped in each other's arms and slept.

Chapter Thirteen

Jessica was up with the alarm on Saturday. This was her time with Rory. The weather looked okay, but there were a few clouds that could be a threat. Taking a light waterproof with her, she set off. The time soon passed and apart from a short shower, the weather had stayed fine. Patting Rory, she told him she would see him tomorrow and then headed for home.

She was just coming out of the shower when she heard the phone. Running down the stairs she picked it up just before it went to voicemail. At first she couldn't make out who it was, or what they were saying. Then she realised it was Gemma and she sounded really upset. It took some time but finally she managed to piece together that some woman had phoned Gemma and told her that Eric was sleeping with her and spending time at her home. Jessica wasn't surprised but could hardly tell her cousin that.

"Oh, Jessica, could you come over for the night and stay with me? Just so I can talk to someone. I've called in sick at work."

"Where's Eric?" That was the first thing Jessica needed to know.

"Gone. We had a big fight when I told him about the woman calling, and he grabbed some of his things and left. I don't know what to do, Jessica. Please say you'll come."

Driving to Calgary was the last thing she wanted to do, but she couldn't leave her cousin on her own in such a state. "Okay, Gemma. I'll get some things together and will be with you in about a couple of hours. If Eric comes back, don't let him in."

Putting the phone down, she called the stables and cancelled her ride the following day. Packing what she needed in a small holdall, she locked the cottage, climbed into the car, and headed towards the highway and Calgary. It was almost ten when she got to Gemma's and it took a further hour to calm her cousin. At least Eric hadn't called or phoned and, as far as Jessica was concerned, that was a good thing. She listened intently to her cousin as she explained all that had happened over the last two days. It seemed that Eric had at first denied it and then tried to brush it off as a one-night stand. This was a story that Jessica was well versed in. Then, apparently, he'd suddenly admitted that he was seeing someone else.

"You should have heard the things he said to me, Jessica. Like how I wasn't much good in bed and…"

Jessica butted in. "Yeah, I know. You're too staid and not adventurous enough and he wants it different and you don't."

Gemma sat silently as her cousin spoke. "How do you know?"

"It's just the same kind of things Tom said to me. But you know what, they're wrong. Both of them are wrong. Because we are good enough and we do like adventure, just not with them. And you know why? Because they were both the wrong man. Believe me, Gemma, in a couple of months you'll be glad he's gone."

"Oh, I don't know. I mean the sex was good. In fact, it was very good. Just too much of it and too often."

"Yes, well, I know about that."

"What do you mean?"

"The walls here are quite thin, Gem. I could hear him, well, both of you."

Gemma put her hands up to her face and looked in horror at her cousin. "You're joking?"

Jessica shook her head. "Sorry, kid. No."

"Oh my God, I hadn't realised. I know he was highly sexed, much more than me. I did try to keep up with him, but it got so hard at times."

They both looked at each other as she said the word *'hard'* and dissolved into fits of giggles. "I didn't mean that way hard," said Gemma when she was finally able to speak.

"I know, but it was funny, though. Seriously, Gem, you do know why he was like that, don't you?" She watched as her cousin shook her head. "He watches porno movies. I saw him one morning after you'd gone to work. He was sitting in the chair over there," she said pointing to the large armchair. "I don't know what the movie was, but he was working himself off as he watched it. I crept away and went back to my room before he saw me."

"God, Jessica, I had no idea. Thank goodness he didn't see you. There's no way of knowing what he would have done."

Jessica knew it was time to tell her cousin the truth about Eric. "Yes, well I have a pretty good idea of what he would have done. Look, I didn't tell you before because, to be honest, I didn't think you'd believe me. But now I think I need to tell you exactly what Eric was up to. Do you remember the weekend I went to Calgary to meet up with friends?" She saw her cousin nod. "Well, there weren't any friends, I just didn't want to be in the apartment with him on my own. A few days earlier, when you were at work, he came to my room and got into bed with me when I was asleep. At first I thought I was still with Tom but then…"

It was some considerable time later when she finished telling her cousin about Eric's assaults on her, including the near rape. Gemma was in tears by the time she finished, and so was Jessica. "So you see, that's why I had to leave so suddenly."

"I had no idea, Jessica. I can't believe that I was taken in by him. And when I think of what he made me do. Things I was uncomfortable with, but I thought that was just me, so I let him persuade me. It makes me want to be sick."

"Yes, well, he'd gone now, so you can forget about him."

"I know but he has stuff here still and he said he was coming back for it tomorrow. That's why I didn't want to be on my own."

This was news to Jessica. But there was no way she would leave her cousin to deal with him on her own. "When's he coming?"

"He said in the morning, about eleven."

"Okay. So we'll both be here and he can get his stuff and go."

They both slept together that night in the main bedroom. By the time eleven came around Gemma was a bundle of nerves. Jessica was only just holding it together but she was damned if she was going to let him see she was scared. They were both scared, but if he knew that he would play on it to his advantage.

It was eleven thirty by the time he arrived. Gemma let him in. He strutted into the room and stopped when he saw Jessica. "Oh, brought out the big cousin. Did she tell you she had the hots for me?" The question was directed at Gemma.

"No, but she told me what you did, or rather what you tried to do." Gemma's voice was firm but there was a slight waver at the end, which showed her nervousness.

He laughed. "Yeah, well you win some, and you lose some. Bet she had fun telling you how bad I was."

Neither of them answered him, so he shrugged his shoulders and went through to the spare room where Gemma had told him his things were. He was ages, and finally Gemma ventured along to see what was taking the time. Jessica offered to go but she declined the offer. "No, I need to show him I'm not scared of him."

Jessica waited at the end of the passage and listened. She could hear talking and then a slight bang. "You okay, Gemma?" she called out.

"Yeah, she's fine. Just dropped something on the floor," the reply came back.

Jessica wasn't convinced. There was something in his tone that told her all was not right. Putting aside her own nervousness, she moved along the passage towards the room. Suddenly, the door flung open and he charged out of the room. It was so sudden that all Jessica could think of was to run. She almost reached the lounge when he grabbed her hair and swung her round. Holding her against the wall, he pushed his face into hers and leered at her. She made to lash out with her hands but he grabbed them and before she knew what he intended there was a belt around them and she was unable to

155

move either hand. She still had her feet and lashed out at him. *Where the hell was Gemma?* He knocked one of her legs to the side and pushed his body between them, pressing her against the hard wall. She was scared now. She was trussed up, her hands now held above her head, and he had her pinned against the wall. She had no way of fighting back. She looked him in the face and glared at him. She wasn't going to speak. She wouldn't give him the satisfaction of begging.

***

He was enjoying this. He'd locked her silly cousin in the closet. Now he would take his revenge on Jessica, for telling Gemma what he'd done. He'd hoped to talk Gemma round but now she knew what had happened with her cousin, there was no way she was going to take him back.

"Not so brave now, are we, Jessica?" As he spoke he pulled the belt tighter, making the leather cut into her wrists. He moved his feet and spread her legs wider. He wasn't going to rape her. He could see from her face that's what she thought he was going to do. That was a risk too far. When he'd tried it on before there'd been only the two of them. But this time her cousin was here, and nobody would believe him if he said it was consensual. But he was going to humiliate her for refusing him in the past and he reckoned she wouldn't want to report that. He put his face against hers and, holding the belt in one hand, moved the other under her top.

Jessica turned her face away. He wasn't going to see how scared she was. There was a smell of sweat and booze on him which was sickeningly putrid. A hand moved under her top but there was nothing she could do to stop him. She kept looking along the passage willing Gemma to come, but all that could be heard was banging. His hand moved, fumbled at her bra, and then he smirked. "Front fastening, Jessica, nice." Then her bra was released. He pushed the cups aside and then pulled up her top, exposing her to him. His laughter was sleazy as he lowered his head, and then he was sucking her. Eric was enjoying himself. He didn't want to take her. Well, actually he did, but statutory rape was a serious charge and he had a woman waiting for him in his new home who would do that and more. This was for him, for his pleasure, revenge for her rejection. "Like this, Jessica?" he said lifting his mouth. She didn't answer and it annoyed him. Moving his hand down, he pushed under the band of her loungers. He felt her flinch and moved his mouth and bit her stomach. Pushing down the briefs he felt underneath and finally reached her groin. Soft hair, but he wasn't stopping there. He moved round and found her clitoris. He played with it, watching her face as she denied any reaction. Then he moved to her entrance and pushed forcefully inside her. This time she did react and gasped.

He pressed his face to hers and smirked. "Like that even more, Jessica?" He still got no reaction, so he continued his assault on her until he finally got the result he wanted as he felt her fluid flow over his fingers.

***

Jessica was humiliated beyond anything she'd ever known before. She had tried to blank her mind to what he was doing and take herself out on the range, on Rory, feeling the cool air as they galloped across the ground. But that didn't work forever. She had no idea that her body would react to Eric of its own accord. She hadn't taken any pleasure in what he'd done. She was revolted by it. But her body had betrayed her. Had convulsed and made her climax. She felt him withdraw and then he held up his fingers and showed her the wetness, laughing as he did, and then he stuck the fingers in his mouth and told her she tasted good. He left her and walked quickly down the passage and came back with a suitcase. Stroking a finger down her face he smirked and loosened the belt. Holding this in his hand, he turned and left.

Why she hadn't screamed, she would never know. It had all happened so quickly, she'd been paralysed by the suddenness of it. But then when she couldn't stop it, she'd taken her mind away, out of the situation. How long she stood transfixed she wasn't sure, but it was the increased banging, and the sound of her cousin's voice, that pulled her back to the present. Pushing herself away from the wall she dragged her top down and ran on unsteady legs to where the noise was. She found the closet door jammed shut by a chair back, and pulled it away.

Gemma almost fell out. She was hysterical. "Where is he, has he gone?" Jessica could only nod.

Then Gemma saw her disarrayed clothing. "Jessica, what's he done to you?"

"Nothing. Well, he's not raped me, if that's what you mean," she said, finally finding her voice.

"No, but he's done something. I can see it in your face." She grabbed her cousin's arms as she spoke and pulled her forwards and held her.

"I'm okay, Gemma, as long as you are. As long as he didn't hurt you?" She said, pulling back.

"No he didn't hurt me, just shoved me in the closet and then jammed the door. But he's done something to you. Please tell me."

Jessica looked at her cousin. She was still trying to take in what had happened. Still trying to understand why she'd not fought. But she'd frozen, and that wasn't like her. Seeing her cousin was waiting for a reply she smiled weakly. "He did the one thing he knew would get to me. He humiliated me. Undid my bra, fondled me and then…well I think the term is, fingered me to a climax."

Gemma's gasp was loud. "Oh my God."

"Yeah, quite a pleasant chap, your ex," she said wryly. "I need to shower and change."

"Jessica. Do you want to call the police?"

She shook her head. "No. I think one humiliation a day is enough. The first thing they'll ask is, if I fought him and did I shout out? And you know what my answer would have to be? No. Because that's the truth. I froze, Gem. I stood there and let him do that to me. Okay, my arms were pinned, but I should have found a way to fight. But I didn't. Any prosecution wouldn't pass first base, and I certainly don't want to re-live it, or read about it in the press."

"Okay. If you're sure?"

"I'm sure. Go and secure the door, Gemma. I'm going for a shower. Need to wash his dirty hands off me." The words sounded braver than she felt. Right now all she wanted to do was to be alone.

Standing under the shower, in a locked bathroom, sometime later she went over the events in her head. She didn't want to talk about it but she needed to analyse it for herself. What disturbed her the most was the way her own body had let her down. How could she climax when she didn't want what was happening? How was it that her body took over and controlled the outcome? What if he had raped her, would the same have happened? Would she have come? There were too many questions going round in her head. Too many that she didn't have the answer to.

She stayed at Gemma's longer that she intended and finally left just before seven. She had to detour because of a road accident and found herself in queuing traffic. Following the signs, she ended up in a part of the city that she wasn't familiar with. She stopped for the lights and was looking around when she saw Frank. He was getting out of a cab and turned back to help out a very attractive blonde. *Sly dog,* she thought.

The traffic started to move and she edged closer. She was watching his companion. She didn't look the kind of woman that would be attracted to Frank. Something was niggling in the back of her mind. The woman looked familiar. She turned her head to get a last look, just as the blonde turned. That's when it hit her. It was Ethan's girlfriend, or rather his ex-girlfriend, according to him. What the hell was she doing with Frank? It certainly didn't look like a business meeting. Not the way he was holding her.

She pulled her thoughts back to the road, manoeuvred the last of the detour, and was soon back on her original route. She was home before she allowed herself to think again about the other problem she had, Frank's plot. Too much had happened today for her to try and think about that as well while she was driving, so she'd put on some music and done her best to concentrate on the road. Once she was inside the cottage, she changed and pulled on her bathrobe. Only then did she allow her mind to go back over the day's events.

She knew Frank was spending time away at weekends, and there had certainly been a change in his demeanour. If that change was due to the blonde, and she was Ethan's ex-girlfriend, then perhaps this was what the plot was all about. He wanted the money to keep her. Perhaps they'd been cheating while she'd been with Ethan, although Jessica couldn't understand why. There was no comparison between the men. So what would attract the blonde to him? Or was the attraction the result of her break-up with Ethan? Was this some kind of revenge, flirting with Frank, to try and make Ethan jealous and take her back?

Switching on her laptop, she listened again to the recent conversations she'd recorded. Even now, when she'd heard them so many times, they still made her feel sick to the stomach. A third person, someone to help them, that's what Frank had told Lacey. Suddenly it became clear. *Who would Ethan trust enough to get close to him? His ex.* She was the other person who was going to help; who was going to drug Ethan. If she felt sick before, she was repulsed now. *How could she do that to someone she'd spent the last two years or so in a relationship with?* Jessica couldn't understand it. But she was certain that she was right. The blonde was the other party to this depraved plot. She would drug him, and then what? Would she drag him to the bed and strip him; or would she have enticed him into the bed before? Then, once he was there, she would drug him. Easy enough in a drink. *Oh God,* she thought. *It all makes sense. They do this, Frank gets control of Ethan's money and the blonde gets Frank and the money, instead of being dumped.*

She put her head in her hands and despaired over what to do. She was certain now that Ethan had ended his relationship with the woman. He was telling her the truth. Now she was the only person who knew about this dreadful plot to bring him down, and he was away. He'd given her his cell phone number a few weeks ago and she'd thrown it away in a fit of pique. Now she regretted the action. She tried to rationalise things. If he was still away, then he was safe. All she needed to do was to find out when he was due back and be there waiting to warn him. After that it was up to him.

She phoned Dan later and told him what she'd seen and that she thought Ethan's ex was the other person involved. "I'm certain of it, Dan. It's cold-blooded revenge on her part."

"Okay, Jessica. Look, I've got this message recording, but I want you to e-mail me all that you've told me, just so we have a full record."

"I'll do that now. You'll have it within the hour."

"Good. And Jessica, be careful. If they're going to these lengths to get control of his money, you don't know how much further they'll go if they know you've found out."

"Yes, I will. I'll be careful. Talk to you soon."

Once the email was sent she made herself a coffee and sat back down at the computer. She was so wound up in the Frank plot that she hadn't given herself time to go over what had happened with Eric. Not that she really wanted to. But she was still bugged by her own body's reaction. She Googled it, using 'involuntary climax during rape.' It was the closest she could get to what had happened. What she wasn't prepared to find out was that it wasn't unusual for orgasm to happen, even when you weren't enjoying the act. One explanation was that the vagina could lubricate itself during the act as a defence mechanism against tearing and pain. She checked out various sites, at the end of which she accepted that her body had simply protected her. She wasn't a pervert, who enjoyed sex even when she didn't want it. What had happened was, to some extent, normal. Or at least that was how she was going to handle it. She'd not betrayed herself, nor Ethan. She couldn't bear the thought of someone else being with her the way he had. Now she knew that wasn't the case.

She was about to back out of the sites when she realised that what had happened with her body was exactly what Lacey was intending to do with Ethan's. To arouse him to ejaculation and then smear his semen inside her. Then she recalled Lacey's query about what she could do if she couldn't get that to work, and Frank's reply. She could simply put him inside her and let the full act take place. That would be rape. Even

161

she knew that. The whole thing was debasing. The thought of someone raping Ethan, or anyone, in that way was too much for her to take in. She needed to tell him the moment he was home. She wasn't about to let this happen to him. Not just because she couldn't let it happen to anyone. But because she cared for him, cared more than she'd been prepared to admit.

Working with Frank that week and knowing what she did was almost unbearable. What had happened with Eric, she pushed to the back of her mind. She didn't want to go there. She could do nothing about that, but she could do something about this. She had managed to find out that Ethan was due home on the Saturday, so she cancelled her ride and planned to drive over to his home and sit and wait. She wasn't going to hang around waiting to hear that he was home. She would sit on his doorstep even if she had to stay there all day.

She thought the wait for the weekend was going to be bad enough, but she'd not anticipated the phone call from Gemma on the Wednesday. Even now she couldn't believe what she'd told her. She'd not given a thought as to the accident that had caused the detour when she'd left Gemma's. She'd wished all kinds of mishaps on Eric after what he'd done but she hadn't expected her wish to be granted. From what Gemma told her, he'd gone to a bar after leaving the apartment and had then tried to drive home. He'd pulled out of an intersection right into the path of a truck, and hadn't stood a chance. Jessica was only thankful that he was alone at the time and nobody else had been injured or killed. Gemma had been upset but told her she was okay. Jessica tried to tell herself that he'd got what he deserved, but even she knew she didn't really mean it. It wasn't in her to wish that much ill on a person. But what had happened, had happened and there was nothing that could be done about it. Not like the situation she had here. That was something she could stop.

Chapter Fourteen

By Friday afternoon she was a wreck. The tension and trying to concentrate on work was getting to her. Even Frank noticed that she was edgy. She told him she had a headache and was surprised when he suggested that she took the rest of the day off. Well, it would be the last few hours of the day, but at least it would get her away from his company. Saying thanks, she took him up on his offer.

Once she was home she couldn't settle there either, so went on the off-chance to the stables and found Rory was free. She spent a couple of hours out on the range and came back much more in control. It was just after eight, and the thought of cooking didn't appeal to her, so she stopped off at the local diner. Sitting at a window table she could look out across the street and watch who was coming and going.

She saw the car drive slowly along the street and then stop on the other side. She thought it was odd because it had crossed over the street and was now parked the wrong way and facing into traffic. *Why hadn't the driver simply stopped on this side? Why risk a penalty?* The door opened, a long leg appeared, and then the blonde got out. Jessica was instantly alert. *Ethan's ex. What's she doing here?* The woman looked around and then crossed back over the street. Leaning into the window space, Jessica saw her disappear into a building. There was only one building along there she could have gone into. Frank's office.

She threw some money onto the table, grabbed her purse and was out onto the sidewalk in a matter of seconds. There was no sign of the blonde, which confirmed that she was in the office. There was no other place open along there. She quickly walked to the office door. There was a light on but nobody in the front office. She pulled out her keys and selected the one for the office. As quietly as she could, she opened the door and then re-locked it. Slipping off her shoes she switched her phone to record and crept along the passage to the storeroom. She wasn't sure what she would find out but she was going to be prepared. She settled on the floor near the vent and listened.

"I don't know why we couldn't have met at your place, Frank?"

"Easy, honey, we need an alibi. Your car is where I told you to park it. Facing the wrong way so it will be spotted. The office is lit and I've just had a long conversation with someone as I was unlocking and coming in. Also I have you down in the diary for an appointment out of hours. So everything is neat and tidy."

"Okay. I guess I understand that. And you get to pay any parking fine I get. So why the other thing?"

"What?" he said, then seeing her raise brow, laughed. "Oh, you mean the little item that's in your purse."

"Yes. What is it with you, wanting me not to wear briefs?"

"I like knowing you're like that, while no one else does. Also I like it that you do as I ask."

"So why am I like this now?"

"Fantasy, honey. Pure fantasy. Now hitch up your dress and sit on the edge of the desk. No, better still, get rid of the dress."

Jessica was speechless. She couldn't believe what she was hearing, or recording. But all she could hear now was rustles and movement.

"That's better," said Frank's voice. Now spread your legs as wide as you can."

"What about you? Aren't you taking your pants off?"

"No. Just unzipping, darling. The full naked thing will come later when we're at home. Now, come right to the edge and lie back. I've wanted you on this desk for years."

Jessica heard the low laugh.

"This close enough, Frank?"

"Yeah, definitely."

"Argh!" the sound made Jessica start. "God Frank, the

desk's cold."

"You'll be hot enough in a minute. Now while I slowly, and I mean slowly, screw into you, I want you to tell me how things have gone up to now. Him coming home early could have ruined everything, but in a way maybe it's worked out for the best. Gets it over and done with and we can spend the whole weekend together. I gather you've dealt with your end of the plan?"

"Yes, went better than I thought. Ah, Frank, harder."

"No, not yet. You can wait for it a bit longer. So you've managed to drug him?"

"Yes, like I said it was easy. He was tired and I don't think he suspected a thing."

"So Lacey is with him now?"

"Possibly not just yet. I drove her over there, well hidden of course, and while I was in the house she got into his car so her DNA is in there. Once I'd done my bit I drove her back along the track a way and Joey was waiting with his pick-up. They're probably at it now. He's going to rough her up good, she says."

Frank laughed out loud. "Oh, how the mighty are fallen. A good night's work, Helena, honey. Now you can have part of your reward. I like the idea of screwing you while he's being screwed over. Soon we can live it up, but right now I want you to come for me."

Jessica felt paralysed where she sat. But she knew she had to get out, and get out fast. The plot was already underway. Ethan had come back early. She had no time to waste. Judging from the noise coming from the office next door, a herd of buffalo could have gone through and they wouldn't have noticed. She was out of the room and out of the office in seconds. Putting her shoes back on, she ran to her car and before long she was heading out of town and towards the Lazy B. She thanked God for her foresight in driving the route to find out where it was. She was approaching the turn-off to the ranch when she saw a pick-up pull out of the side road. Even in the fading light she recognised Joey. So he had finished his part. She needed to get there fast.

***

Ethan had been thankful to get back from his trip a day early. His initial plan had been to go and visit Jessica tonight, but a call from Helena had put paid to that. She needed to see him urgently and had wanted to come over tomorrow, but he wasn't having tomorrow ruined. He intended spending the day with Jessica whether she liked it or not. He was prepared to camp on her doorstep until she relented. Now he had to deal with Helena tonight and that didn't please him.

He had just come out of the shower when he heard her car. Wrapping a towel around his waist, he pulled on a bathrobe and went down to meet her. He didn't want her just walking in. The locks had already been changed since they'd broken up but he'd left the front door unlocked. By the time he got downstairs she was opening it.

"Helena," he said, nodding his head.

"Ethan." Her voice was strained.

For a moment Helena was caught off-guard. He looked good. But then he wasn't Frank, and he wouldn't do the things Frank did. Her breathing evened out, as though she'd decided she was over this man.

"What do you want, Helena?" Ethan said abruptly. He didn't want her here.

"Sorry to trouble you, darling," she said drawling over the final word. "I've lost one of a pair of very special earrings; and I'm sure that the last time I wore them I was here."

"What, you've driven all the way out here for a bloody earring?" He wasn't annoyed about the earring, but about the fact his evening had been ruined.

It seemed she wasn't prepared for the tone of his voice. Blinking, she produced tearful eyes. "I'm sorry. I didn't realise that you cared so little about me and things that mean something to me." She pulled a tissue out of her pocket as she spoke.

He ran a hand round the back of his neck. "Oh hell. Look, Helena, I'm sorry. Clearly they do mean something to you. Where do you think the missing one might be?" The sooner it was found, the sooner she'd leave.

"It will have been in the bedroom. But they're tiny so it could have slipped down anywhere."

The last thing he wanted was her in his bedroom. But she was making it clear there was no way that could be avoided. However, he had no wish to be there with her. "Look, I was about to get dressed and make a coffee." This wasn't quite true but it would give him something to do while she looked. Then she surprised him and offered to make the coffee while he got dressed. It wasn't ideal, it would be better if she simply found the earring and left, not started messing about in the kitchen. But he didn't want a scene so he reluctantly accepted.

"Okay, but just make it instant." He said, making it quite clear he had no wish to prolong this meeting.

He had dressed quickly, and was wearing casual pants and was fastening the buttons on a shirt when she came into the bedroom carrying two mugs of coffee. "I've made one for myself, if that's okay. Don't know how long this will take."

He nodded his head and picked up his coffee and made to leave.

"Oh, I thought you might be able to help. It would get it done quicker," she said, seeming to sense his desire to have her gone. He hesitated for a moment and then agreed.

Helena watched him carefully as they looked in all the drawers and cupboards, and even under the edge of the bed. Eventually the effects of the drug began to show. Just a shake of the head at first and then a slight loss of balance.

"You okay?" she asked.

"Yes. It's probably from flying and being in transit for nearly twenty-four hours."

It had been a long journey, particularly with the delays, but he'd never been affected by flying before or long journeys. Within the next few minutes the symptoms got worse and he began to wonder if there were something seriously wrong with him. He felt distant from what he was doing and his vision was beginning to blur. He sat down on the side of the bed and she told him to drink the rest of his coffee. "It will pull you round," she said closing her hand over his and lifting the mug to his lips, helping the liquid down his throat. Then there was blackness.

***

Helena couldn't believe how easy it had been. Persuading him to stay in the bedroom and help meant she wasn't going to have to get Lacey to help her drag him upstairs to the bed. He was already on it. All she had to do now was to get his clothes off, roll him sideways and pull the covers over him. She put the mugs down on the top, pulled the duvet from underneath him so he was lying on the sheet. She was going to enjoy this, she thought as she pulled on the gloves she had in her pocket. Pulling the shirt open she ripped the top two buttons off. Looking at his tanned naked chest it was tempting to mark him. But that was Lacey's job.

She took her time in undoing his pants and then removing them. She had to keep moving him but she wasn't going to rush the job. His boxers went next and she tried to keep her eyes away from his naked body, but it was almost impossible. She could have seduced him there and then, taken him and he wouldn't have known anything about it. It would have been poetic justice to her, but not to Frank. And Frank was her priority now. And anyway, she couldn't have her DNA on him now. She rumpled the sheets and pillows and then threw the duvet back over him. That was her job done, well, apart from washing up the mugs and remembering her part of the story.

Well, it was like this, officer. I did call Ethan because I'd lost an earring. He said I could go and look for it. Yes, I found it and then I told him that I was with his cousin Frank now. No, he wasn't pleased with that news. Started to drink while I was there. Well, I saw him have one. Then he tried to stop me leaving, but I pushed him away and left. I thought he was following me but I went straight to Frank's office. No, officer, that's the last I saw of him.

Even she had to admit the story was good. But there was one thing she'd forgotten to do and that was the drink. Going to the cupboard she pulled out the bottle of whiskey and a glass and went back upstairs. Pouring drink into the glass she held his head up and pushed the pillow behind to hold him in position. Forcing his lips apart she poured as much of the drink down his throat that she could. He coughed and she thought for a moment he was coming round. But no, he couldn't, there was enough drug in him to keep him out of it for at least three hours. Long enough for things to fall into place. The rest of the glass she poured over his chest and the bed. Pulling the pillow away she laughed as he flopped back onto the bed. She lifted his head and pushed the pillow back underneath him. Leaving the bottle and upturned glass at the side of the bed she made her way outside to Lacey. After dropping her off at Joey's pickup, she drove to Frank's.

***

It seemed like forever before Jessica saw the lights of the ranch house in the distance. She slowed the car to lessen the noise and cruised almost silently to a stop. She couldn't see Lacey so she got out and closed the door quietly. Running up the steps she found the front door open. Remembering the layout from her last visit she went through to the lounge. Empty, then she heard a voice from upstairs. Running silently up the stairs she followed the sound, recognising that it came from the direction of his bedroom.

She hesitated for a moment. What if she'd got this all wrong? What if he had someone in there that wasn't Lacey? But no, she'd heard and seen too much. As she entered the room she could see Lacey kneeling on the bed with her back towards her. Apart from a pair of what looked to be cheap flimsy briefs, she was naked. "Come on. I don't have this problem with my Joey. That's it, get a little bigger for Lacey. Don't want to have to suck you off or put you inside, like Frank said. Mind you, you're good looking so that might not be so bad. But if my Joey found out he'd kill me. So I guess that's not going to happen."

The words hit the back of Jessica's brain like a bomb going off. She could see Lacey's hands working. She knew what she was doing. What she was holding and it tore her apart. This was her man. Nobody had the right to do that to him… except her. The realisation struck her like a force ten gale. God, she loved this man and she was about to fight for him. She wanted to pull Lacey away but the last thing she wanted was a catfight. And who was to say Joey wasn't coming back? She gathered her thoughts and calmed herself. Then she spoke slowly and clearly.

"Get your hands off him."

Lacey swung round as though she'd been shot.

"Who the hell are you?"

"Someone you don't want to mess with."

"I'm not doing anything wrong," said Lacey. "Me and me man here were just having some fun."

"Yeah, right. Fun organised by Frank. I don't think the police will see it that way, Lacey."

"How'd you know my name?" She stepped off the bed as she spoke, and that was the first time Jessica saw the unconscious body. Nothing was moving, well, apart from the part Lacey had been working on. But that now seemed to be deflating. She pulled her eyes away from him and back to the young girl.

"I know a lot about you, Lacey, and shortly the police will too. All about you and Joey, and Frank's plan. Joey's done a good job of roughing you up," she commented, taking in the black eye, the cut to the lip and the developing bruising to her arms and legs.

"Don't know what you're talking about. Anyway, the police will be here soon. Just phoned them. Although I may have done that a bit too early. Got a new phone to do it on. Trouble is I've got to throw it away now." It was almost as if she were talking to herself. Then she looked back at Jessica.

"I know all about Frank's plan," said Jessica. "Not only do I know about it, I have it recorded. You talking to Frank, Joey talking to Frank, oh and yes, Helena talking to Frank. That's where she is now, except they're not talking, they're screwing. While you're screwing Ethan, they're screwing each other. Frank's paid you ten thousand up front, and Joey five thousand for beating you up and having rough sex. Then, when Ethan's convicted, you get another ten thousand."

She could see Lacey getting paler as she spoke, and almost felt sorry for her. She was way out of her depth. "How long since you called the police?" she demanded.

"Bout five minutes. I just had to get some of his stuff and put it in me before they arrived. I would have done it, too, if you'd not shown up."

Jessica didn't doubt it. "Right, well I'll tell you what you're going to do, Lacey. You and Joey have got fifteen thousand of Frank's money. You want a new start. My advice is to take what you've got and run. I presume you've got your own phone on you?" A nod of the head confirmed this. "Well, I suggest that you get dressed, get off the ranch and phone Joey and tell him where to pick you up. Then you and he need to get out of town. Frank's not going to come after you for the money. He can't risk you saying why he gave it to you, and I won't let him. So you can have your new start and Frank gets nothing."

"What about the police?"

"I'll deal with them. You just get dressed and get out," she said throwing the bundle of clothes at her.

"But my clothes are torn. Well at least my top and knickers are."

Jessica had heard enough. "I think the money you've got will more than pay for some new clothes. Get out, or I'll hold you here until the police arrive. And don't forget I have everything recorded. Don't think you'll like being in prison and I don't think Joey will either. Quite a pretty boy, Joey, the other prisoners will love him." She knew that was below the belt but she was mad, not just at the plan, but at this stupid girl for not realising the consequences of what she had been about to do.

It took all of three minutes for her to be dressed and running out of the back door. Jessica had taken the mobile that Frank had given to Lacey, and this was now hidden in the trash. She'd get rid of that later. She could hear sirens. Sound travels further at night, and she guessed she had about ten minutes before she had to put on the acting role of her life. Leaving her shoes in the lounge she grabbed another glass and ran up the stairs. She stripped off as she walked towards the bedroom, depositing her clothes along the way. This needed to be convincing.

By the time she reached the bed, all she had on were her briefs. She poured some whiskey in the glass and drank part of it, grimacing as she did. Not her favourite drink. Then she put the glass down on the floor at the empty side of the bed. Climbing under the duvet, she pulled at Ethan, telling him to wake up. She slapped him about the face then, when she got no reaction, she sat on his chest and straddled him.

"Please, please, Ethan wake up. I promise I won't run away from you again, if you'll just wake up." She was getting desperate. The sound of the sirens was getting ever closer. She pressed her lips to his. She was prepared to try anything to bring him to some level of consciousness. She laid her body on top of his and pressed into him. She felt him moving, or at least a part of him. She felt cheap doing this. It was no better than what Lacey had been doing. She squirmed on top of him and whispered in his ear, telling him who it was. Then she spoke the words she had denied for so long. "Ethan, please wake up. I love you. I want to be with you. But you have to wake up."

He stirred and his eyes opened slightly. "Red?"

"Oh, thank God. Look, you have to wake up. The police are coming. Helena has drugged you." He looked about to drift off again so she sprang out of the bed and into the bathroom. She came back with a glass of cold water and threw it at him. Then she jumped back into the bed.

His arms came round her. "What did you say?" he mumbled.

"I said Helena drugged you and the police are coming."

"No, before that, about loving me?" His words were slurred. "My brain might be mush but I definitely heard the 'L' word."

"Never mind about that. The police are here," she said hearing the cars pull up outside. "Listen to me because I'm all

172

that stands between you and a life term in prison. We have been here together for the last couple of hours. Nobody else has been here. I'll explain it all later. Now just kiss me."

Ethan was wet, his head was all over the place but she was certain he'd be able to comply with that last order. "Anything you want, Red." He put his lips to hers and her body melted against his. The next moment the door was kicked back and they were told not to move. Ethan couldn't have moved if he'd wanted to, and it was now up to Jessica to deal with the situation.

Jessica was shaking when she heard the commanding voice. Shouting back, she said okay and then asked if she could sit up. She told them her name and that she had no weapons. The voice she'd recognised as the local sheriff, and she'd met him in Frank's office.

"Jessica, Jessica Cameron; is that you?"

"Yes, Stan it is. Can I sit up?"

"Who's with you?"

"Ethan. Ethan Slade."

"Has he hurt you?"

Now was the start of her acting career. "What on earth do you mean? Of course he's not hurt me. What makes you think that?"

"Okay, Jessica, you can sit up. Put your weapons away, guys, and apart from Jim go back to the cars. Jim, you wait out in the passage."

While this was going on, Jessica sat up and tucked the duvet under her arms, covering the top of her naked body. Stan looked embarrassed and she felt sorry for him, and also for the deception, but it was necessary. She needed to tell Ethan everything first and let him decide what he wanted to do. She glanced down at Ethan. He was trying to keep his eyes open but she could see it was a struggle.

"What makes you think Ethan has hurt me?" She repeated the question.

"Got a report about thirty minutes ago from some female who said Ethan Slade had raped her at his house."

Jessica looked suitably bewildered. "Sorry, Stan, there's

173

nobody here but us two. And I'm not sure Ethan's all that here. He's just got back from a business trip and jet lag and alcohol don't mix well," she said with a smile. "Hence the early night." She waited while Stan weighed up all she'd said.

"Well, if you're sure no one else is here?"

"I'm sure. But you can check if you like. In fact, I think I would prefer it if you checked through the rooms. Just to be certain."

"I'll do that," said Stan turning away.

"I'll come down in a moment," said Jessica as she watched Stan's retreating back.

She felt the hand on her bare back the moment he left the room. "You can stop that now," she hissed and heard a quiet laugh from the side. "Close your eyes, Ethan."

"Yes, ma'am."

She slipped out of the bed and picked up a discarded bathrobe from the chair. Turning back to the bed, she found him watching her, eyes wide open. "I said eyes closed."

"I know, but I've waited a long time for that sight and I wasn't going to miss it. Sorry, Red." The last words were mumbled as the open eyes began closing again.

Calling her Red made her pulse race, and she turned away before he could say anything else. Going downstairs, she waited while the rooms were checked. The general consensus of opinion was that it had been a hoax call. She thanked them for their trouble and locked the doors. Going back upstairs, she took her time and collected the various items of her clothing. She was going to have to tell him everything, but she didn't know where to start. As she entered the bedroom it was clear that telling him was going to have to wait. He was asleep, or unconscious, and the best thing she could do was to leave him to sleep it off. She longed to climb back into the bed and hold him but if she did that they would both be lost when he woke up. The situation was too serious and she needed to keep a clear head. So she curled up in the chair and kept watch over him until the early hours, when she drifted off to sleep.

Chapter Fifteen

She woke to the sound of the shower. The bed was empty but there were sounds coming from the bathroom. Uncurling her feet, she stood up carefully. She was stiff, and she ached from the cramped position. Venturing to the bathroom door she knocked.

"Come in, Red. We can share." The voice was full of humour.

"Thanks, but no thanks. I'll go and put some coffee on. I'm sure you could do with some." She didn't wait for a reply but ran out of the room and didn't stop until she reached the kitchen. Dealing with coffee and finding eggs and bacon kept her mind away from the thoughts that kept invading her mind. Pictures of them in the shower together, that were driving her insane. It was only when he walked into the kitchen that she became conscious of the fact that she was still wearing the bathrobe with only a pair of briefs underneath. Whereas he was freshly showered, smelled of musky pine and was dressed casually. Joggers with a loose T-shirt and casual shoes.

***

Ethan stopped in the doorway and watched her as she moved from the table to the worktop. This was where she belonged. Here with him and last night she told him she loved him. He remembered that. It was probably the only thing he did remember about last night. He moved into the room and she turned at the sound. He smiled and waited for a response. It took a while but it came. Tentatively at first but then a soft gentle smile that made her lips curl upwards and brought a

175

flush to her cheeks.

"Morning, Jessica." He used her full name. It was time to be serious. He knew where he wanted to spend today and it didn't include putting her offside with him before the day had begun.

"Morning," she replied before turning back to the stove. She flipped the bacon and eggs and then poured two mugs of coffee, handing one to him.

He kept his eyes on her as she stood watching the meal cooking, and slowly sipped her coffee. "So, are you going to tell me what last night was all about?" He asked, as he pulled a chair out with his foot and sat down.

"Yes, but it's a long story so I thought you might like to eat first. I know I'm hungry." She was playing for time and needed to gather her thoughts before relating the tale to him.

"Okay. We'll wait."

It was some time later, after they'd cleared the things from the table, that she started to talk. Telling him of the first conversation that she'd overheard but hadn't been able to record. By the time she'd finished his face was stormy and he was angrier than she'd ever seen anyone before.

"You should have come to me straight away. Do you realise the danger you could have put yourself in?"

That was when she told him about Dan. "Yes, I do know and that is exactly what Dan told me."

"Dan?" There was a question in the word and a flash of something that looked suspiciously like jealousy in his eyes.

Jessica revelled in the thought that he might be jealous, but then pulled her mind back to the seriousness of the situation. "Dan is a former colleague. He knows something about criminal law so I told him what I'd found out." Then she explained how he had copies of everything she had.

He smiled. "Quite the little detective."

"No, just a competent lawyer."

There was something in the way she said lawyer, which made him think there was something else to come. He frowned. "Don't you mean assistant?"

She shook her head. "No. I have a confession to make. I'm

176

actually a fully qualified attorney at law. I just decided to take a back seat for a while after what happened with my ex. Frank's been sailing close to the wind with a lot of things, but this? This is something else. What are you going to do about it? I didn't say anything to the police last night, made out it was a hoax call. I figured you needed to know everything first before deciding what to do."

"Not sure yet. Are you certain Lacey has gone?" Seeing her nod, he continued. "Well, I think we'll let Frank and Helena sweat for a while. I need to work out the best way to deal with it. Did you say you have a recording of them last night?"

They sat at the kitchen table and listened to the recording. Ethan's jaw tensed as he heard the sexual exchange.

"Sorry," she said. "It must be hard for you to hear that?"

He looked up and smiled. "No. It would be a lot harder if I was hearing him with someone I cared about." His eyes held her gaze as he spoke. Telling her exactly whom he meant.

His words brought back what Eric had done to her and she was suddenly sickened by everything that had happened in the past week. It all bombarded into her head and she couldn't cope. Picking up her mug she turned to the machine and began to pour a fresh cup. But the tears started welling in her eyes and then gently slid down her cheeks.

Ethan was waiting for her to turn round when he saw her shoulders shake and realised that she was crying. He was on his feet and with her in a second. Turning her, he held her close while she sobbed. "Jess, Jess its okay. It's over. We'll deal with Frank when we're ready. For now, just let's deal with us."

***

Listening to his words, she wondered how she could ever tell him what Eric had done. Would he feel sickened by it? Would he think less of her? But how could she not tell him? If they were to have any kind of future he needed to know everything. And that included Eric and also the fact that he'd been killed just afterwards. But she felt safe here, held in his

177

arms while he kissed the top of her head and murmured loving words into her ear.

Easing back, she wiped the tears away with the back of her hand. "It's not just the Frank thing. Something else happened last weekend. Something I let happen because I was too stupid to react." She moved back to the table, pulling him with her, and sat down opposite to him. She couldn't tell him this while he was holding her. She started by reminding him of the reason she'd been at the hotel in Calgary, to avoid her friend's boyfriend. Except, she told him, it was not a friend but her cousin. Then she told him what had happened after she returned from Calgary that forced her to leave the apartment.

He listened intently to what she was saying, realising that this was something important, something she needed to do. Hearing how she'd had to leave the apartment and move here. "It's wasn't your fault, Jessica. You can't be responsible for someone else's actions."

"I know, but last weekend I should have stopped him." She saw him pale under his tan, saw the tightening of his jaw and knew he believed she'd been raped. "No, not that. Well not quite that." She continued to tell him about going to Gemma's, and then how Eric had locked Gem in the closet. "He grabbed me, fastened my arms and said he was going to humiliate me." She couldn't look at him and kept her eyes on the table. "He groped my breasts and then he…he pushed his fingers inside me and…he made me come. I didn't want to. It was horrid and I hated it but I couldn't stop it happening." The words were said between broken sobs and she put her head on her arms and cried.

***

Ethan was stunned. The words were ringing in his head. He couldn't take in that someone had done this to her. He wanted to kill this man. He pushed back his chair and walked round to her. Lifting her arms, he pulled her up and held her. "Cry, Jess. Cry it out and then let me make everything alright."

"It can't be alright. I should have stopped him, fought him

or cried out."

"Yes, it can be alright, if we want it to be. Listen to me, what he did was no different to what Lacey was doing to me. And I'm certainly not going to let that ruin things. Certainly not what we have."

She lifted her head and looked up at him. "He's dead. I wished him dead and it happened."

The statement surprised him but he wasn't going to show any reaction. "But you didn't kill him. Did you?"

"No, of course not. But he died in a road accident shortly after it happened. It was too much of a coincidence."

He couldn't help the wry laugh. "Sweetheart, if you think you have hidden powers, let me know. Then I'll be sure not to get on the wrong side of you. What happened was an accident, pure and simple. Nothing to do with you and everything to do with him."

"I know, but it just seems weird. Anyway, what did you call me?"

He grinned. "Sweetheart. Why, are you going to object?"

She shook her head. "No. I quite like it actually."

"Good, because I plan to call you a whole lot more names. But for now, I want you to come with me, Miss Cameron. You look about ready to drop and I know I'm not feeling one hundred per cent. The shower washed the whiskey away, but that's all.

"Where are we going?"

"We are about to start to put things right."

She allowed him to lead her back to the bedroom. But he just collected her clothes that were on the chair and then pulled a T-shirt out of a drawer. Taking her hand, he led her into the guest bedroom and deposited her clothes on a stool. Handing the T-shirt to her, he suggested that she put it on. Pushing her towards the bathroom, he said, "Shower, Jessica. You'll feel better. I'll wait here."

When she came out, she was wearing the T-shirt over her briefs. He'd disposed of his clothes and wearing only a pair of boxers. Holding out his hand, he threw the covers back then drew her down into the bed and wrapped his arms around her.

"Sleep, Jess."

He held her until she drifted off to sleep and then he watched her, as he was sure she'd watched over him last night. He couldn't imagine what she'd gone through finding out what Frank had planned. Then the assault at her cousin's place. He was surprised she was still capable of any thought. But she had been, and she had worked out what to do to save him, and she'd done that because she loved him. Just as he loved her. It was a relief to have the words spoken, if only in his head.

They needed to reconnect, to get back to what had taken place in Calgary. That would take time. Not too long, but he had no intention of making love to her now. And certainly not in this bed. He wanted the first time here to be in his room. The room he hoped they would share for the rest of their lives and where their children would be conceived. Although he was way ahead of her in this plan, there was no way he was letting her go.

He'd realised in Calgary that he cared for her, more than he'd cared for anyone before. If he hadn't been going to the States he would have tracked her down straightaway. As it was, all he'd done when he got back was call in a favour to trace her details from the registration number. He was still waiting for that when he'd dropped in to see Frank. It was then, when he saw her in Frank's office, that he recognised he was falling in love with her. Now everything he wanted was within his grasp and he had no intention of messing it up. Holding her almost-naked body in his arms was testing his resolve and he stole a kiss or two. He didn't think she would begrudge him that.

They both slept well into the afternoon. Jessica woke first, wondering why she couldn't move. Opening her eyes, she found herself looking at his sleeping face. His arms were wrapped around her and she could feel the heat from both of their bodies. There was only a thin T-shirt between them and, much as she'd denied her feelings for him over the past weeks, she could no longer do that. She wanted to put out her hand and touch him. Run her fingers over his face. She could still smell the musky cologne from him and it made her feel safe.

He stirred and rolled onto his back, freeing her. She propped herself up on her elbow, watching him. Willing him to wake. Her other hand was itching to touch his chest, to move slowly through the dark hair. She caught her bottom lip between her teeth. His leg moved and touched hers and she felt the rough hair against her smooth skin. She sucked her breath in. He was doing all kinds of things to her and he wasn't even awake, but she was enjoying this. Enjoying being able to take her fill of him without him watching.

Her fingers moved slowly towards his chest and she felt the first touch of his hair against the tips. Next moment her hand was caught and held and he turned to face her.

"Good morning again, Jess, or is it afternoon? I hope you weren't about to do something that we both might regret?"

She jumped at the sudden movement and was now embarrassed that he knew what she was going to do. "I don't know what you mean."

"Oh, I think you do. If you start it, Jess, it will only have one ending and I don't want that to happen yet, not here, not in this bed. And anyway, you're not ready for it." He put her hand to his lips and kissed the fingertips. "But you do taste good," he said running his tongue across her fingers. "And you feel even better. Which is why we need to get up. That's if you are ready to face the day, for the second time?"

She nodded her head. She couldn't speak. Her stomach was doing somersaults and, somewhere along the way, she'd lost all her inhibitions, again. Why was it that he brought out the best, or worst, in her? She was more than happy to lie here and watch him as he got up and pulled on his clothes. As he disappeared out of the bedroom she followed suit and got up and dressed.

She was downstairs in the kitchen making fresh coffee when he came down. He took the jug out of her hand, held her face, and brought his lips down to hers and kissed her passionately. His tongue teased her bottom lip until she gave him access and then he started an assault on her senses that had her responding to him until her legs threatened to give way. Then he held her, limp against his body, as he drank his

181

fill of her. Finally, he lifted his head and they looked at each other, brown eyes holding grey. They didn't need to speak, what was happening was enough without words.

He pushed her hair back from her face. "I've been longing to do that since this morning."

"Why didn't you?"

"Because I wouldn't have been able to stop there."

"Who says I would have let you go any further?"

"You. The look on your face now, and what I read in your eyes. We are meant to be together, Jess, and no amount of denial will make any difference."

"Who says I'll deny it?"

"Well you've been doing a pretty good job the last few weeks."

"Okay, I'll admit to that. But that was before I knew what they were going to do to you. Then all I could think of was to stop it happening."

"And why was that? Why did you need to stop it?"

She knew what he wanted her to say, but she wasn't going to give in that easily. "I would have done the same thing for anyone." The twist of his mouth told her this was no time for joking. "Okay, because of what happened in Calgary. Because I couldn't bear the thought of anyone else doing that to you."

"And why's that, Jess?" he murmured against her mouth.

"Because I want to be the only one to do that with you." There she'd said it, and she waited for the look of triumph on his face. But there was none, just a look of happiness and something else… love?

He kissed her again, this time letting his hands roam over her body. He was getting harder by the minute and needed to stop. This was not his plan. Pulling back, he sat her down and poured them both a coffee. "I think we need to get some air. So I'm suggesting that we saddle up a couple of horses and go out. Unless you have other plans for the weekend?"

"No, I've nothing arranged for today. I was going riding but I thought you were coming home today so I cancelled. I'd intended driving over here and waiting until you got back and then telling you what Frank had planned. But that all went pear-shaped when I saw Helena and then heard them. But I'm going riding tomorrow, I have Rory booked."

"Then un-book him." The words were direct. "I said 'weekend,' Jess. I have no intention of taking you home today and have every intention of keeping you here tonight."

Her groin heated at the words. She knew what he meant by keeping her here. She met his stare. Should she argue? She wanted to ride out on Rory, but she wanted this even more.

He was watching the emotions crossing her face. He smiled and put out his hand and touched her cheek. "Don't fight me on this, Jess, please."

"Okay." One word that was to seal their future. That was all it took and she couldn't deny the feeling of pure happiness that coursed through her body. Nor could she miss the look of joy that swept across his face at the word.

He saddled up Kohana and a bay filly for Jess. Leading them out of the barn, he couldn't disguise the pleasure he got seeing her coming out of the house towards him. They mounted and rode out of the yard side by side. He took her to a part of the ranch she'd not been to before. They rode along the edge of meadows rich with wildflowers, and where the air was heavy with the scent of flowers and summer grass. The track widened out and he waited until she moved alongside him. Holding out his hand they rode on in silence, completely at one with each other.

It was getting towards dusk when they arrived back. He rode into the barn leading the filly, as Jess went into the house. She was tired but oh, so happy and relaxed. She knew what was going to happen later and she knew it was inevitable. She had no qualms, no inhibitions. She was happy to let things play out as they were meant to be. She only wished she had something smarter to wear than jeans and a top.

She was in the guest bedroom when she heard him come up. Sticking her head out of the door, she called to him. Walking towards her, he didn't think he'd heard anything better than her calling him to the bedroom. He'd remind her of that sometime.

"What time are we planning to eat?" It was a simple enough

question but it was loaded with, when are we going to start this, before or after dinner?

"That depends on when you want to shower?"

She swallowed and grabbed her bottom lip between her teeth and started to nibble it. He was watching her. "I could probably shower now. Get the smell of horses off me before we eat." Her voice sounded strange to her ears.

"That sounds like a plan."

He was giving nothing away. Just standing in the doorway looking at her. No, not looking, devouring, and it was doing things to her insides that nobody should be able to do. His lids were part down over his eyes and there was the hint of a grin on his face, but the stare was intent. This was like Calgary, when they'd started testing and teasing each other. This was the start of it now. There was going to be no waiting until after dinner, they were already part way through scene one. The realisation made her quiver and her heartbeats increased.

He held out his hand and she took it. Leading her into the master bedroom, he went through to the bathroom. Turning her to him, he gently kissed her lips, while his fingers slipped under her top and undid her bra. Then he unfastened the button on her jeans and pulled the zip down. Lifting her hands above her head he pulled the T-shirt off, followed by the bra. She was now naked from the waist up. He put out his hand and touched her, running his fingers lightly over her breasts. His breathing was becoming ragged but she knew he wasn't going to rush this.

He used both hands to push her jeans down and then helped her to step out of them. Pushing them out of the way, he started to unbutton his shirt, but she pushed his hands away and took control. First his shirt was gone, and then his jeans, until they stood facing each other wearing only their briefs. She was shaking. Then he touched her face, trailing his fingers down her cheek, her neck and then her chest until he took one perfect pink breast in his hand. Holding it gently he rubbed his thumb over the nipple, and she felt her body respond. His other hand captured the other breast and she watched as he slowly rolled the nipples between his fingers. She was visibly shaking now and hoped that he wouldn't keep this distance between them for much longer. Her eyes were drawn downward and she could see him hardening, with every touch on her body. Then, leaving one breast, he took hold of her hand and placed it against his erection, keeping his eyes on her all the time.

Jessica held his gaze and gently squeezed him. He shook and enlarged in her hand and she smiled. Putting her hand inside his briefs she felt the soft velvet skin of his penis. It was so soft, but so hard. Carefully she moved her hand, holding him and making gentle up and down movements. He groaned and pulled her nipples and she groaned louder. Apart from this contact, no other part of their bodies were touching, but Jessica felt as though he were already inside her making love to her. She felt her body starting to tremble, to move towards a climax. Her eyes flew wide and she found him watching her carefully.

***

Ethan saw her body move and the sudden look of fear in her eyes and knew what she was remembering.

"Jess, it's me, Ethan. Look at me." He saw her look, but there was still fear in her eyes. He put a finger under her chin and made her look into his eyes. "Jessica, darling, it's okay."

"Ethan," she shook her head as she spoke.

"Yes, me. It's not him. We're going to get rid of him. All you will remember is me doing this. Nobody else. Okay?" She nodded. He wasn't sure about this. But he didn't want her to be hung up on what had happened during the assault. He didn't want to be afraid to touch her in case he scared her.

Pulling her close he held her, kissing her and whispering words of love. As he did his hand moved slowly down her stomach under the band of her briefs and he slipped inside. All the time telling her he loved her and asking her to love him back. She was soft and moist and he wanted more than anything to be inside her but he didn't want to panic her. He knew how badly she must have been affected by what Eric had

185

done, despite her saying she was okay. This was his attempt at wiping that incident out of her mind and replacing it with the same thing, but this time happening between them. He felt her stiffen for a moment but kissed her neck and her face. Then he told her to look at him and was thankful when she did. Holding her gaze, he smiled and then pushed inside her. She gasped. "Keep looking at me, Jess," his voice was soft and low.

***

Jessica had been nervous that she would freak out when he tried to make love to her, but the recreation of what happened in Calgary was wonderful. Well, up to the point she thought she was heading for a climax. Then Eric slammed back into her head. Now Ethan was making her look at him. Making her remember that it was him, Ethan, doing this and nobody else. The first intrusion made her gasp but he was grounding her, reminding her who was doing it. Now, as he pushed inside, she felt her body stiffen, remembering the last time it happened. His words, *keep looking at me,* pulled her back to the present and she saw his face. She smiled faintly at him and saw him nod his head.

Then he started to move and she had to hold his shoulders to steady herself. Holding his shoulders? She wasn't able to do that last time because she was fastened. But she wasn't fastened now, because this wasn't him. This was Ethan, the man she loved. She had an overwhelming desire to push down and quickly looked up at him her eyes wide.

"What is it, darling?"

"I want to push down." She was embarrassed just saying the words.

"Then do so. Take control, you do this. You are in charge of what's happening, no one else." The words were whispered against her cheek.

She was in control, he said. Nothing would happen unless she wanted it to. She wouldn't climax if she didn't want to. But she did want to. She wanted to really badly. Lifting her head, she put her lips to his and kissed him hard. Then she pushed down and then down and down again, before crying out as she felt the climax overtake her. And all the while he moved with her, bringing her to fulfilment.

Ethan kissed her back with everything he had as he felt the violent tremors going through her body. The warm liquid flowed over his fingers and he didn't think he'd experienced anything so beautiful before. He was so hard he could feel the first leaking but held himself in control.

She shuddered as the final throes of the climax raged through her body. It was overwhelming. Nothing like what had happened before. With Eric it had been a tremor, this with Ethan had been an earthquake. She looked up at him and mouthed, *thank you,* before falling against his body. She felt him pressing into her and realised that although she was alright, he was straining. Moving her hand down, she felt the wetness on his briefs. Catching his hand, she led him on shaky legs into the bedroom and to the bed. She crawled across the clean covers, taking him with her and then she pulled off what little clothing they had left on. Then she lay back and held out her arms.

***

Ethan kissed her back with everything he had as he felt the violent tremors going through her body. The warm liquid flowed over his fingers and he didn't think he'd experienced anything so beautiful before. He was so hard he could feel the first leaking but held himself in control.

He hadn't intended this until later, but now she was spread out before him on the bed, like a jewel waiting to be taken. Slowly he lowered his body onto hers. She parted her legs inviting him to take what he wanted. He didn't hesitate, he lifted her slightly with one hand and entered the one place he'd wanted to be for weeks. They made love slowly at first and then, when he could wait no longer, he thrust forward and took her to a second climax and himself to heaven. He sank into her over and over again until every part of his body belonged to her. He was drained, what had been inside him was now inside her.

***

Jessica thought she was going to die. The first climax had been something but this, this was everything she could ever have imagined it would be like. She thought her body was never going to stop. The convulsions took over everything that was happening and she rode with them, not wanting them to end. She felt him come, felt him pour into her and she'd not known anything so wonderful before. In fact, she'd never felt this before. Then she realised that she'd never felt it before, because they'd not used anything. They'd just had unprotected sex. She could be pregnant. She was on the pill, but there was still room for error, and she'd not taken one last night with all that had happened. The thought should have scared her, but it didn't. In fact, it was quite the reverse. The thought of having Ethan's child inside her was breath-taking. She wondered if he had thought of the consequences. But she wasn't going to break the spell by mentioning it.

He collapsed on the bed alongside her as he tried to catch his breath. What had happened had overpowered both of them, and she wanted to capture this moment for ever. She didn't think life could get any better. She turned her head as he leaned over her.

"Well, Miss Cameron, I do believe we have that nightmare well and truly under control."

"Yes, I think we have. Thank you for what you did. I know it might sound silly, but I've never had anyone do that to me before, you know, all the way just with their fingers. When he did it I couldn't understand what had happened. I couldn't believe my body betrayed me the way it did. But then I looked it up and found it wasn't unusual for it to happen. But the climax I had when he did it was nothing. When you did it, it was everything and more."

"I'm glad. I didn't want you freezing in future when I touched you there. Mixing what we have with some nightmare over which you had no control. I need, no I want to be able to touch you everywhere, Jess, and know that it will bring you nothing but pleasure. And hopefully you'll want me to do that to you again?

"Only if you want to. But I'd rather we did the second version."

"So would I. I find that much more pleasurable. And if we're sharing secrets, I've never done it all the way like that before. I hadn't planned on doing it at all, but when I touched you there I knew what you were thinking. I didn't want that memory stopping us from enjoying what we have, it was the only way I could think of to get rid of it."

"I'm glad you did. When he did it to me, it made me feel dirty. When you did it, all I felt was excitement and pleasure, and being able to control what was happening made it... very enjoyable," she said with an embarrassed laugh.

"I hope it will always be enjoyable and exciting between us. I certainly plan for it to be. We've moved forward a lot in the last twenty-four hours and all it's done is confirm that what we have, what we both felt at the beginning, is real. And now that the 'L' word is out there, you realise I'll probably have to ask you to marry me."

"I don't think I recall you saying anything about the 'L' word?" she said teasingly.

"Ah well, I use actions rather than words. But if you want to hear it, Jess, I'll say it. I love you, I think I have done since that first night. It just took a while to persuade you that you felt the same. And last night you told me you did. That's the one thing I do remember."

She giggled. This day was perfect. "Okay, we love each other. I think I can live with that."

"Yes, but can you live with me, Jess? Can you live on a ranch? Can you be with me, be my wife?"

"Is that a proposal, Mr Slade?"

"Too right it is. And I would really love an answer."

"Now let me think," she said teasingly, tapping a finger against her chin.

"Well don't take too long. You do realise you could be

189

pregnant. Don't want to have to carry a heavy woman over the threshold."

"Would you mind if I was pregnant?"

"If I'd minded, I would have put on protection."

"Does that mean you thought about it?"

"Not really. All I could think of at the time was to make love to you, but I can't imagine anything more wonderful that seeing you carrying our child. So before it's born, do you think you can give me an answer?"

She looked at this man whom she'd known for only a short time. But in her heart she knew that they were meant to be together. "Yes," she replied quietly. "I will marry you. But I'll marry you because I love you and for no other reason. As for being pregnant, I'm on the pill." She saw the flash of disappointment on his face. "But I did forget to take it last night. Well, not so much forgot, but I haven't got any with me," she said mischievously.

Chapter Sixteen

They woke almost at the same moment. Their arms wrapped round each other. The night had been amazing. They'd eaten a late dinner and then adjourned back to the bedroom where they had rekindled everything they'd done earlier.

"Well, fiancée, what would you like to do today? Although I do have a few ideas."

"I had booked Rory for today and he'll think I've deserted him."

"What, you're rejecting me for an old hack?"

She slapped him playfully. "He's not an old hack. He's quite young really and he's a sweetie. We understand each other and I enjoy riding him."

"Better than the filly you rode yesterday?"

She nodded. "Sorry. She was sweet, but Rory, well, he's my guy."

"Oh, so I'm blown out by a horse already?"

"No, never, and I don't really want to leave you today."

"Then don't. Leave things with me. You have a shower but don't be too quick. I plan on joining you shortly." He bounded out of the bed as he was talking and she admired the trim muscular body, as he quickly pulled on jeans and a top. He was out of the door before she'd swung her legs out of bed. She was still in the shower when he returned and it would have been a miracle if no one outside heard the shriek as he grabbed her.

After a late breakfast of ham and eggs he informed her they were going to spend the day on horseback. He packed up snacks and water, while she loaded the dishwasher. While she slipped upstairs he went out to the barn to saddle up. Kohana was ready in a short time and Ethan was leading him outside when Jessica came down the steps. His stomach flipped at the sight of her. "Your mount is in the far stall already for you," he said as she walked towards him.

"So, I have to fetch my own horse now we're an item?"

"Yeah, start as we mean to go on. A rancher's wife needs to know her place. And we're not an item, we're engaged to be married," he said with a grin.

She grinned back and stuck out her tongue in a purely childish way, but she felt so happy she wanted to shout it out to the world. Walking to the far end of the barn, she came to a sudden stop. There, tied up against the wall was Rory, all tacked up and ready to go. "Rory," the word burst from her mouth.

***

Rory turned his head as he heard her voice. Thank goodness, he was beginning to get edgy. Taken out of his stall and being put in a trailer wasn't his idea of the best way to start the day. Particularly when he'd not finished his hay and his favourite person was due. Smokey had said he was probably off to the knacker's yard and that had him worried. But he wasn't old, only six and that was still young. Now he felt better but he still didn't know where he was, or why. Snickering and nuzzling into her shoulder as she led him outside, he felt easier and stood patiently waiting while she swung up onto his back. He had a feeling that this would be a good day, but he was going to have to keep his eye on that other horse though, prancing about and showing off.

***

"Oh Ethan, how did you get Rory here?"

"Sent one of the men over for him while we were showering. Couldn't have you disappointed at missing a date with your second favourite guy."

"Thank you. You don't know how happy it makes me that he's here."

"I think I do, if the smile on your face is anything to go by."

They rode for some time towards the foothills. She'd always wanted to get closer to the mountains and it looked as though today that was going to happen.

"How close to the mountains does your land extend?"

"As close as it can. We did own all the land right to the foot of the mountains but gave over several acres to the National Parks quite a few years ago. My land is fenced off now from theirs, but it doesn't stop the bears from getting through, or the elk. They can jump the fence easily but I don't mind. They do little damage this far out and the land is more theirs than mine. The pastures are in the other direction," he said sweeping his arm to the right, "and the valuable animals are kept in the paddocks close to the house."

"So what do you run on the ranch?"

"Cattle and horses mainly. We breed both and sell when we need to."

"So it's a proper working ranch."

"Yes. Why, don't you like working ranches?"

"Oh yes. No, I was just curious. You hear so much about guest ranches I wondered if you did that as well."

"No. The ranch pays its way. But it's not the only source of income. I have a number of investments in oil and gas. I also own several properties in town, as you know," he said with a grin. "I've just acquired a couple of condos on the Waterfront in Vancouver that will bring in a tidy income. So if you're worried I won't be able to keep you, I can assure you I can."

Jessica blushed. "I wasn't thinking that at all. Anyway, I'm perfectly capable of keeping myself. Attorneys are quite well paid, you know," she replied, quite put out at his comment.

He started to laugh. "Oh, Jess, don't tell me we're having our first domestic, and I haven't even got the ring on your finger yet."

"Carry on with those comments and you won't get any ring on my finger." If she'd planned on saying anything else, it would have been lost as he reached across and dragged her out of the saddle and sat her in front of him.

"You were saying?" The laughter could be heard in his

voice before he put his hand behind her head and brought her lips to his.

She was lost. It was all she could do to hang onto Rory's reins. Her head was spinning and all she wanted was for this to go on forever. She was gasping when he finally released her but she only had to look into his eyes and she was melting. Pushing away she pulled Rory alongside and slid her leg across and settled back in her saddle. Her heart was pounding and there was a sensation she had not experienced before in her groin. She squirmed in the saddle to alleviate it and blushed when he leaned over and told her that wouldn't work.

The sun was high when they pulled up close to a shaded area. He lifted packages out of the saddlebags and handed them to her while he ground-tied the horses in the shade. Spreading a blanket out in the open they ate in silence and then drank the cool water. Lying back, she felt the sun on her face. She could smell the grass and the heat of the day. Apart from the odd cry of a bird and the occasional snort from the horses all she could hear was silence.

***

He put the remains of the food back inside the bags and then stretched out alongside her. This was good, but he knew that they would have to talk about Frank and what to do before the day was out. But he didn't want to spoil this. Turning, he propped himself on an elbow and watched her. He wasn't sure if she was asleep. He didn't think so. One way to find out though. His free hand strayed across her stomach and his fingers eased underneath the shirt. He made contact with her bare skin and then crept slowly up towards her chest, taking the bottom edge of the shirt with him. The bare midriff was too much of a temptation and his lips were on it before the thought had fully registered. She groaned and her arms came round him, pulling him to her and their lips met.

What started out as an exploration erupted into an encounter that they would remember for years to come. He stripped off her jeans and briefs and opened her shirt. Burying his head in her breasts it was he who groaned this time. She unbuttoned his shirt and pants and then, when they could wait no longer, she opened herself to him and guided him in. They made love passionately and the orgasms when they came were overwhelming. They came together and she cried his name, the sound drifting away on the breeze. He held her close until the tremors had ceased and then he rolled to the side. He had never felt so contented before in his life. Never felt so much at one with any person as he did with her. He turned to look at her and ran his hand over her stomach.

"If we keep on like this you will be pregnant."

"I don't care. I want you, and if having you like this means I have your child then so be it." The words sounded corny to her but she meant every single one of them.

"I know what you mean. I would like to have you to myself for a while. But I suspect that the last couple of days might have given your body other ideas. Have you ever considered being a mom?"

"Not until now. I've never been with anyone that made me think that way. Not even Tom."

"What about now?"

"I think the idea of carrying our child is something that would be wonderful. But let's not get ahead of ourselves. I may not be pregnant. You may not be that potent, Mr Slade."

"Okay, let's just wait and see what the next few weeks bring. But you could forget to take the pill." The suggestion hung in the air between them. "Anyway, in the meantime, I hate to spoil this romantic time, but there is something we need to discuss. I don't want to wait until we get back, I'd rather talk about it here, out in the open." As he spoke, he fastened up his own clothes and then helped her with hers.

She was instantly concerned. "About us?"

"No, silly. There's no problem with us. But we do have a problem, it's called Frank, and you have to go and work with him tomorrow. We need to decide what's going to happen."

She shook her head. "I don't know if I can work with him. This last week has been bad enough. But hearing him with her in the office. The dirty talk, what they were doing and what

195

they planned to do to you. I just don't think I can go in."

He pulled her back until she was leaning against his chest. "I know it will be hard but I really need you to go in and to act as if nothing is wrong." He felt her stiffen at his words. "I know it's a big ask, sweetheart, but I want him to spend a few days wondering and hopefully worrying about what has happened. I figure he's already trying to find out, but with Lacey gone he'll be panicking."

"Yes, but he'll probably try and find out from the police."

"He'll try, but he won't get anywhere. I spoke to the sheriff yesterday and asked him to keep what happened under wraps. To avoid any embarrassment to the parties involved."

"You mean me?"

"No, I have no problem with folks knowing you were in my bed. But I wanted the sheriff to think that. People will know soon enough that we are, what was it you said? An item."

"I thought I was your fiancée, not an item? Makes me sound like a piece of furniture."

"And a delightful piece of furniture you are. And yes, you are my fiancée and we'll make that official next weekend. We'll go into the city and choose a ring and we'll stay at the same hotel, and if possible the same room."

"931," she answered without thinking. He gave her a squeeze. "So you remember the room number?"

"Of course I do. But we are getting off the subject. I thought we were talking about Frank?"

"Yes, you're right, we need to sort out a plan. What I would like is for you to just go to work as normal, but keep your ears open and watch Frank and what he does. If he asks anything about me, you haven't seen me."

"Okay, but what are you planning?"

"To get back something he should never have had in the first place, and your recordings are going to help me. The problem is I may need you to keep up the charade for a couple of days. I need to go to Calgary and may have to stay over."

"Oh." The disappointment sounded in her voice.

"I know. I don't want to leave you, but I need to do this. I need to get Frank out of our lives for good. Can you put all the recordings on one flash drive and let me have it?"

"Of course. When do you want them?"

"As soon as possible. I want to take them with me."

"I'll do them tonight when I get home."

"Oh, I thought you would stay tonight as well?" The regret was evident in his voice.

"Much as I would love to, I need to prepare for work. You know, shower, wash my hair and I need a change of clothes. Can't go into the office in jeans and smelling of horses."

"Well, I think you smell delicious."

"Now I know that's a lie. All I smell of is your body wash and Rory. I need my own things, my own perfume and creams. And I desperately need my straighteners for my hair."

He ran his hand through her hair. "There's nothing wrong with your hair."

"Typical male comment. I know it looks okay, but it's not perfect. Not how I want it to look for you."

"Okay, but next time you're here, bring duplicates of everything and leave them. Then when you stay, you'll have all you need and I can keep you here as long as I want."

"Oh, Mr Chauvinistic?"

"No, just an ordinary guy whose world you've turned upside down."

She couldn't ignore the comment, and turned and kissed him. "Right, so if I copy the recordings tonight, when will you pick them up?"

"Tomorrow, early, on my way to the city."

They rode back sometime later and Jessica watched as Rory was loaded into the trailer and then taken back to the stables. Going into the house, they had a simple meal of steak and salad, and then it was time for her to drive home. She clung to him until the last minute. She hated the idea of having to go back to the cottage on her own, and even more so going into work tomorrow. As she drove along the highway she couldn't believe all that had happened since she'd last been on it, going in the other direction. Not only had she managed to thwart Frank's plan, but she was engaged to marry the man of her dreams. She felt like pinching herself to make sure she wasn't dreaming.

The cottage felt strange when she got in. But she set to and soon had all the recordings downloaded and put onto one flash drive. She sent a short email to Dan to tell him that she'd managed to stop the plot taking place and would phone him tomorrow and tell him all. Having spent the last couple of days with Ethan she was now at a loss on her own. But she needed to sort things out for work tomorrow so went for a shower and washed her hair. Settling down in front of the television wrapped in a bathrobe, she tried to concentrate on a movie. Eventually, she gave up and turned the lights off and went upstairs. She was about to get into bed when her phone beeped to tell her she had a text. Picking it up, she read the message. *"Missing you. My bed is empty!! Sleep well sweetheart, Love E. xxx"*

She felt the tears well up in her eyes. She'd never had anyone send her a message like that. She sent a reply.

"I know. I feel the same. I wish you were here. Goodnight, my darling. Love J. xxx"

She climbed into bed and put the light out. The sooner she was asleep the sooner it would be morning and she would see him again, if only briefly.

She was dreaming of the time they'd spent together. The way they'd made love. She moaned in her sleep. Turning, she found herself enveloped in a pair of strong arms. This was a lovely dream. It almost felt real. She could feel the hardness of his body against hers and it was exquisite. She sighed and snuggled closer to him, and then the dream became reality as her lips were captured and a tongue invaded her mouth.

She was instantly awake and found herself looking into a pair of grey eyes.

"Ethan," she breathed. "What are you doing here?"

"Morning, sweetheart. Landlord's inspection before I leave. Have to check that everything is in working order."

She started to giggle, which almost ruined the mood. But he knew exactly what to do to bring her back to him. And she gave herself up to him, to his body and to the never-ending climax they knew would come. They were about to be transported to heaven and neither of them could wait.

As he dressed, knowing she was watching, he felt such a rush of love for her. "I couldn't go to the city without being with you one more time." The words were spoken gently, and she nodded. "I'm glad."

Again they'd used no protection and it was as though they were both of the same mind. They wanted her to be pregnant. They wanted a child as a sign of their love and commitment to each other. He turned back to her. She was laid on the pillows, a look of pure contentment on her face. She looked like someone who'd just been made love to, which of course she had. The dreamy look she gave him told him more than words could. Bending over he kissed her and took the flash drive from her.

"I'll be back as soon as I can. Don't let Frank suspect you know anything. I couldn't bear it if anything happened to you. So be careful. You have my cell number in your phone and I have yours. I'll call you as soon as I can. But if there's any problem, or Franks suspects anything, phone or text me immediately and go straight out to the ranch. The lads will take care of you. I don't want you in any danger. If possible I'll be back tonight, but I'm more than certain it'll be tomorrow. I'll go straight home and call you from there. I don't want Frank seeing me here."

"So where's your car now?"

"Two blocks away. So I need to creep out now and hit the road. Take care, darling. I love you."

"I love you too. Drive carefully," she said remembering Eric's accident.

"I will. I have everything to come back for. And possibly more," he said patting her stomach.

Once he'd gone she felt sad, but also excited, if it was possible to feel both emotions at the same time. Getting ready for work was a drag but it had to be done. She had to go into legal assistant mode and keep her wits about her.

Frank was already in the office when she arrived and greeted her with a smile. That threw her. She thought he would be worried. Perhaps he didn't know his plan hadn't worked?

She forced herself to concentrate on the work in hand. It was almost lunchtime when the door opened and Helena walked in. Telling Frank she was there, Jessica watched as she went through. Picking up a file she slipped into the storeroom and turned on her phone.

"So have you heard anything yet, Frank?"

"No, nothing yet. Don't want to appear as though I know something is wrong. I'll saunter down to the police office at lunchtime and see if anyone they pulled in over the weekend needs a lawyer. I often do it so they won't think it odd."

"Did Joey do his bit?"

"Yup, showed me a lovely photo on his phone of Lacey all bashed up."

"How do you know it was taken that night?"

"Honey, give me credit. She was holding a copy of that day's paper. Told him I wouldn't hand over any money until I was convinced. Anyway I was, so Joey got his five grand in his hand and no doubt he's lying low."

"How long do you think it will be before you can get your hands on Ethan's money?"

"Well, it will take some time, but I can always cream some off and use credit. Thought we could take a trip to the Bahamas, just to get us in the spending mood."

"Oooh, Frank; that would be delicious. I've always wanted to go there."

"Good. You deserve a treat, particularly after the weekend we've had. Never thought spending the whole weekend in bed could be such fun. Well, okay, not the whole weekend, but being naked all the time and going to bed whenever we wanted was something else."

"I enjoyed it too, Frank. You do things to me that I really like."

"I know. Right now I'd like you to do something for me."

Jessica heard the giggle and then the rustling of clothing, followed by gasps and grunts. She knew exactly what they were doing and shook her head in disbelief. Neither of them gave a damn that they thought they'd ruined someone's life. All they were concerned about was getting Ethan's money and screwing each other. One thing was certain, at this point in time they weren't worried, but they soon would be. She left the storeroom and went back to the front office. Collecting her jacket, she took an early lunch. She didn't want to be in the same building as them.

She struggled that afternoon being around Frank, but she thought of Ethan and his request that she act normally. It was almost nine when he called her and she was beginning to think that something had gone wrong. He assured her it hadn't, that everything was working out well and he should be back late the next day. She had hoped that he would come to the cottage but he said he was intending to go straight to the ranch but would see her the next day. She was disappointed, and it must have shown in her voice.

"Don't worry, darling. It's only one night and hopefully it will be the last night we spend apart."

"What do you mean?"

She heard the humour in his voice. "As your landlord I'm giving you notice to quit.""Oh, and where am I supposed to live once I've been evicted?" She asked the question but knew the answer. But she wanted to hear it from his lips.

"At the Lazy B Ranch, with me. I'm not giving you chance to disappear. And if you're looking for something to do tomorrow night, you could start planning our wedding. I don't intend waiting."

His words sent a thrill through her body. To live with him, be married to him and sleep with him every night. It was all too much for her to take in. She needed some time out, but all he was giving her was twenty-four hours. But time out for what? To procrastinate, to be reserved and predictable. What was she hesitating for? She loved this man and wanted nothing more than to be with him.

"Okay, so what do you want, large or small?"

Now it was his turn to be puzzled. "Large or small what?"

She laughed and felt the sheer joy of the moment. "Wedding, idiot."

"Idiot, you say. You'll pay for that when I see you. But whatever you want, although the whole town will probably

201

turn out for it. You work out a rough plan and we'll talk about it later. For now, I'm going to have to go. I need a shower and my bed, it's been a long day and there's still loose ends to tie up tomorrow before I leave."

"Okay. I guess I'll see you Wednesday. Drive carefully."

"I will. Like I said, I have a lot waiting for me. Goodnight, sweetheart. I love you."

"I love you too. Goodnight." She held the phone in her hand for a long time after the call had ended. Holding onto the connection she'd had with him. Finally, she closed up and went to bed. Reminding herself that, after tomorrow night, she wouldn't be sleeping on her own again. She drifted off to sleep with a smile on her face.

Chapter Seventeen

He'd spent a restless night. He hadn't wanted to say too much to Jess about what was going on. Although he desperately wanted to be with her, at the moment he needed to lie low. He wanted Frank to think his plan had succeeded. He'd already called the sheriff and, whilst he'd not told him everything, he had hinted that someone was out to discredit him and for the time being he wanted them to think they'd succeeded. It had taken some persuasion to get Stan to agree to hedge over his whereabouts and say he couldn't disclose where he was. Telling him that he didn't want anyone to know his whereabouts, including Frank, had made Stan suspicious, but he told him that he was handling it and everything was above board. Now he had another meeting with his city lawyer. The one Frank knew nothing about.

Two hours later he was back in his hotel room, frustrated. They needed a further deposition and he cursed himself for not thinking of it beforehand. He was due to check out in thirty minutes and he needed to do some quick thinking. He'd promised Jess that they'd come to the city this weekend, now it looked as though he was going to be here until then. This meant a change of plan. Pulling out his Blackberry he phoned the hotel where they'd first met and was relieved that they had accommodation. He specified the room number he wanted and made it clear that another room was not an option. Now all he had to do was phone Jess and break the news to her, but he thought he would wait until tonight to do that.

***

By the time Jessica got home she couldn't help the smile

that kept appearing on her face. He would be home soon and this would be their last night apart. She was excited and happy. She hoped he would call early as she wanted to hear his voice, but not only that, she needed to tell him that Frank was now looking worried. He'd been in and out of the office for most of the day and on the phone. Helena had come in to see him but she'd been on the phone with another client so had no idea what they'd talked about. By the time she'd got to the storeroom all she could hear was panting so she knew exactly what they were doing. She would never have thought he was like that. But there again, who knew what went on behind closed doors? Although on this occasion she did.

It was almost seven when the phone rang and she answered it on the second ring. "Hi," she gasped, out of breath from the dash from the kitchen.

"Hi, to you. You sound out of breath. Do I need to be worried?"

"No. I was in the kitchen and just ran through from there. Are you home?"

He'd been anticipating the question. "No, darling. I'm still in the city." The line was silent. "Jess, are you still there?"

"Yes," her voice was quiet. "I was hoping you were home and that I could drive over."

"Oh God, don't say that. You have no idea how I wish you could do that. I wish I was home as well, but there's been a slight hitch. Nothing to worry about, but I need you to swear a deposition about what you heard and recorded. Or rather, my lawyers do. I should have thought of it and brought you with me..."

She interrupted him. "Deposition, lawyers. What are you doing, Ethan?"

"I'm trying to get Frank out of my life for good and, after what he's tried to do, out of town. Look, I'll explain everything when you get here."

"I can't come now."

"I know, but I thought you could perhaps get away early on Friday. Or even Thursday evening, if you can take Friday off?"

She couldn't miss the pleading in his tone. Well, she could

finish on Thursday and drive to the city on Friday morning. "I'll see what I can do. In the meantime, Frank is starting to worry. He's been running about all day looking anxious, and then Helena came in and swept straight through to his office. I couldn't hear what was said, as I was on the phone to a client. By the time I got there they were doing other business, if you know what I mean." She heard the groan and laughed.

"You mean he's been doing what I want to do?"

"What, you want to screw Helena as well?" she said feigning horror.

"No, I damn well don't. You know exactly what I mean, and I don't screw you. I make love to you."

"I know you do. And you do it very nicely, Mr Slade."

"Jessica," the name was said as a warning. "Don't push me too far. I can still be with you within the hour. Under cover of darkness no-one will see me, but you won't get any sleep. And that would be a bad thing, as you need to keep your wits about you. I don't want Frank suspecting you have anything to do with this. Well, not yet anyway."

They talked some more and then agreed that she would phone him the next day with details of when she would arrive.

Telling Frank that her cousin had a minor emergency and she needed to go to the city was easy. He grumbled but agreed that she could take Friday off. Telling Ethan that night that she would drive to the city on the Friday morning, she was met with a complaint as to why she couldn't go on the Thursday night. Convincing him that she would prefer to drive when she was fresh and not after a tense day in the office quickly brought about a change of heart. He didn't want anything to happen to her, so Friday morning it would be.

***

Frank was beginning to worry. He'd been to the sheriff's office but couldn't find anything out. He'd dropped into the conversation that he'd not been able to contact Ethan and had watched Stan's face close over as he replied. "Can't say where he is." That had given Frank some hope. Was he unable to say where he was because he was in custody in the city, or did he simply not know where he was? He drove out to the ranch, but the foreman had said no one knew where he was. They were just getting on with what needed to be done. That had given him more hope and he'd gone home to Helena in a better frame of mind.

"I think our plan must have worked," he said as he walked in the door. "Just been out to the ranch and nobody knows where Ethan is."

"So you think he's under arrest?" she said wrapping her arms round his neck and pressing her naked body against him.

"Possibly. I reckon he's been taken to the city for processing. They'll be taking statements and I guess that's where Lacey is as well. I've been into the diner where she works but no one has seen her all week. The police will be carrying out tests and keeping her there."

"Were there any police at the ranch?"

"No." He thought for a moment. "But then maybe they have all they need from there. After all, they have Lacey and they'd only need the bedding and so on to show she'd been in the bed. No, I reckon he's in the city jail with a smart lawyer trying to get him out. But no amount of money is going to work this time. He's going to get all that's coming to him."

"Come on, Frank. Don't think about him. It's party time for us. And what is the first thing you do when you come in from work?"

He laughed. "I know, get naked and dirty with you. I never thought life could get this good," he said grabbing her and kissing her lips, while his fingers eagerly made their way between her legs and thrust upwards.

Leaving work on Thursday, Jessica was a mass of excitement. She was meeting Ethan at the hotel, their hotel and in their room. She could have gone tonight, it was very tempting, but she wanted to prepare herself. A long leisurely bath, painting her nails and toes, washing her hair. She was preening herself for her mate, the way any female would do, and she intended to make a good job of it. He phoned her cell phone while she was in the bath and she took the greatest pleasure in telling him what she was doing when he asked. She loved to tease him and she was getting bolder by the day. He reminded her to make sure she brought her laptop and phone, as the lawyer would need to take details.

"Darling, I do know what lawyers need. You are intending to marry one." The dig wasn't lost on him and he apologised for overlooking the fact, telling her that he certainly did intend to marry her, and the sooner the better.

The drive to Calgary took just over an hour, due to a hold up with construction work. It was just after ten-thirty when she arrived at the hotel and he was waiting in the lobby. Her heart somersaulted in her chest as he walked towards her. He was every inch the businessman today. Mid-grey suit, white shirt and deep blue tie. And the smile on his face told her everything she needed to know. He gave her a brief kiss and took the holdall from her and they went to their room. Room 931; the room that had changed her life forever.

Once inside, he threw the holdall on the bed and pulled her into his arms and gave her the kiss he'd been saving from the moment she'd walked in the hotel entrance. He deepened the kiss and his hands were taking on a life of their own, but they couldn't do this now. They were due at the lawyers shortly. Backing away, he held her at arm's length taking in every detail. The dark hair, glossy and sleek, the pale pink shirt underneath a tailored jacket and a matching pencil slim skirt. The heels, not quite killers, but enough to finish off his rational thinking. "God, Jess, you look…you look sensational. I could just sit here and watch you, deciding which part of you I was going to undress first."

She didn't speak but raised a questioning eyebrow. She was beyond words and waited.

"Perhaps I would start with the skirt, and then the jacket. After that I'd slip my hands under the shirt and remove the bra, then…"

"Back up, Slade," she said teasingly. "So how do you get my bra off without removing the shirt?"

He groaned and held his head in his hands. "Why did you have to spoil my illusion?"

"Lawyers always have to work out all the details."

"Okay, so how would *you* get the bra off without removing the shirt?"

"That's for me to know, and for you to find out later. If you're good, that is."

He kissed her again. "Jess, for you, I'll always be good. But now I think we need to go. We'll take a cab, see the lawyer and then grab some lunch somewhere."

The lawyers were meticulous in their questions and took details from her hard drive as to when the various conversations were downloaded. They took a full and detailed statement from her, while Ethan waited outside. She had to apologise for deleting all the messages from her phone, apart from the final few, in case someone had got hold of it. But her deposition together with the copies was sufficient. Eventually they were finished and all that needed to be done was for them to call back later for the statement to be signed and to collect her laptop and phone.

They stopped in a small restaurant for a light lunch since Ethan had booked a table in the hotel restaurant for them that night. Returning to the hotel they held hands as the elevator took them up to the ninth floor. When the doors opened she held back, and grinned mischievously at him. He put his head on one side and gave her a look that said *'no way,'* and she allowed him to pull her gently out of the elevator and along the passageway. By the time they reached the room door she was shaking with anticipation.

Holding the door open he allowed her to pass. Every part of his body was under tension. She went into the bathroom, saying she wouldn't be a moment. He hung his jacket up and took off the tie and undid the top buttons on the shirt. Then rolled up the sleeves and sat down on the small sofa and waited.

Inside the bathroom Jess quickly took off her jacket and undid the buttons on her shirt before slipping it off. Removing the straps from her bra, she then re-dressed and went back into the bedroom. He looked up as she came in and then looked puzzled. She smiled and held out her hand and pulled him to his feet. He was about to discover multiway bras.

"You were saying earlier about what part to undress first?"

Now he understood her. She'd taken off her bra. So the way to remove it, was for her not to wear it in the first place. "Well, I seem to recall it was the skirt," he said as he slid the zip down. "Then the jacket." He eased this off and put it on a hanger with the skirt. All the time she stood waiting for him. Now he took in the long legs still with the heels on and the briefs and shirt. Reaching forward, he put his hand under the shirt expecting to find her naked, but the bra was there.

He frowned and looked at her, but she just smiled and raised an eyebrow. So this was some kind of test. He moved his hands to the back and undid the fastening, and peeled the bra away. It came off and he pulled it out from the bottom of the shirt. Hearing her soft laughter as he did.

"I think you're teasing me, Miss Cameron?"

"Only a bit, Mr Slade."

A quick move of the fingers and the first button was undone, then the next and the next until the shirt hung open against her body. He put his hand forward and touched her skin, moving up to cup the soft breast in his hand. The shirt gaped and he could see the white of her breasts when the sun hadn't been. He moved his head forward and, pushing the material aside, moulded his lips round the pink nipple. She shuddered violently and he put his other hand out to steady her. She grasped his forearm and he heard the moan from her lips. Lifting his head, he moved his thumb slowly over the soft tip and she threw her head back and then her eyes met his. The passion he saw was almost the undoing of them both, but he held back. Held them both in check.

***

For Jessica what was happening was beyond ecstasy. Every part of her body was quivering and screaming for him. She wanted rid of the remaining clothes she had on and wanted him naked as well. But she wasn't in control of this and at this point she wasn't capable of taking control. His thumbs rubbed gently over her nipples and her legs threatened to give way. "Please, Ethan?" The words came out on a groan.

"I know. Don't fight it, Jess. Go with it. Let it happen."

The shirt slipped slowly off her shoulders and he threw it onto the chair. Now there were just the briefs and the shoes. He dealt with the briefs first until she was standing before him with only the heels on. He'd never thought himself kinky but the sight of her like that had him fantasizing over what they could do. But all he wanted to do was to make love to her.

"Lose the shoes, Jess," the words were low and husky.

She stepped out of the shoes and dropped at least three inches. As she watched he pulled off his shirt and pants and then everything else. They stood facing each other, naked as they'd done the first time. But this time it was different. They weren't strangers anymore.

He put out his hand and cupped the back of her head and pulled her towards him. His tongue invaded her mouth and her arms went round his neck. Then they fell backwards onto the bed and after that it was difficult to say who did what. But they made love. In the middle of the afternoon in a hotel room, she gave everything to him and he gave the world to her. They exploded together and she felt him pouring inside her and wrapped her legs around his waist until he was fully drained.

They lay in bed, sipping champagne from the bottle he'd had in the fridge, and talked. Away from the town and everything that had been happening, and was still to happen, he opened up to her, and she to him.

"I was only three when my mom died," she told him. "And I was six when my dad remarried. Not quite the wicked stepmother. But she didn't have too much time for children, and she and my dad never had any of their own. But I was happy. I had my dad and my friends. And there was my Aunt Margaret, Gemma's mom. She was my mom's sister and was divorced and I used to spend a lot of time at their house. Gemma's only a couple of years younger than me so we got on really well. That's why I was so upset when she was with Eric. I knew he was no good for her before anything ever happened. Gem is an angel. She works on the children's ward at the hospital and the kids adore her." She paused, thinking back to her family and then realised that he was waiting for her to continue.

"Anyway, as I was saying, I was happy growing up and went to college and then university. When I was in my final year, my dad died. He'd had cancer for a couple of years and did well to survive as long as he did. It was hard after that going home. It never felt the same. Then a couple of years later my step-mom met a guy who was here on holiday, married him and moved to New Zealand. After that there was just Gemma and me, as her mom had passed away the year before my dad. When I qualified, I got a job for a year with a local firm and then applied for the job in Lethbridge, and that's where I met Tom. When that fell apart I decided to take a step back from the pressure of being an attorney and that's when I saw Frank's advert. So I sent off an application, and I think you know the rest."

Ethan had listened carefully as she opened up about her family. They'd teased each other, made love and committed themselves to a future together, but they'd not spoken about their past or their families. Now it was his turn. And lying in bed with her body close to his was the right time. Filling up their glasses he draped his arm around her and tucked her in close.

"I guess I was lucky. I had a very happy and settled childhood. Grew up on the ranch. My dad had taken over from my granddad and he and grandma had moved into what is now the foreman's house. Still on the ranch but away from the everyday hustle of work. I was riding horses before I could walk and roping young calves by the time I was five, according to my late mother. She used to tell me that once school was out I was out on the range with the men and she had a devil of a time getting me to do homework."

"So Frank and his family didn't live on the ranch?" She had to ask the question that had been niggling at her ever since she heard Frank talking about taking back what was owing to him.

"No. Frank's father, Nate, was three years younger than my dad and what you would call a wild one. He had no interest in

211

the ranch; only the money that came from it and, from what dad told me, he and granddad had no end of rows. He got engaged to the daughter of one of the other ranchers in the area, but he played away. Eventually he got one of the local girls pregnant. There was hell to pay when it came out, apparently, and when granddad found out they had one hell of a bust-up and Nate left. Didn't come back for over five years. Granddad was apparently so disgusted with him that he changed his Will and left everything to my dad. Said the continuation of the ranch was the most important thing and in my dad's hands it would be safe. Dad and my mom were already married by then and they lived in the main house with gran and granddad, until they moved out, and that's where I was born."

"So Frank's mother raised him on her own?"

"Not entirely. Uncle Nate came back and they lived together for a number of years, although they never married. But he and granddad never spoke and granddad had no interest in Frank. That was mainly because of who his mother was. Let's say she entertained a lot. Nate didn't stay around. When Frank was about eight he left, never came back. My dad never saw him again. Never heard anything from him, either, until he got a call to say he'd died somewhere in Colorado.

No-one ever mentioned him when he'd gone, grandad wouldn't have his name spoken. Then one day, granddad took a tumble from his horse and, although it wasn't serious in itself, he suffered a stroke a couple of days later and died within the week. Grandma was heartbroken. They'd just celebrated their golden wedding anniversary and had been together since they were teenagers. After that, she moved back into the main house with us, and stayed there until she died about ten months after granddad. I was about nine when that happened. After that it was just mom, dad, and me. I learned to run the ranch from the bottom up, working with the men and taking orders from them. Once I left school I did on-line university degrees in ranching and business management, and worked alongside my dad during the day."

He took a mouthful of champagne before continuing. "I was

twenty-two when dad died. A sudden heart attack. There was no warning, he just dropped where he stood and there was nothing anyone could do. It was the worst time of my life. Although I did what I could for mom, she was never the same. Dad left the ranch and everything to me, apart from a twenty percent interest in the ranch. I didn't know until the Will was read that he'd given twenty per cent to mom as a gift on their silver wedding anniversary. But his Will stated that he trusted it would revert to me when mom died. I had no doubt that it would and never discussed it with her. Sadly, she took dad's death badly and gradually people began to notice changes in her. Forgetting things and doing things that were out of character. It was a couple of years before the doctor diagnosed Alzheimer's and the deterioration after that was swift. It wasn't safe for her on the ranch, even with someone trying to keep an eye on her. So eventually I had to take the decision to move her into a nursing home. That was the hardest decision I ever had to make." He broke off, deep in thought.

Listening to him, Jessica felt her eyes filling with tears. "I'm so sorry, darling," she said, resting her head against his shoulder.

He nodded. "She died five years ago." His voice broke the silence. "That was when I found out that just after dad had died she'd changed her will. Everything came to me but she left ten percent of her share in the ranch to Frank. Apparently she felt sorry for him having missed out on his share but, in her kind but misguided way, left me with the problem of Frank. He can't change anything, I have ninety percent of the ranch, but he does make life difficult. Now I have the chance to get him off my back and out of my life for good."

"How do you plan on doing that? Although I suspect that I may have some idea, but you'd better enlighten me."

He kissed the top of her head. "Easy, or at least I hope it will be. I have more than enough evidence for him to go to jail. For all of them to go to jail, but that's my leverage. His freedom and theirs, in exchange for his share in the ranch. Oh, and he leaves town and never returns." He gave a bitter laugh. "Never thought I would be reduced to blackmail to recover

213

what should never have been lost."

Jessica didn't know what to say. He'd just opened up his heart to her about his family. "So that's what the deposition was all about. The lawyers have all the information to make a prosecution, either through the police or privately."

He nodded. "Yes, and at this moment Frank suspects I'm being held in the city jail. I asked Stan to say he didn't know my whereabouts, and the men have been told to say they haven't seen or heard from me all week, on pain of their jobs, if he asks. Leaving him feeling secure for a couple more days will make his downfall even harder."

"He will take it hard. He had it all worked out, how to get control of your money."

"So I gather. And that's the funny part of all of this. It would never have worked."

"Oh, I don't know," she said butting in.

"Ah, but I do, sweetheart. You see once I knew he had a share in the company, no matter how small, I took action to protect everything. I didn't trust him, never have. Mark, the lawyer you met today, he's had Power of Attorney to act on my behalf since just after my mom died. So, you see, his plan would have failed. Mark would have looked after everything and done so in accordance with my instructions. Whether they were given from a prison cell or not."

She sat upright, holding the sheet under her arms. "So all of this has been for nothing?"

"No. Not for nothing. This is setting me free and means that the ranch, and all the other assets he tried to get his hands on, will pass to our children in due course. Which reminds me," he said changing the subject abruptly. "How are things in that department?"

She laughed. "What do you mean, department? If you mean, am I pregnant? then the answer is that it's too soon to say."

"Well, I guess we'd better keep trying." He took her glass and put both down on the bedside table and pulled her down under the sheet. All that could be heard were her giggles as he started a delicate assault on her body.

214

Chapter Eighteen

Waking up in his arms the following morning was everything and more than she thought it would be. They'd enjoyed a wonderful dinner in the hotel the previous evening which had reminded her of the first meal they'd shared in the restaurant, when he'd first called her Red. Returning to their room they'd showered together and then slept until he woke her in the early hours, when they made love again.

Now she was watching him as he slept. They were going out to choose a ring but she also wanted to go and see Gemma while they were here. She wanted to tell her they were engaged, wanted her to meet Ethan. Looking at the clock she saw it was just after seven-thirty. She knew her cousin was working until two so they would have plenty of time to shop before then. In fact, she really needed to get herself some more casual clothes. As the wife of a rancher she couldn't parade around in designer suits or killer heels. She closed her eyes and pictured it and smiled at the thought of mucking out a stall in killer heels.

"Care to share the joke?"

The voice made her start and she opened her eyes. "Just imagining mucking out in killer heels." The statement made no sense whatsoever and she watched as he frowned.

"Is this a trick question? Or are you getting kinky?"

"Neither. I was just thinking that I need to get some more casual clothes. I can't be on the ranch in the kind of clothes I wear to the office. So while we are out this morning I'll do some clothes shopping. You don't have to come if you don't want to."

"Of course I do. Clothes shopping isn't all we're doing. Is it?" He left the question hanging in the air.

She shook her head. No, they were shopping for something really special this morning. The one thing that would tell the world that they were together. That she was his and he belonged to her.

They ate breakfast in their room and then set out to buy the most important thing of all. She thought it would take a long time to find the ring she wanted, but in fact she found it in the third shop. Three square-cut diamonds on a gold band. She loved it when she saw it and prayed that it would be the right size. It was, and as she held her hand out for Ethan to see, he agreed with her choice. They then chose wedding rings. Ethan took some persuading, as rings and ranch work don't go well together. But they compromised; he would wear it on a chain when working. They stopped for lunch in a small café, sitting outside in the sun, and that was where he slipped the ring onto her finger and they became officially engaged.

They took a cab to Gemma's apartment. She'd already phoned her cousin to say they were intending to call but had staved off her onslaught of questions when she told her that she was bringing her fiancé with her. Going back into the apartment sent a shiver down her spine and she gripped Ethan's hand tightly. He frowned but she smiled tentatively back at him. There was no time to say anything as Gemma was firing questions at her, at both of them. Where did they meet, and when was the wedding going to be? Telling her she wasn't sure, Jessica glanced quickly at Ethan, who was sitting back in the chair with a smile on his face.

Ethan knew women could talk, and talk over each other. But these two were something else. "Remind me to make sure I'm needed somewhere else when you two first meet up, so you have plenty of time to catch up on all the feminine stuff without me," he joked. Jessica grinned. She could see he wasn't serious. "I have a feeling, Gemma, that you're going to be a regular, and very welcome visitor to our home," he concluded. Jessica could have kissed him for what he said. He could see how important her cousin was to her, and how much their friendship meant. They opened a bottle of wine, not that Jess had more than half a glass since she was driving home later. Ethan was happy to finish the bottle with his new soon-to-be cousin-in-law.

Although Jessica was happy, and with the two people she loved, she was also aware of what had happened last time she was here. She needed to go to the bathroom and had been putting it off for some time, but now necessity took first place. Excusing herself, she walked along the passage towards Gemma's bedroom. It was the closest to the lounge and she had no intention of going to the guest bathroom. She almost ran past the spot in the passage where it had happened and shot into Gemma's bedroom. Locking the bathroom door, she took a few moments to compose herself. Coming back out of the bedroom she took a deep breath and started to walk back, past the spot, keeping her eyes looking straight ahead. She felt the touch on her hand and her name being spoken at the same time. Swinging round she didn't know what to expect, but she was ready to strike out.

**

Ethan had used the other bathroom, following Gemma's instructions, and thought Jess would have been back with her cousin, so was surprised to see her ahead of him in the passage. Moving quickly, he touched her hand and said her name. What he wasn't prepared for was the look of sheer terror on her face as she turned. "Jesus, Jess. What's wrong?"

She didn't or couldn't speak. Then it hit him. This was where it happened. Where Eric had assaulted her, and now he had just come up behind her suddenly. "Jess, sweetheart, it's me," he said, as he pulled her into his arms. He felt the shudder that went through her and cursed himself for forgetting this was where it had happened. "Where was it?"

She turned a white face to the wall and put out a shaking hand. He took her hand and led her to the spot. Placing her against the wall he cupped her face in both hands. "Darling, there's nothing to fear. This is just a piece of wall that from now on will have nothing but a happy memory for you." He lowered his lips to hers and teased hers until she opened to

217

him. His tongue played a seductive dance with her own and gradually he felt her relax. Then he pulled her into his arms and deepened the kiss.

She was breathless when he released her. But he hoped the bad memory was replaced with something wonderful. From now on every time she was here he hoped she would concentrate on what had just happened and nothing else. Smiling, he took her hand and led her back to where her cousin was waiting. Another demon, he hoped, had been exorcised.

***

Leaving Ethan later was the hardest thing for Jessica. He rang down and had her car brought around to the front of the hotel, and then carried her holdall out to the forecourt. She hated having to go and wished she could have stayed another night but she knew that if she did, there would be no way she would be back in Longville for nine. He kissed her tenderly before she drove away and she kept the feel of that kiss with her long after she'd left the city limits. All she had to do now was to keep up the charade tomorrow until Ethan came home. He'd told her he would come straight to the office and deal with Frank.

She was in the office early. She wanted to get as much work done as she could before it all kicked off. Because kick off it would. Every time the door opened her heart was in her mouth. By lunchtime she was beginning to think something had happened. What if Frank had found out and had done something to Ethan? It didn't bear thinking about. She slipped out at twelve for lunch and was back by one. Frank wasn't back so she presumed he was still at lunch. He came back at two looking agitated and went straight through to his office, saying he didn't want to be disturbed.

The office door opened and her head shot up. It wasn't Ethan, but another player in the game. Helena swept straight through to Frank's office before Jessica could pick up the phone to say she was there. Grabbing a file from the desk she crept into the storeroom.

"Are you sure nobody knows anything? Helena's voice came over loud and clear.

"I just said so. I've tried Lacey's phone but there's no answer, just the bloody machine."

"What about Joey, have you tried him?"

"Of course I have. Same thing, voice mail and nobody's seen him around town all week."

"Look, Frank, sweetie, it's probably just a coincidence. Maybe Lacey's phoned him from the city to go and stay with her while the police take statements."

"No. We should have heard something by now. And Stan's being secretive."

Jessica longed to stay and listen some more but she knew Ethan should be arriving any time so she needed to get back to the front office. Closing the storeroom door, she crept quietly along the passage back to her desk.

It was almost three when the door opened and he walked in, and she heaved a sigh of relief. The last few hours had been torture. Pressing her finger to her lips, she whispered that Frank wasn't alone. "Helena arrived some time ago. I listened to some of what they were saying. She's trying to calm him down." Ethan listened to her but then he picked up her left hand, frowning at her bare ring finger. "I couldn't wear it to work or Frank might have spotted it," she offered by way of explanation.

"Where is it?"

"In my purse."

"Put it on, Jess, please."

She took it out of her purse and handed it to him and held out her hand. He slipped it back where it belonged and then bent down and kissed her lips. "Seeing it there makes me believe that this is real and we are going to have a happy-ever-after. Which is more than Frank is. So, the delightful Helena is with him. Do you think I dare interrupt?"

She couldn't help but giggle at the thought of Ethan bursting in when they were in a compromising situation. "I don't know. As I said, I was listening in up until about fifteen minutes ago. He's getting anxious because he can't find out anything."

"Good. Well, I think I'll go and add to his anxieties. Do you want to come in with me?"

She shook her head. "No, but I'll eavesdrop from the storeroom."

She followed him along the passage and slipped into the storeroom. By habit, she took her phone and switched it to record. She heard the door open and then the gasps as presumably they'd seen Ethan.

"Afternoon, Frank. And you have the delightful Helena with you, how convenient." His voice sounded clearly through the wall.

"Ethan," Frank stammered. "What are you doing here?"

"Got some business to discuss with you. You don't look well, Frank. Is something wrong? And you don't look much better, Helena. In fact, you both look as though you've seen a ghost. Or is it that you weren't expecting to see me, Frank?"

He left the question hanging. He was enjoying this. Watching them squirm. When he thought of where he might have been now if it hadn't been for Jessica, it made his blood boil. He wanted to smack Frank in the face, but it wouldn't serve any purpose. What he had in mind would be retribution enough. He lounged against the open doorway and watched the conflicting expressions going across both their faces.

Frank looked stunned. Not only by his sudden appearance, but also by the fact that he didn't appear to have a care in the world. Ethan smiled inwardly. Frank was no doubt now having serious misgivings about the success of his plan. Helena had remained silent until now, but she moved into action.

"Ethan, darling," she said drawling out his name. "Where have you been? Frank has been really worried when nobody seemed to know where you were." She slid off the edge of the desk and made to touch him.

"Whoa, hands off, Helena," he said putting his palms up in front of him. "You'll make Frank jealous. Not that he has any reason to be. My feelings are firmly elsewhere and I know that yours are too. Well, from what I've heard anyway. Mind you,

Frank, you'll need to be careful, letting her make you coffee packs quite a punch." He waited, while the comment hit home. And it did. Helena backed right up to Frank and his arm went protectively around her.

"Don't know what you mean," said Frank, now on the defensive.

"Oh, I think you do, Frank. Let's cut out the bullshit and get down to business. I know exactly what you planned to do. You and Helena, with help from Lacey and Joey." He saw Frank whitening by the second and Helena looked about ready to pass out. "Glad you're not denying it. So here's the deal, Frank. You sign over your shares and interest in The Lazy B, and in this practice, and leave town. In exchange, I won't go to the cops with what you tried to do."

Frank saw everything he'd been working for slipping out of his grasp. But he wasn't finished yet. "It'll be your word against mine. Nobody would believe you."

Ethan had been expecting this. He opened the folder he had in his hand and dropped a bundle of papers on the desk. "Copies of recordings of your meetings with various people. Oh, and some of them could be a bit embarrassing," he said, looking at Helena. "How you could agree to such a plan is beyond me, Helena. I didn't think you capable of anything so devious."

"It was your fault," she flung back at him. "You dropped me when that…that person came to work for Frank. I spent two years with you and expected marriage, not to be dumped for a pen-pusher."

"She's not a pen-pusher," he said firmly. He wasn't going to have any slur made against his fiancée. "In fact she's as qualified as Frank, but that's another story and not one that's any concern of yours. But if you thought I was going to offer marriage to you then you were delusional. Any relationship we had has been dying for the last twelve months. And I didn't drop you when Jessica came to work here. Our relationship ended before then. It ended before I left for the States. That's when I met Jessica, before I flew out. Her coming to work for Frank was coincidental but, as it turned out, she saved my life.

221

Or at least saved me from a life behind bars for something I didn't do."

Frank had been reading the papers, his face going red at some of what he was reading. The discussions with Lacey, with Joey and with Helena, all recorded. And some of the things with Helena were embarrassing but, if he was losing this war, he didn't intend to lose her. "So what do you plan to do?" He directed the question to Ethan.

"Exactly what I said. You sign over all your interest in the Lazy B and the practice and leave town and don't come back. In exchange, the originals of these papers and the depositions that support them stay with my lawyers."

"So you won't prosecute any of us?"

"No. I think you've got your just desserts, Frank. You've lost, what is it, oh yes, fifteen thousand to Lacey and Joey, but you've gained Helena, and presumably all the screwing you can get."

"Didn't hear you complaining," snapped Helena.

"No, in the beginning it was good. But the kinky stuff left me cold, and eventually what was between us left me cold. I don't want to be cruel to you, Helena, but what we had was nothing. What I have now with Jessica, is everything."

Sitting in the storeroom, Jessica was feeling quite put out listening to the conversation between Ethan and Helena. She knew they'd been together but hearing them talk about it, well, it brought it home and made it real. She didn't want to listen to this any more, so left the phone on the floor and stood up. But she caught his last words and that made her smile.

"Well, what Frank and I have is everything as well," said Helena. "He likes the stuff you didn't and he pleases me more than you did."

"I'm glad," said Ethan, failing to rise to her bait. "I think you two are perfect for each other. In fact, when Frank leaves town, I think he should set up in the city and you two should live together."

Frank, having heard enough of this exchange, spoke up. "That's exactly what is going to happen. I don't care what you do to me, you leave Helena out of it."

"I'll leave you both out of it. All you have to do is sign the papers I have with me. I'm sure Jessica can get us a witness from outside. Can't you, darling?" he called out, knowing that she was listening.

The question was an invitation to Jessica to join them and she was only too happy to oblige. She'd had enough of listening to Helena. Coming into the doorway she stood next to Ethan and slipped an arm around his waist, staking her claim on her man.

Frank knew when he was beaten. He'd read enough to know the game was up. Ethan knew everything he'd planned to do. And he was right about the money; he was fifteen thousand out of pocket. But at least he wasn't going to jail and neither was Helena. But he was losing his business here, and his home, since both properties belonged to Slade Enterprises. He would have to start up again in the city, that was providing Ethan wasn't planning on reporting him to his professional body.

"So if I sign and leave town that's it. No other repercussions. You're not going to report me and have me disbarred?"

"Much as I would love to, Frank, you are family and I figure if you have to keep Helena, you'll need a decent income. So no, I won't report you. This stays strictly between my lawyers and us. I have little stomach to drag the family name down."

"Okay, I'll sign the bloody papers."

Jessica went next door and brought the owner of the hardware store and his assistant to witness the signatures and then, thirty minutes later, Frank had cleared his desk of his personal belongings and was about to leave.

"How did you find out?" Frank asked before he left.

Ethan looked at Jessica so she took over. "I overheard you talking while I was in the storeroom. There's an air vent behind the filing cabinet and I heard every word that was being said. I just recorded the conversations. It was as easy as that."

Helena's face was red. "So you listened in while Frank and

223

I were… well, you know?"

She nodded her head. "Not one of my better recordings."

"You bitch," she spat out.

"Helena," Frank and Ethan spoke together. Up to now, things had been civil and they didn't want this turning into a brawl.

Seeing she was to be quietened, Helena couldn't resist one last dig. "He'll get fed up with you before long, move onto somebody else. Then you'll be on your own."

Ethan spoke up before Jessica could. Picking up her hand he displayed the diamond ring. "Didn't we say? We're engaged so that won't happen. Sorry to disappoint you, Helena."

"Helena's not disappointed. We're getting married as well." Frank interjected. He wasn't having Helena put down. He only hoped she would agree, although looking at the smile on her face he didn't think that would be a problem.

"Glad to hear it Frank. At least something may have worked out for you."

He watched as his cousin packed the last of his things into his briefcase. In a way, he almost felt sorry for him. He hadn't had the easiest of lives but what he'd had was good, compared to some people. For him to throw it all away for greed was something Ethan couldn't understand. But then again, he'd never been in Frank's position, nor did he have Frank's apparently devious mind. There was one thing that he hadn't told Frank yet and figured that now was the time.

"You know, Frank, it was quite an ingenious plan you worked out. Very legal-minded, thought you'd crossed all the t's and dotted the i's. But there was one flaw in your plan."

"Oh yeah, and what was that?" Frank was getting beyond needing to be civil. The reality of what lay ahead was only just hitting home.

"The plan would never have worked. Oh, you could possibly have had me put in prison, but that's as far as it would have gone."

Now Frank was curious. He thought he'd done his homework. "Okay, so why wouldn't it have worked?"

"My lawyer in Calgary, the one you know nothing about, holds Power of Attorney for me. Has done for several years. So you wouldn't have got control of anything." Frank looked about to combust. His face went almost purple. "So it was all for nothing, Frank. You risked everything and ended up with nothing."

Frank smiled. "No, not nothing. I got one thing you had that I wanted." He took hold of Helena's hand and walked towards the door.

Closing and locking the door behind them, Jessica leaned against the glass and looked at Ethan. "Well, that's it. It's over."

"Not quite, darling. I need to have these papers filed and to do that I need to get them back to the lawyers. Do you feel like a trip to Calgary tonight?"

Jessica looked at the open files on her desk. Now that Frank had gone, she would have to step up and revert back to being the attorney that she was. There were some depositions that needed filing with the court that she couldn't leave and, much as she wanted to go with him, the responsible lawyer in her told her she had to stay.

"Sorry, darling, I'd love to, but I can't. Now Frank isn't here I'll have to step in and deal with some matters that need filing today." She saw the disappointment on his face and reached up and kissed him. "But I'll be waiting for you when you get back. That is, if you are coming back tonight?"

"Yes, I need to be back. I've been away longer that planned and there are things that need doing. But mostly I want to get back to you. Where will you be, the cottage or the ranch?"

"Where would you like me to be?"

"I would love you to be at the ranch but I doubt there'll be anyone around and I don't want you there on your own. So I guess it's the cottage. I'll come there when I get back and then go home in the morning. If that's okay?"

"Oh, I don't know. I'll have to check with my landlord about taking in lodgers," she couldn't help teasing.

"Well, I think your landlord will approve of the lodger. So there should be no problem. I'll drop these off with Mark and turn straight around and come back. Should be back about eight."

"Okay, but please drive carefully. I don't want anything to happen to you, and make sure you have a coffee before you set off back."

"Yes, ma`am," he said giving her a mocking salute before giving her a hug and a kiss and telling her not to work too late.

"I'll get something from the store and we can have a late dinner." She called after him and saw his hand come up in a wave. She heaved a sigh of relief. They could now relax and get on with their lives. Well, once he'd done this last job.

She spent the next hour filing the various papers online with the court and then decided to phone Dan and tell him the outcome. She tried his home but got no answer so phoned the office. He was glad to hear that everything was sorted and that she had managed to keep herself safe.

"How come you're still working?" she asked.

"Oh, had a couple of cases passed to me by…" he hesitated and Jessica knew who he was referring to, so she said it for him.

"Tom. It's okay, Dan, you can mention his name. In fact, I have some news myself. I've just got engaged and I couldn't be happier."

"Oh, Jessica, that's great news. And yes, it was Tom. Apparently he's got behind with things. Out partying with you-know-who. Seems to spend a lot of time passing work to other people nowadays. Now he's a partner he can get away with it. And daddy isn't going to refuse his little girl anything, particularly with the wedding only a couple of weeks away."

"Gosh, that's quick, even for Tom," she said, not feeling a flicker of sadness, just relief. If he hadn't cheated on her she wouldn't have gone to Gemma's, and she wouldn't have met Ethan.

"Yes, well, any longer and she'll start to show."

Jessica started to laugh. "Oh no. You mean she's pregnant? Oh that'll please Tom, he never factored children into his relationships."

"Well, he's got one on the way now. So I can only imagine

that things will get worse on the work front for us underlings."

Jessica thought for a moment. "Dan, are you happy working all hours in the city? Or would you like to be your own boss?"

"Where would I get the money from to set up my own firm?

"What if there was a practice already set up in a small town? Plenty of clients and certainly enough work for one lawyer. Won't be the same money as in the city but you would be your own boss, work your own hours and manage a work-life balance. Anyway, think on it and let me know if you're interested."

"So whose practice is it?" Dan sounded curiously interested.

"My fiancé's cousin. But he's had to leave town suddenly and there are clients to be dealt with. For the time being I'm doing that. But I don't want to do it full time and I'm not sure I want to do it at all. Married to a rancher, I'll have enough to do without working full time. So let me know and we can discuss it further."

She felt quite pleased with herself, thinking of Dan. He would fit in perfectly here and she had no doubt that he would enjoy the job. Locking the office door, she turned along the sidewalk and headed for the restaurant. She would get something to take home and then have a long soak in the tub before Ethan arrived.

She was so wrapped up in her plans that she didn't see the car until it was too late. Her last thought was that she had right of way...then blackness, and pain that reminded her of falling from Rory.

Chapter Nineteen

Ethan was half way home when he got the call to say Jessica was in the hospital. She'd begged them not to call him, but the doctor was insistent that someone be informed. She'd taken the phone from the sister and spoken to him herself, assuring him that she was fine, just cuts and bruises. What she didn't tell him was that Helena was in the sheriff's office being processed for dangerous driving.

Frank had come into the emergency room in a state of panic, begging her not to tell the police everything. He assured her that he hadn't known what she intended and that he didn't really think it was premeditated. "It was a spur of the moment thing. She saw you crossing over and just turned into the side road. All I could do was pull on the wheel and steer away from you. She's sorry, and she's in a terrible state. Please don't let Ethan do anything to make matters worse, Jessica. I love Helena and I will do anything for her, but I can't help her if I'm locked up as well."

Jessica couldn't believe his audacity, asking this of her. She was in pain and, for a moment when she'd come round in the ambulance, she'd been terrified that she might be seriously injured. And the question before they X-rayed her caused her some concern. *Was she pregnant?* It had made her hesitate, and was enough for them to take precautions in case she was. If she was pregnant, would the baby have been harmed by the accident? She hadn't wanted to think about that possibility, at least not yet.

But the doctor had since assured her that she seemed fine, apart from some bruising that would take a few days to develop, and some cuts. "Reckon someone was looking out for you, Jessica," he said, as he walked into the cubicle. "You were very fortunate."

She shook her head in a daze. "I know. Did the X-ray show up anything else?"

"Not that I'm aware of. There's nothing on the report other than what I've told you. But it could be that something else just wasn't detected. So I'll leave that one with you."

She smiled. "Thank you." So she probably wasn't pregnant, but it wasn't certain. But the way they were behaving, she would be before long. The thought had made her smile.

Now, listening to Frank, and with the doctor's words still echoing in her head, she realised that she had everything she could possibly want. Frank had nothing, apart from Helena, and if they told the police he wouldn't have her. Suddenly she wanted it to be over. Wanted to look forward to the future with Ethan and eventually with their child. She still could be pregnant and wanted to hang on to the possibility. With all that had been going on she'd completely lost track of her monthly cycle but now she began to hope. After all, they'd not been taking any precautions, and she had enough unused pills in the drawer for it to be a possibility. What she needed to do was to buy a testing kit as soon as she could and find out for certain.

Looking at Frank, she saw the tears in his eyes but she hardened her heart. "Okay, Frank, I'll speak to Ethan when he gets here. I can't promise but I will ask him. After that it's up to him."

"Thank you. I'm sorry, Jessica. I need to get back to Helena. I hope you recover well." With that he was gone.

She knew Ethan was there before he appeared through the closed curtains. The sister's voice booming across the room made her smile.

"No one runs in my department, and that includes you, Ethan Slade."

She was sitting up in the bed with the biggest smile on her face when he arrived. He came into the curtained-off section like a whirlwind and didn't stop until he reached the bed and was able to hold her gently. "What the hell happened? Thank God you're alright." The words were muffled into her hair.

Now she would have to start the hard bit. Trying to get him to overlook it. His face told her this would be difficult. "Look, darling, I'm okay. Just a few bruises and cuts and the doc says I can go home. I was waiting for you. Didn't think I should drive myself," she said attempting to lighten the atmosphere. The look she got told her exactly what he thought of her idea and her joke.

"If anything had happened to you I don't know what I would have done." He gently touched her face and then kissed her.

"Can we go home please, Ethan? Oh, and I didn't get a chance to buy anything for dinner." She was desperately trying to make light of the situation, knowing the serious conversation she was going to have to have with him.

Even he had to smile at that. "I don't care about food. I only care about you and that you're okay. But yes, we can go home, as long as the doc says you can."

Walking in through the cottage door, she thanked God that things had not been any worse. If she had been badly injured in any way, she would not be able to stop him from venting his full anger on Frank and Helena. Now she had to tell him who was driving the car and persuade him not to take matters further. While he put a meal together, she explained about Helena and then about Frank's visit.

"Please don't make it worse, Ethan. Let it go. I'm okay and what has happened has probably brought things to a permanent close." She waited for his reply.

His face was like thunder. "How can you ask me that, Jess? If she did it on purpose who's to say she won't do anything like it again? I can't take the risk of you being hurt, and neither can you."

"Frank won't let it happen again. He loves her and he intends to marry her and he'll keep her happy. He doesn't think she thought about it before she turned the car. Fortunately, Frank was able to pull the wheel otherwise I may have come off somewhat worse. He's positive it was a spur of the moment thing, and I'm willing to let it go." Even as she spoke the words, she knew she wouldn't have been able to do so if she had been seriously hurt. That would have put a whole new outlook on it.

He came through with a couple of bowls of pasta and handed one to her. "I don't know."

"Look, if we make a fuss, and anything of what they tried to do comes out, that will be the end for them both. And as you said, Frank is family, and it would drag the Slade name down. Just think how we will feel starting our married life, knowing we had destroyed their future. Let them have a chance at happiness. What they do with it is up to them." She waited while he digested her argument.

"They deserve all they get. But, if you're sure that's what you want? Although I'm not happy about it."

"I know you're not. But yes, it is what I want. Just let the police handle it, she'll have to plead guilty. I don't want any more worry, or stress."

"No, I guess you'll have enough to do planning our wedding."

"Yes, now about that. How about two weeks' time, if we can get it all arranged?" She smiled as he just about choked on his food. He hadn't expected her to give in to an early wedding so quickly.

"Two weeks. Are we in a rush? Not that I'm complaining. As far as I am concerned the sooner the better."

"No, not really in a rush," she said, while her mind was already forging ahead. If she was pregnant she didn't want to be walking down the aisle and showing. She wanted to be slim and sexy for him and to let him see what he was getting. "But I can't see any reason to wait, unless of course you do?"

"No way, I'd be married tomorrow if it were possible, but we can delay for a couple of weeks. So, as you say, we need to plan a wedding. And if you're certain, we'll let the Frank situation remain between us. Helena will have to face the consequences with the police but that's out of our hands, and I wouldn't have stopped the prosecution anyway, even if we had the chance."

"Oh, darling, thank you and yes, we will have to start planning but before we get caught up in that, I may have found

231

a new tenant for Frank's office and a new attorney for the town." She then proceeded to tell him about Dan and how good he would be.

"I wasn't sure whether you would want to take on the practice," he said between mouthfuls. "You know you can if you want. The office is there, so are the clients."

"I know, and I did think about it. But I've been disillusioned with the profession and there's something else that I have ticking away in the back of my mind."

He looked at her warily. "Do I need to be worried?"

"I don't think so. But I was wondering if we could possibly set up a visiting centre for disabled and sick children? A lot of children in the city have never seen a ranch, or baby animals, according to Gemma, and it would be lovely to offer them the chance to share that experience."

He took a deep breath. This had come from way offside. "Clearly you've given this some thought, and I guess I wouldn't be wrong in thinking the idea has come from Gemma. So what are you thinking of?"

"Not sure yet. Gemma has told me about the children on the ward, but this is my idea, I've not mentioned it to Gem. I was thinking something along the lines of a petting area and some docile ponies they could sit on and be led round a paddock. We could do a barbeque and get someone in with a guitar to make it like a camp. I initially thought if it worked out we could offer an overnight stay, but I don't think that would work because of their various disabilities. It may be that a day trip is the only way it will work. If I set it up, I would be able to work it with Gemma, and it would mean that I would be working from home. And that would be a plus when we have a family," she said, pleadingly.

"You seem to have given it a lot of thought?"

"Well, it's been ticking away in the back of my mind. My focus has been on other things, which is why I've not made any of the necessary enquiries yet. I'm sure Gemma would be on board."

"Okay, I'll think about it. But for now you need to rest, so eat up and then I'm going to put you to bed."

"Don't you mean take me to bed?" She queried with a mischievous look.

"No, definitely not. I said put you to bed, and that's exactly what I intend to do. Any plans I had in that department for tonight are postponed."

She pouted her lip and stuck out her tongue. "But what if my plans aren't postponed?"

"Tough. I intend to keep an eye on you all night to make sure you have no further problems. Those were the conditions when they let you come home. That someone would be here to watch you. And that someone is me."

"Okay, but couldn't you watch me from the other side of the bed? I would sleep much better if you were holding me."

"I'm sure you would. But I wouldn't. A chair in the corner of the room will be fine. At least for tonight," he said softly. "Tomorrow night is another matter altogether."

Despite her protests, he carried her up to the bedroom and once there had the enjoyable but torturous task of helping her to undress. Settled in the bed, she looked the picture of innocence as he gave her a quick kiss. As he pulled back, the sign of his arousal told her he was going to have a very long and uncomfortable night.

***

He crept down to the kitchen and started to make coffee and something to eat, but all he could find was a pack of chocolate muffins in the fridge. Shaking his head, he put a couple on a plate and then set them on a tray with a couple of mugs of coffee. She was still asleep when he returned upstairs and he set the tray down on the top. Bending over he lightly kissed her lips and found himself wrapped in a pair of arms and pulled off balance. Managing to avoid landing on top of her he gazed into the mischievous eyes that were now wide open and staring at him.

"Minx," he said trailing his tongue across her bottom lip. She responded immediately, opening to give him access, and he took it. In fact, he was ready to take everything she was

233

offering. He couldn't fail to notice that the demure nightdress of the night before was missing and all that covered her body was the duvet. He deepened the kiss, moving his arms under her shoulders. The feel of her soft silky skin was torment. He wanted to wait until tonight, until they were at the ranch and in his, no, their bed, but she was intent on making it difficult for him.

"Jess, I've brought coffee and it's getting cold." His attempt at pulling the situation back met with only an, "mm." "Jess, you need to give yourself time to recover. At least until tonight." He tried again to pull things back, and thought that he'd succeeded when her hands dropped away and she lay back. Sitting upright, he groaned inwardly. She looked delicious. She had that drowsy look on her face and her hair was tousled from sleep.

"So you're turning me down, Ethan Slade?"

The groan was loud. "No, just postponing. If that's possible?"

She pulled herself upright, letting the cover drop down to her waist. He closed his eyes. "That's cheating, Jess."

"I know. So, still want to postpone?"

Very slowly he opened his eyes. She was settled back on the pillows displaying her naked upper body to him. He saw the look in her eyes and knew that he'd lost this battle. Standing up, he shed his clothes and slipped into the bed alongside her.

**

Jessica knew she'd won the moment she'd dropped the cover. "That's better, Mr Slade. I don't like having to ask twice." She was shaking as she spoke. His body, displayed magnificently for her pleasure, was sending a heat to her groin that was about to alight. His erection told her that he wanted her and a soft smile played on her lips as she thought of what she wanted to do to him.

"You'll never need to ask twice, Jess. Never." His voice was husky as he pulled her gently down the bed. "I just don't want to hurt you."

"You won't." Those were the last words she spoke before she ducked under the covers and took him in her mouth. She'd not done this since that night in Calgary, when she'd lost all her inhibitions. Now she was taking control of this part of the foreplay. Settling between his legs, she pushed them wide apart and let her tongue tease his tip. Swirling and turning, she was bringing him to the brink. Her hand gently moulded his testicles and squeezed. She thrilled at the sound of his cry and took him deep into her mouth. Sucking and stroking, she felt the first drops escape and licked them away. This was another world to her and one that she was eagerly willing to embrace. But she didn't want to bring him to a climax. She wanted that to happen inside her and she was almost ready.

Moving her mouth away she held him in one hand, running her hand up and down the length of him. She crept her body up his inch by inch until she was holding him between her legs. She rubbed him over her clitoris and moaned at the sensation. He was leaking and this made the movement glide over her. His hands were holding her shoulders. His neck was arched upwards and his head thrown back. She could see the moisture glistening on his chest and gave in to the urge to run her tongue through it.

Moving her hand, she teased herself with his tip. She couldn't believe she was doing this. She was pleasuring herself with his body and she was loving every minute of it. Her clitoris swelled with the movement and her sex clenched, wanting fulfilment that she would give it in time. Any aches she was feeling were lost in the erotic sensations going through her body. She could feel the perspiration on her own skin as she rubbed him from back to front between her legs. He was hard and leaking more with every movement.

"Please, Jess…" The cry was almost wrenched from him as he gripped her shoulders, his buttocks thrusting upwards, trying to find the way inside her. But she still held him back. Her own breath was coming in gasps and the pulsating in her sex was almost unbearable but she didn't want to stop this. Then suddenly she was turned over.

"Sorry, darling. You're killing me." The words came thick and heavy as he moved above her and thrust forward with one movement and sank deep inside her with a groan that echoed round the room.

She was still recovering from the sudden change of being in control when he entered. Her body arched up and then thrust back at him. She looked at him, brown eyes on grey as they pushed and thrust, rolled and turned in the bed until finally they reached an orgasm that left them beyond breathless. Even when he was emptied and they were both fulfilled, she came at him again and again. She wanted more, her body was on fire for him. This was when he moved to her groin and, flicking his tongue and sucking, brought her to a second and then third climax.

They showered together some time later and made love again under the hot steaming water. Then he took her out for breakfast to the diner, their first public outing together as a couple. The ring secured on her left hand made it quite clear what the state of play was and there were lots of offers of congratulations.

Early afternoon, they packed up most of her belongings and drove out to the ranch. He insisted that she drove in front of him so he could keep an eye on her.

"Worried I'll run away, Ethan?" she joked.

"No. Even if you did I would find you."

"You didn't find me, after Calgary," she quipped back at him.

"Wrong. I had started looking. But I just hadn't had any feedback and then, I didn't need to look, because you were here, exactly where I wanted you to be."

"How could you have found me when you didn't have my name or know anything about me?" She was curious for his answer.

"I didn't have your name, I couldn't persuade reception to give me that, but someone at the hotel took pity on me and gave me some information, like your car details and registration. It wouldn't have taken long for an investigator to find you. Trouble was I was out of the country, so I couldn't call in a favour until I was back, and then when I came to see Frank, there you were. So I just called off my search. Destiny, Jess. It was meant to be. We were meant to be."

The conversation had sent a thrill through her. She hadn't thought it was possible to love someone as much as she loved him, and to be loved back equally. Arriving at the ranch, they pulled up outside and he quickly picked her up and strode into the house. Depositing her in the hall her held her face in his hands and kissed her.

"Welcome home, Jessica."

She was moved to tears and had to wipe her hand across her eyes. "Thank you. I hope I make you happy?"

"You will, sweetheart. You being here makes me happy. It's about time this house heard the sound of laughter and, in time, children's voices again."

That night they made love in his bed, which was now their bed. He was tender and gentle. There was none of the erotica they'd shared that morning. This was pure and simple lovemaking. A worshiping of each other's bodies, of getting to know every part of them and those parts that gave the most pleasure. He stroked and touched her, telling her what a wonderful life they were going to have, and then he made love to her again and she opened up to him, giving him her body and her heart.

As soon as she could, she made a journey to the next town and bought a couple of pregnancy tests, which would give an early reading. She was sure that she was late and she could hardly contain her excitement as she waited for the result. She was doing them at the cottage while she was on her own, as she needed time for them to show the results. When they both said 'positive' she sat and cried from sheer happiness. She was longing to tell Ethan, but wanted to choose the right moment. But she also wanted to take another test, just to be sure, before she said anything.

Over the next few days she contained her excitement and moved the rest of her things into the ranch, leaving her cottage empty. She was still overseeing the work at the office but Dan had indicated that he might be interested in the practice. He was going to come out and have a look around next weekend, and as far as Jess was concerned, life was getting better by the day. The wedding plans were well underway and the local minister was happy to conduct their wedding, despite the short notice.

She spent a couple of days in the city staying with Gemma while she looked for a wedding dress. Gem was to be her maid of honour, so they had a hilarious time shopping and came home with exactly what they wanted. She also bought another test kit, just to be certain. But she knew she was pregnant, she was definitely late. Ethan phoned every night and texted during the day, telling her how he was missing her. She'd never had this kind of love before and it was amazing to her.

Returning to the ranch, she was again stunned by the beauty of it. The green pastures on either side of the road. The fences running along the side that were keeping in the horses and cattle. It looked and felt like another world, and then the house and buildings came into sight and she felt such a rush of love for this place that she stopped the car. Getting out, she stood in the open door and gazed around, drinking in the sounds of birds and insects. The lowing cries of the cattle and the occasional whinny from the horses drifted across the fields. She could smell the grass and feel the heat of the sun on her bare arms, it was all telling her that she was home. She remembered his words, *one day you'll be as eager to reach my home.* He was right, she was eager, and this was home. Sliding back behind the wheel she put the car into drive.

Epilogue

He thought his heart was going to stop. As it was, it just missed several beats. The sight of her standing at the end of the aisle blew his mind away. Jess caught his gaze; she knew the effect she was having. She'd loved the dress the moment she saw it and was fully aware of the impact it would have on him. It was pale ivory, and moulded her figure before flaring at the back into a short train that caressed the floor as she walked. Sleeveless and strapless, it showed off her smooth pale golden skin. She wore a simple tiara in her hair encrusted with pearls and mock diamonds. She refused to have her hair re-styled and, seeing the tiara in place before they left the ranch, she'd been glad of that decision. Around her neck she was wearing a single strand of pearls that had been loaned to her by Gemma, pearls that had belonged to Gemma's mom. The only other adornment was her engagement ring, which for the moment was sitting on her right hand. The flowers she carried were pale pink roses and white stephanotis in a cascading bouquet.

She started the walk towards him placing her ivory shoes carefully down onto the floor. She would hate to fall or wobble but the slender four-inch heels, although they were the perfect match for her dress, made that a distinct possibility if she lost concentration. She'd been practising all last evening, walking around the house in them until Gemma had taken them off her feet and hidden them away. Gemma had been such a support, and now she was walking down the aisle in front of her. The dress she wore was deep pink, sleeveless with two thin straps holding the top. She carried a smaller bouquet of pale pink roses and white carnations. Around her neck she wore the gold locket that had been their present to her.

Taking her eyes off her cousin, she looked at the man waiting for her and a soft smile curved her mouth. He looked delicious. The dark grey tuxedo with an ivory vest and cravat set off to perfection his dark hair and tanned complexion. She couldn't wait to discover what lay beneath and took a deep inhale of breath. As if reading her mind, he ran his tongue across his top lip and his eyes flared. They held each other's gazes until Gemma stepped to the side. They had reached the altar. Passing her bouquet to her cousin, she placed her now shaking hand into Ethan's and the service began.

The music was playing *Lady in Red* as Ethan swirled his new wife around the dance floor in the community centre. He'd hunted the song down. He'd heard it a few days after their meeting and couldn't get the tune out of his head, and to him it was the most appropriate song for their first dance.

Almost the whole town had turned out for the wedding. As he looked deep into her eyes his unspoken words made Jessica melt inside. Nobody else had any idea of the significance of the song, and the red dress, well, that was packed in her suitcase ready to go on honeymoon.

***

It was just over four weeks since the accident, and in that time they'd arranged the wedding with the help of the community. The two-week plan had gone out of the window within a couple of days. They could have had it in a posh hotel somewhere and had caterers in, but this was a town, a community into which their children would be born and then grow, and they wanted to share this special day with everyone. So the wedding was in the small church and the reception held in the community hall. Jessica's step-mom had send a card and check but had declined to attend, due to the distance. Jessica didn't mind, she had Gemma and friends from the city, including Anna and Dan, but more importantly she had the man she wanted.

As she swayed in her husband's arms, she let her mind drift back over the last few weeks. She'd spent most days in the office keeping the work moving. Dan had been impressed by the set-up and said he just needed to convince his bankers, and he'd done that within a couple of days. The offer of the house at half rent for the first two years had been a generous gesture on Ethan's part, but she knew he'd done it to sweeten the deal. He wanted her at home for a short while before she started on her new project.

Two days before the wedding they held a huge barbeque on the ranch for all the hands and as many townsfolk as wanted to come. It had been a great success. The country music had flowed, as had the alcohol. She'd come up with an excuse as to why she wasn't drinking that seemed to satisfy her future husband. The local tour bus had been commandeered to take people back and forth. They spent the evening socialising and mixing with their guests, wandering hand-in-hand amongst the crowd and, at every opportunity, he'd pulled her into a dark corner and kissed her.

By the time the last guests had gone, the whole place seemed like a ghost town. After the music and laughter, it was silent. The fairy lights were still lit, trailing from barn to barn, but the main floodlights were now out. She looked up at the sky, seeing the stars twinkling brightly as they walked slowly, their fingers interlinked, until he drew her into the stables. This was her idea of heaven.

"I'll just check on Kohana, before we turn in." The words were said casually as he went to the bin at the end of the stalls and brought out a couple of apples. Cutting them both in half he proceeded to feed one to Kohana and suggested that she gave the other to the nag in the end stall.

"You don't have nags, Ethan. You shouldn't say that, you'll hurt its feelings." She walked towards the box as she spoke. Then she stopped. She found herself looking at Rory's rear end. His head was turned partly round and he looked most disgruntled. Ethan's hands came onto her shoulders.

"Thought you might like a wedding present, since I seem unable to compete with this guy."

She turned and flung her arms around him. "You mean he's

mine? My own horse to keep?"

"Sure is. Although I don't think he looks too happy about the red bow around his neck. Perhaps you'd better put him out of his misery, sweetheart."

***

Rory was most indignant. He'd been taken out of his stall yet again and put in that bumpy trailer. Then he was here, but that was okay because he knew she was here. But the bow around his neck. Well, that was just beyond a joke. Although the prancey guy across the way thought it was hilarious. He'd tried to pull it off with his teeth but all they'd done was shorten his rope. Well, he'd got his own back for that. Gave that young chap's backside a nip as he walked away. But now she was here and he knew she would rescue him from this predicament. He gave a low whinny, begging her to help him.

***

"Oh Rory, what have they done to you?" she cried, as she walked towards him, a piece of apple held out on her hand. He took it greedily while she undid the ribbon. He snickered and pushed his nose into her arm and was rewarded with the rest of the apple. Patting his neck, she folded the ribbon and then gave him a hug.

"See you in the morning, big guy."

Walking back towards Ethan she gave him the biggest of smiles and then promised to show him just how much she loved her present. He had, in fact, made her own announcement easier, not that she was worried about it, but she had wondered how to broach the subject. Now all she had to do was wait until they got back to the house.

Once inside, she ran upstairs and pulled the wrapped package out of its hiding place. She'd done the further test this morning while he was outside with the men putting up the lighting. She'd known the result before it had shown. In fact, she'd known for over a week when she had worked out that she was at least four weeks overdue, and that had made her visit the doctor just to check that the accident hadn't caused any problems, which thankfully it hadn't.

Going back down into the lounge, she saw him relaxing on the sofa so crept up behind him. Dropping her hands over his head she placed the package on his knee. "You're not the only one who can give early wedding presents."

He caught one of her hands and held it while she walked round and sat next to him.

"So I guess I'm to open this very pretty little package."

She nodded and watched as he undid the white ribbon and then unwrapped the paper. "Okay, I'm no genius, what is it?" he asked holding the plastic item in his hand.

She leaned forward and turned it round to the front, with the blue line showing clearly. Then she looked at him and grinned. She couldn't not grin, as he looked completely perplexed. But then again, he'd probably never seen a pregnancy test kit before. She couldn't contain herself any longer. "It's telling you something, or rather about something that's going to have a big impact on our lives for around the next eighteen years." She watched as the realisation hit him.

You're pregnant?"

Beaming she nodded her head. "I hope you're pleased?"

"Pleased? I'm beyond pleased. I just never thought…"

"Never thought what? That the unprotected sex we've been having wouldn't have any consequences? Anyway, I thought that we were both in agreement about pregnancy. If it happened, it happened?"

"Oh God, sweetheart," he said throwing the plastic kit onto the table and gathering her into his arms. "I can't find the words to say how I feel." His hand wandered down over her stomach. "I can't believe my child is there."

"Not only there, but probably listening to every word you say. Well, perhaps not yet. But soon."

"But I thought you were on the pill?"

"I seem to recall someone suggesting I didn't need to take it. Hope I made the right decision?"

"Definitely, darling," he said with a grin. "So when is

junior due?"

"Possibly in about seven months. We'll know more once I get into the system. And before you start worrying, the accident hasn't caused any problem. I've already seen the doctor about it."

She spent the next few hours showing her future husband just how grateful she was for his present and he was more than eager to express his delight at her news and tell her how much he was going to miss her tomorrow night. While she would be on the ranch with Gemma and other friends, he was spending the night before their wedding in the local hotel.

Everything had worked out well. Dan was due to take over the practice on Monday and was moving into Frank's old house. He'd had the option of taking the cottage but chose the house instead, it was larger and meant he could have a home office.

***

She sighed and brought her mind back to the music. Looking across at Dan, now dancing with Gemma, she had a feeling that it wasn't only the practice and the move that would work out well for him. She'd watched them both at the barbeque and, if the looks passing between the pair of them were anything to go by, her cousin would be spending a lot of her spare time in the town.

"Hey, Mrs Slade. Do you think you could concentrate on your husband instead of ogling the new attorney?"

She slapped his arm playfully. "Not ogling, darling, just plotting. See how well Dan and Gemma look together? And see the way they are looking at each other?"

He swung her round with a throaty laugh. Burying his face in her hair he whispered, "I'd rather concentrate on the way you'll be looking at me shortly."

"Is this when you're dressed or undressed, husband?"

"Both, and I can't wait to get you out of that wonderful creation. Are you wearing a bra or can I let my thoughts run wild?"

"Wearing one. You remember Calgary, when we got engaged?"

"Ah yes, the bra with no straps. Can't wait to unwrap you, sweetheart."

The music stopped and they walked back to the high table. Time to cut the cake was the call. This was done amid cheers while they fed a piece to each other. He leaned forward and gently licked a small piece of icing from the side of her mouth. "We need to get out of here…quick," he whispered.

The look in his eyes told her why. Moving to the front of the hall, she stood in the centre with her back to the crowd. Holding her bouquet in both hands she threw it high in the air behind her and then turned to see who the lucky lady, or gent, was. It couldn't have worked out better. It was heading right for Gemma, but then Dan moved forward and caught it. There were cheers and jeers, so he held his hands up in surrender. Then he turned and, with a devastating smile and bow, handed it to Gemma. Jessica felt her own heart flip at the sign. If that wasn't a declaration of, *I like you,* then nothing was.

She grabbed Ethan's arm to tell him but found her hand captured and she was propelled out of the door and into the waiting car. Not one of the ranch cars, but a low, sleek convertible. Opening the door, he waited while she gathered up her dress and slipped into the passenger seat. Their bags were in the trunk and, with a wave of the hand, he put the car into drive and they roared away to a scattering of rice and flowers.

Once out of town he hit the button and brought up the roof. He didn't want that dress damaged in any way. He had plans for it. Tomorrow they would fly out, but tonight would be spent in the city. He knew the hotel, and the room in which that dress would soon be adorning the floor. The honeymoon suite was reserved for Hawaii; the room tonight was for them. They would begin their marriage in the room where it had all begun.

He touched his hand to hers and she turned, the sun catching on the diamonds in her hair. Moving his hand, he placed it against her stomach, against their child. She stretched out her hand resting it on his thigh, and felt the taught muscles tense. The smile she gave him turned to a wicked grin and he moved his hand and pressed the control, taking the speed up to the maximum. This was the start of their new life.

THE END

Fantastic Books
Great Authors

CROOKED
CAT

Meet our authors and discover
our exciting range:

- Gripping Thrillers
- Cosy Mysteries
- Romantic Chick-Lit
- Fascinating Historicals
- Exciting Fantasy
- Young Adult and Children's
  Adventures
- Non-Fiction

25175804R00150

Printed in Poland
by Amazon Fulfillment
Poland Sp. z o.o., Wrocław